Bello:

hidden talent rediscovered

Bello is a digital only imprint of Pan Macmillan,
established to breathe new life into previously published,
classic books.

At Bello we believe in the timeless power of the imagination,
of good story, narrative and entertainment and we want to use
digital technology to ensure that many more readers
can enjoy these books into the future.

We publish in ebook and Print on Demand formats
to bring these wonderful books to new audiences.

www.panmacmillan.co.uk/bello

B E L L O

30130505342620

Winston Graham

Winston Mawdsley Graham OBE was an English novelist, best known for the series of historical novels about the Poldarks. Graham was born in Manchester in 1908, but moved to Perranporth, Cornwall when he was seventeen. His first novel, *The House with the Stained Glass Windows* was published in 1933. His first 'Poldark' novel, *Ross Poldark*, was published in 1945, and was followed by eleven further titles, the last of which, *Bella Poldark*, came out in 2002. The novels were set in Cornwall, especially in and around Perranporth, where Graham spent much of his life, and were made into a BBC television series in the 1970s. It was so successful that vicars moved or cancelled church services rather than try to hold them when Poldark was showing.

Aside from the Poldark series, Graham's most successful work was *Marnie*, a thriller which was filmed by Alfred Hitchcock in 1964. Hitchcock had originally hoped that Grace Kelly would return to films to play the lead and she had agreed in principle, but the plan failed when the principality of Monaco realised that the heroine was a thief and sexually repressed. The leads were eventually taken by Tippi Hedren and Sean Connery. Five of Graham's other books were filmed, including *The Walking Stick*, *Night Without Stars* and *Take My Life*. Graham wrote a history of the Spanish Armadas and an historical novel, *The Grove of Eagles*, based in that period. He was also an accomplished writer of suspense novels. His autobiography, *Memoirs of a Private Man*, was published by Macmillan in 2003. He had completed work on it just weeks before he died. Graham was a Fellow of the Royal Society of Literature, and in 1983 was honoured with the OBE.

Winston Graham

GREEK FIRE

First published in 1957 by Hodder & Stoughton

This edition published 2013 by Bello
an imprint of Pan Macmillan, a division of Macmillan Publishers Limited
Pan Macmillan, 20 New Wharf Road, London N1 9RR
Basingstoke and Oxford
Associated companies throughout the world

www.panmacmillan.co.uk/bello

ISBN 978-1-4472-5529-1 EPUB
ISBN 978-1-4472-5528-4 POD

Visit **www.panmacmillan.com** to read more about all our books
and to buy them. You will also find features, author interviews and
news of any author events, and you can sign up for e-newsletters
so that you're always first to hear about our new releases.

Chapter One

The Little Jockey was not much more than a converted cellar. Vanbrugh found it at the second attempt, down an alley just out of reach of the seedy lights of Ommonia Square. But here twenty yards was enough to pace out a thousand years—from hissing trolley-buses and neon lights and chattering crowds, past two doorways, a Greek and a Turkish, past a garbage can with its lid aslant like a mandarin's hat, across a gutter half choked by the mud of yesterday's rain, to an arched entrance and twelve stone steps cut before Charlemagne, rubbed smooth and treacherous and leading down into the dark. At the bottom an attendant dressed like an Evzone took his coat and pulled aside a curtain to see him down a second flight to the main room.

The place was about two-thirds full, but they found him a table in a good position in a sort of upper cellar which formed a terrace on a higher level. Eight or ten tables up here led to six break-ankle steps and a larger domed cellar where there were more tables and room for dancing. The walls were of rough stone and inclined to sweat; curtained arches led to service quarters; and lights from candles in old glass lamp-holders lit up the statuary which stood defensively in recesses: two tired Byzantine madonnas, a stray apostle lacking an ear, St. Francis with a lamb.

The newcomer waved away a couple of the house girls who drifted across to help him with the bottle in the bucket, but when a tall Lithuanian Jewess stopped by and said, "Amerikani?" and slipped into the seat opposite, he raised no objection, and a waiter hovering near quickly put another glass on the table.

Vanbrugh was the sort of man you wouldn't notice in the street:

he could have been twenty-five or forty, and his tight rather craggy face, his deep-set, pale-eyed inner containment made no substantial first impression. He didn't talk to the girl, but she re-filled his glass once or twice, and her own with it, and when she stretched forward a hand for his package of cigarettes he absent-mindedly shook one out for her and lit a match with his thumb-nail.

At a table in a corner was a middle-aged stout man in a black alpaca suit, with a fluff of untidy beard worn like a bonnet string under his chin. Vanbrugh frowned as at an uneasy memory. The fat man was eating; he was the only person so occupied; he paused now and then to brush crumbs from his shiny shabby suit, and with a sort of sham gentility he raised the back of his hand to hide a belch; once a piece of shell fish slid out of his mouth and hung like mucus from his beard; his companion, a tall youth with a narrow nose and a girlish mouth, watched him with bright malicious eyes.

The orchestra of four were perched in an odd wire balcony to the left of the steps like canaries in a cage. They were playing a western dance rhythm, and half a dozen couples moved like sleepwalkers about the dance floor. Beside the band was a fair copy in bronze of the third century B.C. LITTLE JOCKEY WHICH GAVE THE CLUB ITS NAME.

"Who is that man, d'you know?" Vanbrugh said to the girl opposite him. "The fat man eating at the table in the corner."

"Who? That one? No. I have never seen him before."

"I have. But it doesn't matter."

"You know Greece, honey?" she said.

"A little."

"I am quite new here. You must tell me."

"Where are you from?"

"Memel."

"It's a long way to come."

"I travel light. And you?"

He said: "I'm far from home too."

The band had stopped and the dancers were dispersing. Two couples climbed the steps and took seats at a table nearby—wealthy young Greeks, both men handsome but running to fat, one girl ordinary, the other a beauty.

Vanbrugh eyed her through his smoke-screen. Her raven black hair was caught together with a diamond clasp at the back; ivory profile with a slender, almost too slender, nose, eyes lit with exceptional brilliance; the classic conception of beauty—by Byron out of Polyclitus—but all on a twentieth century basis, from the peach finger-nails holding the long amber cigarette-holder to the brilliant worldly-wise smile.

With that sixth sense that women have, she soon knew she was being looked at, and her gaze moved to Vanbrugh's table, took in the thin undernourished-looking American, the cheap girl, the waiter changing the bottle in the bucket. A glimmer of amused civilised contempt showed in her eyes before she turned away.

"How long have you been here?" Vanbrugh said to his companion.

"Eight weeks, honey."

"What's this new cabaret you have?"

"The three Tolosas? They are Spaniards. They dance like all Spaniards."

"This their first week?"

"Last week was their first week. They come from Paris. They have been good for business. Before that we had singers from Macedonia. It was very awful."

"When does the cabaret come on?"

"Almost any time now. Like to dance, honey, before it begins?"

"Thanks no, if you'll excuse me."

"You are not very bright, are you?"

"Maybe there's someone else who'd dance with you."

"Does that mean you want to get rid of me?"

The fat Greek had stopped eating to draw breath, and he took his handkerchief from the corner of his collar and wiped it across his mouth. His heavy glance seemed to linger on Vanbrugh's table. Vanbrugh said: "No, stay if you'd like to."

"The floor show's just beginning."

One by one the candles were blown out, and shadows fell on the company like a secret retinue of waiters. Towering wine barrels and weather-born statuettes were sucked up into the darkness, and light played on the circular dance floor.

Vanbrugh said: "D'you happen to know—maybe you won't—but d'you happen to know the name of the girl on the next table but one—the girl with her hair in that diamond clasp?"

"I tell you, honey, I know no one. We do not see the same faces often. Ah, but that one . . . Stonaris, isn't that her name? Anya Stonaris. I have seen her photo in the weekly papers."

Her voice was drowned by the clash of cymbals. Four girls in traditional Spanish costume came out and performed a Flamenco, to the clicking of castanets and the vehement stamping of their feet, while in the back-ground a thin lithe man dressed like a matador crouched before a harp and touched it in a casual way from time to time with his hands. The first thing Gene Vanbrugh noticed about him was that he was in a sweat of fear.

When the girls went off, dragging perfunctory applause after them, the thin Spaniard stayed where he was, his short nervous fingers barely touching the strings. Once he raised his bloodshot eyes to sweep them in a quick semi-circle, meeting the darkness and the waiting faces.

"Who is she?" said Vanbrugh. "What does she do?"

"Who?"

"This—Anya Stonaris."

His companion shrugged. "Who knows? That one with her—that man—is called Manos. He is a politician. He has been here often before, but then he has come alone. . . ."

A woman stepped through the curtains on to the dance floor. She was young, about twenty-two, and fat, twelve stone or more, and short, not over five feet. The broad nose and thick flattened lips weren't negroid, not even Moorish. She was pure Spanish. Hands on hips, in perfect ease and confidence, she sang a comic song in a harsh broken powerful voice.

Nearly everyone in the cellars knew French, and those who did not were jollied along. Her eyes, small as diamonds and as bright, and the good-tempered shock of her white teeth, made you ready to laugh before the joke was out. She was all fat, healthy young fat, mainly in the breasts and behind. Her black crêpe dress fitted her like a sausage skin. And when she began to dance she used her fat as a comedian uses a false nose: with it she laughed at you and then at herself.

At the table where the Greeks were the girl, Anya Stonaris, put out her cigarette. The politician Manos, deferential and attentive, offered her another; she took it, twisted it slowly with pointed nails into the holder, thoughtful lashes black on cheeks, glinted a smile across the lighted flame at her escort, flickered her glance back across the American before turning again to watch the show.

Down below the harpist, who, after the end of the applause and while the fat girl stood aside, had been hinting at the sad nostalgias of Seville and Castile, suddenly set fire to his harp with great chords and discords of a new kind. In the sudden silence which followed, El Toro himself stepped into the ring.

Welcoming applause was discreetly led by the waiters, schooled in the dangers of anti-climax, for El Toro, dressed though he was in all the magnificence of a toreador, was tiny, no taller than his girl partner, fine featured, dapper, the perfect lady killer—and perhaps bull killer—but in minuscule.

The man and the woman began to dance. It was the dance of the bull-ring, hot and bloodstained, to the shrill pulse of the harp. They swirled and twisted to the shouted rhythm, she charging, he adroitly avoiding her with his muleta, sword point to ground, enticing and evading, side-stepping and, body swaying. For *she* was the bull, not he. She looked like a bull, heavy shouldered, broad nosed, dark curled, she breathed and snorted and charged like a bull, at his delicate, precise almost feminine evasions, his perfect slender body leaning this way and that. Here was some inner truth from Spain stated in terms of the dance, an allegorical picture of the relationship of the sexes, spiritual more than physical but partly both, a statement of a racial anomaly which had existed for two thousand years.

As the dance reached its climax, the harpist in a sort of frenzy produced unheard of sounds. If a harp was the instrument of angels, then this was a fallen angel, perverting his gifts to the expression of the noise and cruelty of a blinding Andalusian afternoon.

Vanbrugh sipped the indifferent champagne. The bull was tiring, faltering now and stamping in hesitation, watching the toreador who flicked his muleta with small poised formal movements. She lowered her head to charge, El Toro drew back his sword. As she ran at him he turned slightly aside and plunged the sword between her arm and shoulder. She sank slowly, her attitude the conventional posture of the slain bull. In a moment he had drawn away and she was on the floor before him; his foot rested lightly on her shoulder.

There was loud applause at the end of this dance, and the partners, toreador and slain bull, stood bowing side by side.

"You see," said the Lithuanian, "it is not bad after all. Of course, that fat woman, Maria Tolosa, she is the best."

Vanbrugh looked at the harpist as he went off. He was still sweating. The band came back to their cage and a few dancers drifted on to the floor. Manos asked Anya Stonaris for a dance, but she said something smilingly and they did not get up.

Vanbrugh nodded or answered in monosyllables as his companion chattered away. He was debating in his mind one or two things, the least of which was how he might most easily get rid of this girl and go. The most important was whether he should attempt to see Juan Tolosa tonight. He had only landed at Hellenikon three hours ago. Rushing one's fences. Also he thought he had been recognised tonight by the fat man, whose name he thought was Mandraki, and if that were so it was a disadvantage to any move now.

So he made no move now.

He didn't realise then the importance of the decision, because he did not then know that by tomorrow it would be too late.

6

Chapter Two

George Lascou was taking his mid-morning coffee when Anya rang him.

"Good morning, darling," she said. "I suppose you have been up hours."

"Since six. But, that's no reason why you should be. Four weeks and it will all be over."

"Or all beginning. I can't imagine in either case that you will learn to relax."

"I relax when I'm with you. That's why you're so good for me."

"It must explain why you have been seeing so much of me lately!"

"Darling, I'm *sorry*. I hate it as much as you do. I wish I could do something about it, but you know what it is at present. This morning we have a press conference at twelve. At five there's a meeting of the party executive. Then this evening there is the manifesto to consider in full session. It will be easier when the campaign is in full swing. What will you do today?"

"I have a press conference with my hair-dresser at twelve. At five I shall buy a hat. This will pass the time until seven when I'm to take cocktails with Maurice Taksim."

"And what did you do last night?"

"Had dinner with Jon Manos and two of his friends. Afterwards we went to the Little Jockey and danced for a while. It wasn't much fun without you."

"You went where?"

"To the Little Jockey."

"Did Manos take you there?"

"Yes. There's a new cabaret. Quite good. I got home about two. My sweet, it's a perfectly *respectable* night-club. One is in far more danger of being bored than corrupted. We must go together sometime."

"Yes. Yes, of course. I know it." As he poured himself a second cup of coffee, the morning light glinted on the heavy silver coffee-pot and on the big emerald-cut diamond in the ring on his left hand.

"But are you being disapproving just the same?"

"Nothing of the sort." He dabbed at a spot of coffee which had fallen on the tray-cloth and sucked the damp tip of his fingers.

"Then what? . . ."

He said in slight irritation: "Perhaps one has to be specially careful at a time like this. The opposition press are always out for snippets of scandal, and they know of our connection. A photograph. A chance of involving me———"

"You can always disown me."

"That I may do in my coffin but not before."

"Darling, a gallant speech before midday."

He laughed politely. "One has to keep up with the Taksims of this world. What did you think of the cabaret?"

"It was Spanish."

". . . Is that all?"

"No. I hate their singing but love their dancing."

"I prefer Greek. What was it, all women?"

"No. A man. Two men. One danced and one played a harp as if he'd sold his soul to the devil. Then there was a woman. They're known as The Three Tolosas."

"Good. Good. I'm glad you enjoyed it. But I must talk to Jon Manos."

"You quite astonish me. I'll go into purdah for the next four weeks."

"Nonsense, darling, you exaggerate. Tell me when you are next going down to Sounion. . . ." He began to talk easily, smoothing over what he had said.

When they had rung off George Lascou sipped his coffee. From where he sat two reflections of George Lascou aped his movements

8

and were a constant reassurance that he was still personable and still in the early forties. All the same, he was angry with himself now for having allowed himself to be surprised into an emotion which she had detected.

His secretary came in.

"Where had I got to, Otho?"

"Shall I read the last piece? 'It was Aristotle who said that Virtue consists in loving and hating in the proper proportions. The danger of a too-civilised approach is that we become afraid of the positive emotions. If this election——' "

"Leave it now." He made an impatient gesture. "Before we go on I'd like you to get Mr. Manos on the phone."

Otho put away his notebook, but as he was about to go out Lascou said: "And also Major Kolono."

"Sir?"

"Major Kolono. You'll find him at police headquarters. Tell him I'd like him to call round here about four-thirty this afternoon on a personal matter."

"Very good, sir."

While he waited, George Lascou re-read a report he had received that morning from a man whom he occasionally and reluctantly employed. Having done that, he put it in his wallet and began to slit open with a bronze dagger some letters that Otho had brought in. The blade of the dagger was three thousand years old and a lion hunt was inlaid on it. The handle had long since rotted away and been replaced with a modern ivory one. He read the letters, made an emphatic note in the margin of one, got up, lit a cigarette, and went to one of the windows which looked out over Constitution Square. He was high enough here to be undisturbed by the bustle and noise and all the clamour of the morning traffic below, high enough too to see over the new budding trees to the Tomb of the Unknown Soldier and to the Old Palace, where Parliament had recently been prorogued. Beyond were the trees of the National Garden. Along the further rim of the square three trolley-buses were crawling like centipedes surprised by the lifting of a stone. A handsome man, with that shadowed pallor that comes to some

Greeks; the pince-nez he wore softened the strong cheekbones and the strong skull, gave an uncertain studious look to a face otherwise purposeful. As Otho came in again he let the scarlet-and-white-striped satin curtain fall.

"Sir, I phoned Mr. Manos at his office but he was in court. I left a message for them to ring when he came back."

Lascou put the end of his cigarette in an ash-tray.

"Then get him *out* of court. I want to speak to him."

It was then nearly 11 a.m.

Chapter Three

At three o'clock that afternoon a short stout young woman was walking through Zappeion Park. Her mane of hair was dragged back and fastened under a scarlet head-scarf. Her cheeks were puffy with crying but she was not crying now; her face was set like iron; it was a good-tempered face riven by lightning, hardened by storm. She walked any way, not looking where she was going and not caring; but after a while she came opposite a statue and hesitated staring at it, not really seeing it but uncertain whether to go on or turn back. As she stopped, a man who had been following the same path stopped also and looked at the statue. After a moment he glanced at her and said in English:

"He died here too."

"What? Who?" She stared at him with blind, angry eyes. "What do you say?"

"Byron. That statue. He loved Greece more even than his own land."

She focused the speaker properly for the first time, saw his slight figure and down-pulled hat. "If you are from the police I will spit in your face."

"If I were from the police that would land you in trouble."

"And you are not?"

"I am not."

"Then get out of my way!"

She turned her back on him and walked off. There were not many people about and he followed her a few paces behind with his easy cat-like walk.

"Tell me one thing," he said, catching her up. "How did the

accident happen? I was coming to see him about midday when I heard."

She strode out of the park but at the entrance stopped, breathing again like a bull, formidable for all her shortness, quite capable of knocking him down in the street.

"Who are you?"

"A friend. My name is Gene Vanbrugh."

"What is your business?"

"I was at the Little Jockey last night. This morning I had a certain business proposition to put to your husband, but I was too late."

"So you were too late! Well, I am sorry. But that's the end of it, isn't it."

"Not necessarily."

"Why not?"

"I might put the proposition to you, Mme Tolosa."

"Do I look or feel in a condition to listen to business propositions? Get out of my way."

"How did the accident happen? He was run over, wasn't he? What did the driver say?"

"Clear off or I will call the police. See, that one."

"Your husband perhaps took to many risks."

That stopped her. "What are you talking about?"

"Take a coffee with me and I'll tell you."

She hesitated, fingered an ear-ring, glanced up at him again, looked him over, taking in the lean slant of his jaw, the bony hands he kept thrusting in and out of his pockets, the old suit.

"How do you know I have English?"

"Most cabaret dancers do."

She looked behind her. "I do not want for coffee. But if you have something to say I will sit down."

He nodded, his mouth still tight, but with a gleam of approval in his eyes. "I've something to say."

They sat at a table part protected from draught by a glass screen. It was a chilly day. There were very few people about at this time of day, and a waiter, yawning, came and swept the table-top with a perfunctory cloth. Gene Vanbrugh ordered coffee for himself and a brandy for her.

She said: "Well?"

He looked at her! It might be she was easy-going most times, but once roused she was a fighter. He was a fighter himself and felt drawn towards her.

"How did the accident happen?"

"Accident nothing."

"Tell me."

"He had a phone call at nine this morning. I do not know who it was from, he did not tell me. But as he left the house he was run down by a waiting car. I saw it all because I went to the window to call after him. The car came from up the street, not very fast. You know. There was a lorry turning up the street blocking it to other cars, and the street was empty. It went on the pavement behind Juan. He turned at the last minute and tried to jump out of the way, but it caught him against a wall—crushed him. I . . . I saw his face. . . ."

There was silence. "I'm very sorry. . . . There was no chance of its being an accident?"

She thrust the tears off her face. "The police pretend to believe it was. But they are fools or liars."

"What happened to the car?"

"It was—damaged at the front. It turned quickly round and went off the way it had come."

"Did you see the driver?"

She shook her head. "Now what have you to say?"

He offered her a cigarette but she shook her head again, impatiently. He struck a match and lit his own cigarette. She watched him suspiciously. He looked like a man who lived on his nerves, but his hands were steady with the match.

He said: "I was coming to see your husband because I think he had something to sell."

"I don't know what you are talking about."

"Have the police searched his belongings?"

"No. I don't think so. I am not sure. You know. I have been so distracted since it happened. I came out, I had to come out, just to walk, to breathe, to think."

The waiter came with the brandy and the coffee, clacking the glasses and saucers. Gene stirred his glass, but she put out one of her small fat pointed hands and pushed hers contemptuously away.

The coffee was thick and sweet. He frowned as he sipped it. "Two weeks ago you and your company were in Paris. Right?"

"Well?"

"At Katalan's. I live in Paris."

"You saw us dance?"

"No. I have to tell you I don't go much for night-clubs as a normal thing. Maybe I've grown out of them—or through them—I don't know. But a friend of mine met Juan Tolosa. El Toro played a lot of poker, didn't he?"

"So?"

"They met in a poker game more than once. Your husband lost. Once he drank too much and got talkative. He dropped a hint of something he was going to do when he came to Athens. He mentioned a name. My friend knew I was interested in that name. When he saw me a week or so later he passed the information on. By then you'd left. I work in Paris, and it took me a couple of days to put my things in order. I got to Athens yesterday."

She picked up her glass now, frowned at it, contorting her flat lips, then abruptly she drank the brandy at a gulp.

"Give me the name of the man who killed Juan. That's all I want to know."

"I have no proof that would satisfy the police."

She said: "Tell me the name and I will not go to the police."

He studied her. "I believe you. But it wouldn't help. You'd only be putting your hand into the same snake's nest——"

He stopped. A pale shadow had fallen over the table. In the flood of Castilian that followed he could only pick out a word here and there. He got up.

"Join us. I was hoping you'd come."

Philip Tolosa said in English: "I have no wish to talk with reporters. Maria, come."

Gene said: "You play the harp superbly."

The Spaniard's sallow face was drawn and dirty, and there was cigarette ash and stains on his coat. He was a good lot taller than his brother, being about Gene's height. Maria got up and there was another sharp, explosion in their own tongue. He had been looking for her everywhere, he said, couldn't think why she had gone out; she was explaining about this man. Tolosa looked at Gene, eyes cagey and bloodshot. He couldn't keep his fingers steady.

Vanbrugh said: "Are you sure you're going to get out of the country? Are you sure they'll let you go?"

The girl pushed her chair aside, nearly upsetting it. "What is this you are threatening us with?"

"I'm threatening you with nothing. Perhaps your brother-in-law knows what I mean."

"I know nothing except that we have no word to say to anyone. Come, Maria."

"This man tells me——"

"Come, Maria."

She shrugged and glanced again at Gene, hesitating between them.

"If you want me any time," Gene said, "I am at the Astoria. Ring me or call round."

There was nothing more he could do now and he watched them go, Philip Tolosa holding the girl's arm. After a few paces she jerked her arm free. But she did not look back.

Gene sat down again to finish his coffee. Then he took out a couple of notes and put them beside the printed bill.

Chapter Four

As a clock was striking five Vanbrugh crossed Kolonaki Square and made his way up one of the avenues running off it towards the slopes of Lycabettus. This was a good neighbourhood, the houses individual and distinguished, some set back from the road with wrought-iron gates and balconies.

It was raining now, a fine drizzle falling like nylon across the city; but towards the sea, towards Piraeus, the grey day was illuminated with broken blue. He walked with the collar of his jacket turned up, hands in pockets, easy slouch, as if the iron pavements were not his natural home at all. He looked like a hobo or a trapper, and had never been either.

At the house where he called the half-coloured maid was new to him and seemed doubtful whether Mme Lindos would see him. He gave his name and waited at the door.

When he went in he was shown in to a small morning-room where a handsome old woman sat before an open fire fingering a book of photographs. There are certain architectures of forehead and nose and cheek-bone which defy the erosions of age. She had them.

He kissed her hand and then her cheek, while her gentle sophisticated gaze went slowly over him, noting that he had lost weight and carried like a monogram his familiar air of strain.

"So. We cannot keep you away, Gene. Have you no home?"

He smiled. "No home. Are you, well?"

"When one is as old as I am one is modestly grateful for being alive at all. Let me see, have you ever met M. Vyro?"

Gene turned to the short elderly man with the grey imperial who had been standing by the window.

"*M.* Vyro is the proprietor of *Aegis*, one of our oldest morning papers——"

"And one of the most distinguished," said Gene.

M. Vyro bowed. "That is too kind. You are English, sir, or American?"

"American."

"Am I up to date with your occupation, Gene?" Mme Lindos asked. "The last time you wrote you were——"

"Yes, still in publishing."

"—M. Vanbrugh is European representative of Muirhead and Lewis, the New York publishers."

"Then we should have much in common," said M. Vyro. "You are here on business?"

"Partly, yes. We have two Greek authors on our list, Michaelis and Paleocastra——"

"Ah, Michaelis, the poet. Yes, yes. His is the true voice of Greece——"

"And partly I come to see old friends—among them Mme Lindos, who always knows so much about all the things I want to know."

"If that was ever true, Gene, it is far less true now. Fewer people come to see me."

"Except the most important ones," said Gene.

"Ah, only my oldest friends. I have known M. Vyro for nearly fifty years. What brings you at this particular time, Gene?"

"Your elections interest me. I wanted to ask you who is going to win this one?"

"There is an astrologer round the corner. My maid will give you an introduction to him."

Gene's face changed when he smiled—the narrowness, thinness, tightness eased and broke up. Lines crinkled across it in a peculiar and original way. "Maybe M. Vyro will hazard a guess. I imagined *Aegis* will support the Government?"

"Yes—but tending to move right of the Government. It is not a tendency I approve, but two years ago I handed over direction of the paper to my eldest son. He must go his own way."

"What of this grouping of all the opposition parties against Karamanlis?" Gene said. "And this new party of the centre, EMO, led by George Lascou?"

"I see you are up to date in some things," Mme Lindos said dryly.

"What sort of a man is Lascou?"

The question was addressed generally, but for a minute neither answered. The question appeared to have been dropped into an empty room. Then Vyro said:

"Intelligent, cultured. His money makes him influential. But I doubt personally if he's dynamic enough for a popular leader. There's something of the dilettante about him."

"You'll stay to tea, Angelos?" Mme Lindos said.

"No, thank you, I must go. You will be here some time, M. Vanbrugh?"

"A week or so. I haven't decided."

"Next week—a week today—is the fiftieth anniversary of the founding of my paper. I am proud to have begun it in a back street of the town when I was twenty-three. Next week we are celebrating the anniversary by setting in motion two new printing presses. I came to see Mme Lindos today about the reception which she is holding here first. It would be very fitting—and a pleasure to us—if you could come, having regard to your profession."

"I shall be glad to. Thank you."

"My very oldest surviving friend," said Mme Lindos when Vyro had left. "My husband's friend too. A man of such integrity. His sons are poor copies."

"Talk Greek to me, will you, Sophia?" Gene said. "One gets out of practice."

"Are you likely to need practice?"

"Sometimes it's convenient."

Mme Lindos got up. Arthritis made her moving ungainly, but once up she was as erect as he was. "You must come into the drawing-room for tea, and then I want to know what you are here for."

"I believe you don't trust me."

"Not very far."

The maid came in and opened double doors into a very large airy drawing-room. The old crimson wallpaper had faded rectangles on it of varying shapes and sizes. One handsome mirror still hung over the Louis Seize fireplace. Tea was set on a small table, a fine tea-pot in a silver cradle, cups as thin as egg-shells, spoons with the Lindos crest.

She said: "And do you really love your publishing now?"

"It enables me to live in Paris."

"It's the longest you have ever stayed anywhere, isn't it? Always before you have been wandering, restless—homeless, perhaps? It's the faculty of your type. You moved too much, saw too much when you were young."

"I still get around, but on my job—to Germany, England, Italy . . ."

"And sometimes to Greece. Does anybody here know you have come?"

"Who is there to know or care? Tell me, Sophia, what do you know about a woman called Anya Stonaris?"

"George Lascou's mistress?"

Gene stirred his tea. "Is that what she is?"

"You have met her?"

"What's her history?"

"I know very little. She is still very young but they have been together a long time. She gets photographed often because she is beautiful and smart. A hard brilliant person, and a thoroughly bad influence on him, I'm told. He of course has a wife and two children, and he poses to the electorate as a family man. But most people in Athens know of the connection."

Gene said: "I've heard of Lascou for a good many years, but until he entered politics I wasn't interested in him."

"And now?"

Their voices, though not raised, had been echoing in the sparsely furnished room. The maid came in with hot buttered toast, and the conversation lapsed till she left them.

Gene said: "One gets different opinions. Some say he'll soon be the most powerful figure in Greece."

While they talked the clouds had broken, and the room brightened and darkened as the sun intermittently came through. The Venetian blinds had not been lowered, and Mme Lindos looked at her visitor whose face was lit with a reflection from the mirror on the wall. She thought again how young he looked in spite of his hollow cheeks: his was the youth which sometimes comes to people with singleness of mind. She remembered her first meeting with him twelve years ago, in the middle of the civil war; he had appeared on her doorstep in rags speaking Greek then with an accent she had thought Anatolian, had warned her to go into the cellar and stay there: the fighting was coming up this street. Sten gun under arm he had said this apologetically, like someone calling about the gas, and then, as it seemed summing her up in a glance, had asked her if she could care for a woman who was dying and needed attention and water. After that she had not seen him for nearly two weeks, when, during the worst famines and the worst massacres, he had come suddenly again with a few tins of food he had stolen from somewhere and left them in her hall.

Gene said: "Things are still bad here?"

"You do not need to listen to the politicians to discover the problems of Greece, Gene. Under the surface prosperity we have a food shortage, except for the rich, and the old, old bogy of inflation—and unemployment, or underemployment, everywhere. Many of our people—perhaps two million, perhaps more than a quarter of us all—have to live on less than two thousand drachmae a year. What is that in your currency? Seventy dollars? That is what we have to face and have to cure."

Silence fell for a while. "How do you plan to spend your time here?" she asked.

"I have to see Michael Michaelis. And I shall wander round meeting some old friends."

"Go carefully. Don't get into trouble like last time."

"I was of use."

Her grey worldly-wise eyes flickered up to him for a moment. "I *know* you were of use. I know that, Gene. But you made enemies in high places as well as friends."

"It's an occupational risk."

"That's just what it's not. If you are here on publishing business I'm sure no one will interfere with you. But if you start dabbling in our politics again ... Besides, it is perhaps not altogether a pretty scene but it could be worse."

"Do you have friends who know Anya Stonaris?"

She made a gesture disavowing responsibility. ". . . I have some."

"I want to meet her. Could it be arranged in some casual way?"

"I suppose it is human nature that if you tell a man a woman is bad it makes him more eager to meet her."

He said: "I've met a lot of so-called bad women. They bore me to death. This one probably will. But I've other reasons for wanting to get to know her."

"Well, make no mistake. She is George Lascou's woman without question."

"That too," said Gene, "is something I'll be interested to discover for myself."

Chapter Five

The day ended well. Towards evening the last of the clouds split and a vivid sun fell on the scene like an arc light on a film set. The temples clustering at the foot of the Acropolis were like things drawn out of themselves by a stereoscope, and above them the great Parthenon stood crowned against the sky in four-dimensioned light.

Below it the modern city pullulated, a city of no visible connection except that of locality with the marble ruins of Cimon and Pericles, a city separated from the Hellenic age by two thousand years of neglect and non-inhabitation, a mushroom town grown in a hundred years from 5000 people to 1,250,000, spawning, sprawling, raucous and decentralised over all the great plain, ringed by mountains and stretching to the sea. Handsome boulevards and nineteenth century squares stood between the escarpments of the Acropolis and the Lycabettus; and around this central conglomerate a thousand featureless streets segmented to a German design stretched away until they deteriorated into rows of drab concrete boxes on the fringe of the plain.

It was in this sudden brilliance that Gene Vanbrugh walked back to his hotel. The Astoria in spite of its name was small and in a dark side street and rated B class. Gene had known the proprietor for years. As he entered the proprietor's wife said in an undertone: "Oh, M. Vanbrugh, there is someone waiting for you upstairs."

"Name?"

"She wouldn't give a name. But she said you had asked her to call."

"Where is she?"

"In the writing-room."

Gene took his key and turned away.

"And M. Vanbrugh, Paul told me to tell you . . ."

"Yes?"

The woman glanced round. "The police came while you were out, checking over our register. They said it was a routine call . . ."

"Yes?"

"But they asked for a description of foreign visitors. You are the only one. It is unusual for them to come like this. Paul said you should know."

"Thank you. How long have they been gone?"

"About an hour."

Thoughtfully Gene went up the stairs and into the writing-room. After the brightness outside there was nothing at first in the semi-darkness but dusty rexine furniture and the smell of mildew and moths. Then a foot scraped on the bare floor and a voice said in English:

"I have come to call on you, M. Vanbrugh."

"I'm glad you've been so prompt." He went to the window.

"Leave the shutters for just the present."

He could see her now, braceleted, head-scarved, sitting at the table in the centre of the room, her hand moving among the tattered dog-eared magazines like someone reading braille. "Well?"

"You have here the name of the man who killed my husband?"

"I didn't say that. I think I know the name of the man who drove the car."

"Tell me that."

Gene said: "What's the good of trying to revenge yourself on a paid nobody? I'm interested in the man your husband was interested in. Do you know who that was?"

She got up. "Gene Vanbrugh—is that your name?—let me tell you that today I am not a happy woman. I loved Juan. Does that mean anything to you? Yesterday I was—in amity, do you say?—a married woman, a successful dancer, known all over Europe, happy. You know. Today I am a widow. In losing Juan everything is lost.

Tonight I have no wish whether I live or die. It is so or it is so—well, who cares? For only one thing do I want to live—d'you understand?"

"Yes, I understand. But there are more ways——"

"Wait. You have understood that. Now understand this. You came upon me this morning saying you know much of this affair, *knowing* much, and saying you have the name of the murderer. What am I to think? Either you tell me that name or perhaps you are the murderer yourself."

In the narrow street outside, some children were playing, and their shrill excited voices echoed in the room.

Gene said: "Juan Tolosa must have known what he was doing. You're his wife. Why don't you?

"Well, I do not."

"Perhaps you know what he had to sell."

She hesitated. "He did not have it here. Was he such a fool? He left it safe in Spain."

He took out a cigarette and offered the packet to her. She shook her black-maned head and watched him break a match head and carry the flame to his own cigarette.

He said: "Does Philip Tolosa know you have come here tonight?"

"No."

"He didn't want you to have any contact with me."

"He thought you were a reporter."

"Perhaps he knows more than you do."

"Perhaps."

One of the children outside had hurt himself and was crying. Maria went across and wrenched open a shutter. Sunlight came in like a rich visitor slumming, falling on dusty leather and unfamiliar floor.

She said: "I will go, since you have nothing to tell me."

He said: "The man driving the car was probably a silversmith called Mandraki. There are only one or two such in Athens, since in the main Greeks like to fight their own battles. But he was there at the Little Jockey last night with a younger man I didn't know. He is not the night-club type. I thought it strange at the time."

"So?"

24

"But he's just a hired man, a go-between. Can you remember what sort of contacts your husband has had since you came?"

"He was out a lot."

"And Philip Tolosa?"

"Philip knows *nothing*. I have asked him."

"You say this thing you were trying to sell is still in Spain?"

She turned, hands thrust deep into the pockets of her scarlet mackintosh. "Juan was not born yesterday. What was the name you heard in Paris?"

"Avra."

She shook her head. "It means nothing. Who is he?"

"A man I have met. . . . What are you going to do now?"

She said: "I don't know how it is that you are interested in. this. Even if you are—what is the word?—level, what have you to gain?"

"It's a personal matter. But I want to help you. Shall you stay in Greece for some time?"

"I—don't know. The funeral is tomorrow. It will depend on Philip and the others. You know. Soon I shall go back to Spain."

"It would be better."

"Why?"

Gene put out his cigarette, screwing it slowly round. "I've already told you, Señora Tolosa, I think you may be in considerable danger yourself—and your brother-in-law."

"Ha!"

"If one accident can happen, another may do. Tell me, is it letters you have in Spain? Or a diary? Or photographs? What will you do with them when you get home—burn them?"

"Why should I trust you? You may be for the people who killed Juan."

"I don't think you believe that or you wouldn't have come here."

She stared at him, her face like a rock. "No, I don't think I believe that."

"Will you trust me?"

"I can't do that."

"Then will you come and see me again tomorrow? I think I can help you more than anyone else."

"There is only one thing I want, and that is the life of the man who killed Juan."

"First you have to be sure of his identity."

She said: "This man Mal—Mandraki should know."

"I doubt it. One like that only knows the next step above him."

She was silent, but even her silences were combative. The more he saw of her the more formidable he realised she was. She was hardwood: hammer a nail into her and the nail would bend.

As she went to the door he said: "You haven't told me what you came to tell mey have you?"

"I came to tell you nothing. I came to ask you what you don't know."

"If you want my help during the next few days, don't come here again. Go to the first newspaper kiosk in Constitution Square, in the north-east corner. Ask for Papa André. He will tell you where I am staying."

That appealed to her, not because she was a romantic and welcomed conspiracy but because it somehow convinced her that he was not on safe ground himself.

"Philip will wonder where I am."

"Don't trust him too far."

"Why do you say that?"

"A hunch."

After a moment she said: "I can trust only myself."

It was still daylight when she left. Through the blinds in his bedroom he watched her go off down the street. So far as he could tell nobody followed her.

He packed his grip and when dusk fell, paid his bill and left the hotel. He turned due south and was soon in the huddle of mean streets and tumbledown houses which mark the old Turkish quarter at the foot of the Acropolis. Unerring as a dog making for a buried bone, he pushed his way through the lanes of antique dealers, shoemakers, junk sellers, food stalls and second-hand clothes merchants; as the lights came on all this bazaar district was coming to life, people thronged, chattering, arguing, fingering the goods, elbowing each other out of the way. He got through the busiest part and turned into a narrow unpaved way with a gutter down the middle and wooden balconies nodding overhead. At the end of it he stopped and rapped at a door.

Somewhere near, hens were cackling sleepily. He knocked again. While he waited the floodlights were switched on for the Parthenon, and the great temple suddenly stood out like a prophecy above the noisy city.

A light came on and the door was opened by a middle-aged dark-skinned woman who frowned at him and pushed back her lank hair with nails as black-rimmed as a mourning envelope.

"You have accommodation?" he asked in Greek.

The woman made no reply but stepped aside to allow him in.

Chapter Six

The next morning Gene telephoned Mme Lindos.

"I've changed my address, Sophia. The Astoria couldn't keep me. My present place isn't on the phone, but I'll put a call through to you from time to time in case you are able to do anything in that matter we were talking about yesterday."

She said: "You are not in trouble already?"

"No, no, of course not."

"Angelos Vyro rang this morning. He seemed very taken with you and wanted me to be sure to confirm his invitation to you to the fiftieth anniversary of his paper next Tuesday."

"That's very kind of him. I hope I shall still be here."

Mme Lindos said: "I'm glad you have rung because by chance I have been able to arrange that meeting you desired."

"*Already?* But that's a miracle."

"No, just good fortune. Do you know the Comte de Trieste?"

"An Italian?"

"No. A Corfiote. Certain of the old families there cling to the Italian titles conferred on them long ago. He is taking a party to the gala performance of *Electra* tomorrow evening. Mlle Stonaris will be one of the party."

"And? . . ."

"You also will be one of the party."

"But dear Sophia, how have you fixed it?"

"De Trieste was once under an obligation to my husband. And one of his party is sick. You will go to his house at seven-thirty. He knows all that it is necessary to know."

"It is exactly what I wanted. Tell me one thing—is George Lascou to be one of the party?"

"No. It is a formal occasion. The King and Queen will be there. George Lascou will take his wife and sit with certain other members of the party."

"I can't thank you enough."

"Let me warn you that this may be no occasion for thanks. Promise me you will go carefully."

"I'll go carefully," said Gene.

Chapter Seven

I'll go carefully, he thought, until he saw her again. He noticed first her bare arm and hand as she put her glass down, and wondered in a detached way why he instantly knew it was hers. Something in the colour of the skin. Then he followed his host and saw again the eyes he had seen before, the lips like painted petals, the elegant fastidious nose. The diamonds round her throat weren't worth more than ten thousand pounds.

The Comte de Trieste said, speaking English for his benefit: "Allow me to introduce M. Vanbrugh to you. Mlle Stonaris. M. Taksim. General Telechos. Mr. Vanbrugh is visiting us from Paris."

M. Taksim was a cotton millionaire from Istanbul, big and middle-aged and fair. General Telechos was older with a face pitted like a map of the moon. Gene remembered he had served under Metaxas.

Telechos said: "This is your first visit to Athens, sir?"

"No, I've been here before," said Gene, using more accent than normal, "but it's all quite a while ago, shortly after the war."

"Ah, yes, you would be here like many of your countrymen. Helping us to our feet again. Rehabilitate, is it; your American Mission. You like Athens, then, to return?"

"The air suits me. It has a kind of harsh clarity. There are no illusions in Greece, are there?" He turned to the girl. "Are there, mademoiselle?"

Her expression as she looked across the room was polite but uninterested. "I should have thought many."

"Maybe a foreigner is entitled to sentimentalise."

"It's a common mistake."

"But excusable?"

"If you're looking for excuses." She opened her bag. He said: "Please smoke one of mine."

"Thank you, no. I don't very much like the tobacco from Virginia."

"Or the people either?"

"Are you from Virginia?"

"Quite near—as those kind of distances go."

"Then it would be polite to say only the tobacco."

"But not polite after that question."

She looked at him then with her great dark eyes before lowering them to fit her cigarette into its amber holder. After a few moments, as she was about to move off, he spoke to her again.

"We've met somewhere before, surely?"

"I don't think so. What was your name?"

"Vanbrugh."

"Oh. No. Have you been in Athens long?"

"This time a few days only. It's quite something to be back again."

"Quite something," said M. Taksim. "Quite something? Is that English? It's also many years since I am in London."

"They don't say that in London," said Anya Stonaris. "It is what they say in Virginia."

"We grow phrases with the tobacco," said Gene. "Rotation crop."

"I am afraid," said the Turk, "this is an argot, is it not? I was in London three years and it is there also. The Cockerney. Very difficult."

"You understand the language well," Gene told the girl.

"I learned it in a hard school. Maurice, don't you think——"

"What school was that?"

"For a year I helped at a canteen, after the liberation."

"You must have been very young."

"Well," she said, "not old enough to know better."

The party was getting ready to move off. There were ten of them—all the women superbly dressed. Gene might have felt conspicuous in his hired suit if it had been his nature to care. He had heard of one or two of the others before: a Yugo-Slav ballerina called Gallanova; a French marquis visiting the city; a Greek tobacco king.

Gene found himself sharing a car with Anya and the Turk and the wife of the tobacco king. While he was making casual conversation with the girl, while he was taking in everything about her, her cool challenging indifference towards him, he was also listening to the conversation in Greek between the other two in the car.

"If the Government had resigned in a normal way without attempting to change its colours . . ."

"But why did Karamanlis dissolve the Greek Rally? It is playing into the hands of the extremists."

"Or the new Centre. EMO prospers. Ask Anya."

"Some say the Army is restive. General Telechos no doubt could say if he would."

"Is he back in favour?"

"Oh, very much so. Anya, Telechos is very much in favour with the Army again, isn't he? It is spoken of everywhere."

"My dear Maurice, I only know he is very much in favour with me, because he sent me orchids yesterday."

The Turk laughed. "Your innocence deceives no one. What does George think of it all?"

"You'd be shocked to know how little he confides in me."

They were approaching the theatre. As they drew into the queue of cars waiting to give off their occupants, they could see the crowds of sightseers at the entrance to the theatre.

Taksim said to Gene: "I think, monsieur, you will be bored tonight. A Greek tragedy, in the language of Greece—could anything be duller for you?"

"I've a kind of family interest in it," he said. "My grandmother's name was Electra."

Anya glanced at him then. "Was she Greek?"

"Yes. Electra Theroudakis. She went to the States when she was twenty-two."

"And never came back?"

"No."

"What a calamity."

They drew up at the door of the theatre. "Perhaps you speak Greek, then?"

He shrugged deprecatingly. "Just a smattering."

They went in. The Comte de Trieste had followed his briefing admirably, and Gene found himself between Mlle Stonaris and Mrs. Tobacco King. They were in the eighth row of the stalls and the theatre was blooming with the flower of Athenian society. Programmes fluttered, arms and shoulders gleamed, jewels and orders winked. There was a hum like bees on a lazy afternoon. Most of the ex-Government and the diplomatic corps was there. He saw the girl glint a smile across at one of the boxes, where a dark very pale man sat beside a plump woman whose attention just then was on the two young children behind her. George Lascou in his role of family man and representative of the people.

Then everyone stood and the National Anthem was played as Royalty came into the opposite box. After it was over there was some applause before the audience rippled back into its seats and the lights were lowered for the play to begin.

In the first entr'acte Gene said to the girl: "She's a fine actress but I've seen others I've liked better. For one thing, she's too old for the part."

"Electra has to be at least fifteen years older than Orestes. Would you prefer Marilyn Monroe?"

At least he'd got his reaction. "Have you been to the scene of the crime?"

"Mycenae? Of course."

"The most impressive thing in all Greece."

"After Delphi."

"I've not been there. But I shall be going next week. You know of Michael Michaelis."

"Who doesn't?"

"My firm publishes him in America. He lives near Delphi, and I have to see him there."

"I envy you the experience."

"You're interested in archaeology, aren't you?"

They moved through the crowd of people. "Who told you that?"

"There was a paragraph in the paper a couple of days ago."

"I know nothing whatever about archaeology; but through a friend I'm able to take an interest in some diggings at Sounion. That was what you read of?"

"Yes."

"In a *Greek* newspaper?"

"Well, I guess I can pick out the words if I go slow."

"I guess you can follow everything that's been said on the stage tonight."

"Tell me, do you know everyone in this foyer?"

"No. They're always changing the door-keeper."

A brief smile broke across his deeply preoccupied face. "Who is the man talking over there?"

"The Mayor of Athens. He is leading a party at the election. Were you in the Army during the war?"

"Kind of. You would be too young to remember it."

"I was nine when the Germans invaded us. I have the most vivid recollections of it all."

"You were in Athens right through?"

"Yes. Where did your grandmother come from?"

"Kifissia."

"She was rich?"

"No. Nor was my grandfather when he came over here and met her and married her."

"Could she have been happy in America?"

"It's not impossible, you know."

"I suppose not quite."

"Anyway, she left me a legacy."

'A legacy?"

"Not of money but of blood. Who is that going up the steps now?"

"George Lascou. He leads the EMO party at the election."

"Anyone here who isn't leading a party?"

"Personalities count in Greece. Perhaps you don't understand our politics."

"I'm always glad to learn."

"It is time we were going back."

At the second entr'acte she said: "Thank you, no, I'll sit here."

"Then I'll stay too—if I'm not in your light."

General Telechos on the other side had not gone out either, and for a while he took her attention. It left Gene free to watch her quietly and to collect his thoughts. She was as hard as nails, he could see that. Her brain was as sharp and as cutting as the diamonds round her beautiful throat. And it *was* beautiful. She might be a *femme fatale* but at least if you were fool enough not to care about the danger it would come awfully easy being one of her fatalities. Her eyes weren't black, they were brown but made darker by their lashes, they had a sort of fronded brilliance which was quite devastating.

As he thought this she turned her head suddenly and met his look. They stared at each other then for several seconds.

She said: "Why are you looking at me like that?"

"I remember where I've seen you before."

"That must be very gratifying for you."

"At the Little Jockey on Monday."

"You were there?"

"I was there."

"Now I remember you. You were sitting two tables away from us. Do you like cheap night-club women?"

"They're terrific."

Her eyes didn't move for a second longer, they seemed to deepen with an expression they did not or could not hold, then a flicker of the lashes and they had moved beyond him.

But it was as if they had looked at each other just too long. Some inner content of the look—though it was over—superimposed itself on what they were saying.

"Well, if you do not like cheap night-club women, why do you sit with them?"

"You know how it is when a man goes to a place like that alone—all the girls run away."

"Then why go alone?"

"To see the show."

"You are interested in dancing?"

"I'm interested in dancers. Did you know that the Spaniard, Juan Tolosa, was killed in an accident the following day?"

"I read it in the papers."

The others were coming back. General Telechos spoke to Anya again. George Lascou was re-entering his box. He stared down at the stalls before he took his seat. Gene stood up to let some of the party past. The whole glittering company was moving and murmuring about them.

He said: "Does it strike you—being Greek—as much as it does an outsider, that the first night of this play—first day of this play—when it was first performed two and a half thousand years ago, was on a site probably not a mile from where we're sitting? Or is it left for the foreigner to get sentimental and excited about it for the wrong reasons?—as you implied when we first met."

"Some Greeks think about it."

"It's hard to imagine what that first performance ever would be like—probably connected with some Dionysian festival—people squatting round with their baskets, seeing it – on a dais against a plain backcloth. The author would be here, even though he was getting up in years; but what would his critical audience be? Euripides probably, come to see this new work by his great rival. Aristophanes too? Socrates would be here. Pericles, maybe, if he could spare the time from questions of high policy. No, I think Pericles would just have died by then. Plato may have been brought by his mother and father. And Democritus, who first put forward the atomic theory. . . . And that at a time when my ancestors—or most of them—were crouching over smoky fires in damp northern caves."

She looked at him. "We have gone down the hill ourselves since then."

"I shouldn't let that depress you."

"It doesn't. Go on."

He said: "My speculations haven't run any further. Except to wonder if you'll lunch with me one day this week?"

Her expression suggested she'd had fifty such invitations before, all put in just that way.

"Thank you, but I think I shall be busy at present. How long will you be staying in Athens?"

"Not as long as that."

She opened her programme again. "Tomorrow afternoon I shall be driving to Sounion. If you have not seen it . . ."

"I have not seen it."

"Then perhaps you would care to come." It was a statement, not a question.

"Thank you. I'd very much care to come."

Chapter Eight

She was in bed when the phone rang.

"Anya?" Lascou said.

"Yes, darling. Did you enjoy the performance?"

"Good enough in its way. The evening was a social success."

She said: "Did you get to talk to him?"

"To them both for three or four minutes. It was a good *occasion*, before the fight begins. And you?"

"The usual crowd, as you saw. I think Solaris stole the play."

"Otho told me you rang me about twenty minutes ago."

"Yes. You weren't back. I have a little news that may entertain you."

"Oh?"

"Oh, I mustn't forget. General Telechos paid you one or two agreeable compliments. I think he is ready to make a deal."

Lascou listened to the compliments. "Good. And your news?"

"Did you see the man sitting beside me?"

"On your other side? Yes. I didn't know him."

"Klaus was ill, Leon de Trieste invited this man in his place. An American called Vanbrugh."

"Ah. . . ."

"Did you say something?"

"Just ah."

"That's what I thought you said. A coincidence after your telling me about him the other day."

"If it was a coincidence."

"I was wondering; but I should think so . . . I asked Leon about him afterwards and he said he met him first some years ago."

"What is he like?"

"So-so. More grown up than one expects. You haven't told me exactly what you've got against him."

"I tried to."

"Oh, pooh, some fracas in Piraeus five years ago. That's an old wives' tale."

"Not altogether."

"But you were not involved in some fracas in Piraeus five years ago."

"Of course not. He's really nothing to me. As you gather, I never saw him until tonight."

"But you are interested in him."

"So are the police."

"What do they want him for?"

"Some irregularity over his passport, I expect."

She laughed gently. "Couldn't we be more original than that?"

"No, seriously. . . . He's a trouble-maker and always will be. To get rid of him is a simple insurance at a time like this."

"Well, if you won't tell me you won't. Perhaps I shall discover for myself tomorrow."

"You're seeing him again? It might be of use."

"That's why I made the arrangement."

"Find out where he is staying, for one thing."

"Apparently he's a publisher or represents a publisher. Did you know that? He also speaks Greek and reads Greek; I'm not sure how well. He has lived in Paris for the last three years. His firm publishes Michael Michaelis. He knows quite a lot of people here; but he doesn't seem anxious to be recognised. Two or three times in the foyer tonight he changed his direction to avoid people, including his own ambassador."

"It shows he's up to no good."

"Even that doesn't make him attractive."

"Go on."

"By the way, did you know the chief dancer at the Little Jockey had been killed in a street accident?"

"No. One of those you saw?"

"The chief male dancer. I wonder why this Gene Vanbrugh was at the club the same night as I was."

"When was the fellow killed?"

"The following day."

"Find out as much as possible when you meet Vanbrugh."

"I'll listen carefully to everything he has to say."

"And of course," added Lascou, "he will say so much more to you."

Chapter Nine

They met as arranged outside the King George at three. There was still no great heat although the sun was brilliant. It fell on a square strangely silent after the abounding life of two hours ago.

She was sitting in a grey Silver Phantom Rolls. A chauffeur was standing beside the car, but when Gene came up he stepped respectfully back and opened the door. As Gene got in she looked at him thoughtfully but did not smile. She'd done her hair in a different way and was wearing Chinese jade ear-rings and a frock of grey jersey.

He said: "You should have warned me."

"What of?"

"If I'd known we were travelling the hard way I'd have put on battle dress."

She lifted a half-ironical eyebrow and started the engine. The chauffeur stood back and saluted as the car turned off into Venizelou Street. It was not until they had gone some way that Gene spoke again.

"You must be very rich."

"Why don't you talk Greek?"

"You must be very rich," he said in Greek.

"Scarcely any accent. It is as if——"

"As if I came from one of the neighbouring νομοι. Never from the one I'm in."

"How do you speak so well? You have relatives still here?"

"Nobody here."

"You are staying with friends in Athens?"

"No, I have rooms."

She waited but he said no more. They left the suburbs of Athens and skirted the barren eminences of Hymettus, travelling fast through olive groves and vineyards. Once they were out of the town there was practically no traffic except for the occasional farm cart piled high and drawn by donkey or mule moving ponderously on businesses known only to the black-dressed, black-scarved peasant woman between the shafts. An occasional village street saw them by, inevitable café, inevitable yellow mongrels, tiny Byzantine church, eucalyptus trees, tattered buildings, black-clad idlers staring.

He said: "Tell me about these excavations."

"You will see them for yourself."

"The paper said you were closely superintending the work."

"That's because it was a paper which favours the people I am friendly with. I act in this for my friend, who is too busy to come down."

"Tell me what you have found."

She said: "Tell me why you went to the Little Jockey on Monday."

He stared out at the road with his grave, craggy, withdrawn face. "Why not?"

"Why did you say at the play that Juan Tolosa had been killed in an accident the following day?—putting on an emphasis as if you didn't believe it was any such thing."

"Did I? No. . . . But it's a little strange, isn't it, that the car which killed him was badly damaged but hasn't yet been found."

"Who told you that?"

"I went along to the police inquiry this morning."

"It was interesting?"

"His widow said the car mounted the side-walk and deliberately crushed him against a house."

"She must have been hysterical."

"Quite hysterical."

She glanced at him. "You don't think so?"

"The police did. That's all that matters, isn't it?"

As they came near Lavrion the green fields and vineyards gave place to old mine machinery, grey heaps of slag and rusty iron derricks. Then they were through the area of the silver mines and the brilliant sun lit up the low cliffs and ultramarine sea of Cape Sounion, with the white temple of Poseidon like a tall nun brooding on a hill. The girl drove up to the Acropolis and stopped the engine. They got out.

He said: "When I was a student we used to come here at the week-ends to bathe."

"You said last night you had not been before."

"I've not been before with you."

He stood by the car for a while looking about him, and she glanced once or twice at his face.

He said: "Fruitful study of aesthetics as well as of ancient history."

"Why?"

"Where does the impact come from? Thirteen pillars. Half a dozen rectangles of fluted marble with the sea as a drop curtain. If you analyse it, it's nothing."

She said: "A rag and a bone and a hank of hair."

He turned. "*Exactly.*" Then his eyes focused on her. "Except that there's a physical as well as an aesthetic element in a woman's beauty."

She didn't seem put out by his stare. "What is physical?" she said. "Where does it become only emotional? And what is emotional? Where does it become only aesthetic? I don't think you can separate them."

"Well," he said, "let's say the difference with marble pillars is that there's no wish for personal possession."

A sea breeze was stirring her hair and she put up a hand to it. "Personal possession is always unwise. What you grasp you destroy. Taste your pleasures and let them go."

He said: "I'm glad you agree with tasting them."

"I'm glad you are glad."

After a few moments he said: "Where are your excavations?"

"Down there, down nearer the sea. Last year a great statue was found here, of a warrior. They think it is of the seventh century B.C. and they think there is more yet to be found. There was of course a temple here long before this one was built."

"Can we go down?"

"The siesta will not be over."

The promontory of Cape Colonna slopes down on its western side into a sandy bay, and they walked to it through pine trees where the ground was littered with the shells of hard-boiled eggs left behind by week-end picnickers. Near the sea just where rock and soil and sand met, there was the usual paraphernalia of archaeology: trenches, rubble, and beside it a disused 'tourist pavilion' in the shade of which a dozen Greek labourers crouched and slept.

"Here we began, you see, and here the statue was found. The head with its great helmet was broken from the body and the body was naked. But they fitted together. It couldn't have been broken naturally or they would not have been so far apart."

He said: "You must be rich to have financed these diggings."

"I didn't finance them—I told you. I have rich friends. It is the way we live in Greece."

An elderly man came forward, hastily fastening his tie, and was introduced to Gene. He and the girl talked for some time on the progress of the operations. They stayed about half an hour. When they were alone again Gene said: "Have you any of the things that have been found here?"

"The big things, like the statue, are in the National Museum, but I have a few of the smaller articles in my flat."

"I'd like to see them sometime."

They stopped, looking out to sea. The rocks showed copper and purple and green through the glass-clear water. A lip of white, inches wide, nibbled at the edge. Gene lingered on when she would have moved.

She said: "Is it true that you really have some affection for Greece?"

"Yes ..."

"I mean true affection, not just empty sentiment."

"Yes ... But I don't think I like your politicians."

"Do you like your own?"

"Maybe they're not the most admirable people in any country."

"Well, they are no worse here."

"This morning I was hearing about that man you pointed out to me last night. Lascou, was it? Someone I met this morning said that Lascou was the most dangerous man in Greece today."

She opened her green lizard hand-bag. "Have you a light, please? I haven't smoked this afternoon."

"A match. We'd have to get in the shelter of the trees . . ."

They walked across to the pines. He flicked a match alight and held it to her cigarette. When he got close to her—a few inches from her face, he thought, yes, there really is danger. Her skin at close quarters had a faint luminosity. Nonsense, of course; so one's senses played one false. A rag and a bone and a hank of hair. A rag and a bone. . . . It was her own estimate.

She said contemptuously: "When an election is due one man will say anything about another in the hope that it will win him a vote."

"And this is untrue?"

"You have told me nothing; how can I say what is true or untrue?"

"My friend, who is I think an intelligent man, said that there are plenty of hypocrites in the world who try to deceive others. George Lascou, he says, is that much more dangerous type, a hypocrite with visions of greatness who begins by deceiving himself."

She looked down at her cigarette. "Your friend no doubt is of an opposing party. Did he not also tell you I was George Lascou's mistress? You surely must know that too."

Four or five ragged boys had been staring at the car, hanging on the handles, feeling the polished wings; at the sound of footsteps they scattered and ran off down the cindery track.

Gene said: "I knew he was a man of infinite taste."

She opened the door of the car. "It is time we started back."

"Whenever you say."

She got in and flicked the steering wheel once or twice with her green velvet gloves while he shut the door and walked round and slid into the seat beside her. She started the engine and drove off the way they had come. Behind them the sun was getting lower and the delicate tapering pillars of the temple seemed to support the sky.

He said in Greek: "I owe you an apology."

"That must have needed a lot of hard reasoning on your part, Mr. Vanbrugh."

"I wonder if you could bring yourself to call me Gene?"

"I thought that it was a girl's name."

"Not the way I spell it."

They drove on.

She said: "Perhaps sometime you would be interested to meet this hypocrite, this shady politician."

"I'd be delighted."

"Write down your address. I can arrange it."

"Could I call you? I'm changing rooms and haven't yet decided where to stay."

"Well, where will you be tonight?"

"Out on my ear, I expect, if I don't get back. I promised to vacate my room by five, and have forgotten to pack my case."

She didn't press any more, and silence fell again. He thought; a rag and a bone, a rag and a bone; stick to that; hold on to it for dear life. Plenty of women before but only two like this and both brought shipwreck. How often does the sailor put to sea? Not now; for Pete's sake certainly not now, knowing who she is and already something of what she's like, and who her friends. You don't have to be an optimist, you have to be a lunatic to set sail when all the storm cones are hoisted.

She said: "What have Greek politics to do with you?"

"If I explained that it would take a time."

"I could listen."

"You can't avoid it, can you? Sharing a car with a bore is one of the worst things. There's no escape except the end of the journey."

"Well, you could try not to be boring."

After a minute he said: "It isn't all that easy to explain. You asked me if I was fond of Greece. But it isn't really a question of liking or disliking the country; it's a question of having it in my *blood*. I told you last night, but I don't know if you understood."

46

"No, I don't think I did."

"When people are born in a place they normally accept it as part of their inheritance; they take it for granted; they're all of a piece. I'm sure you are—in that respect anyway. You're Greek, and Greece comes first and the rest nowhere."

"Maybe."

"I'm American. Many Americans are 'all of a piece'. But some are not. America's a young country—its roots go often into other people's soil. Mine do . . . Make no mistake, America's my native country and I wouldn't change it for any other on earth. Just the smell of it the minute you get in takes and holds you like a new experience, however often you return. I enjoy going there. My family and my friends are there." He paused. "Do you mind if I stop talking Greek?"

"No. I don't mind."

"But when I'm in the States, however hard I try, I feel myself there as a *visitor*. I'm a soldier on leave, a commuter, a dog on a chain. And the stake the chain's attached to is right here in Athens. Maybe I'm some sort of a throw-back, who knows, it can't always work the other way. For every hundred Europeans who go to America, maybe three or four—of them or their children or their children's children—travel the other way. I never thought I'd be one."

"And are you?"

"I'm trying to explain. You asked me why I care about Greece and what is happening here. I'm trying to explain because I want you to know."

He glanced at her. She was listening with a vigorous intelligence that went much deeper than good looks. It might be hostile but it was not sham.

"But don't think I have any glamorised view of your country, Anya. In spite of its history and in spite of all the glitter of Athens that makes it look like a carbon copy of Manhattan, I know the other side all too well. I know it's badly governed, poverty-stricken, unenterprising; part East, part West with a dash of the Balkans shaken in to make it more difficult."

"You're too kind."

"But that may be one one reason why I can't get it out of my system. I want to do things about it, just as I would for a lame child that's always falling in the mud. I'm never as content as when I'm here, never as much at home, never as conscious of a *root*. I tell myself it's nonsense, this preoccupation, a sort of blinkered self-hypnotism; I've got to stop it. At most I'm only one-quarter rooted here. My life's to do with the new world, not with the old. But it doesn't wash. I'm still the dog on the chain."

There was silence for a time. He said: "Maybe even that isn't quite the truth. One's got to be honest sometimes in one's life, and if I'm honest now I have to say I don't really *want* to change. I only tell myself I should. Deep down in my guts—or whatever intestinal part knows best—I *welcome* the chain."

She stubbed her cigarette in an ash-tray and frowned at the road ahead. "You have thought a lot about this?"

"Yes. I've thought a lot about it."

"And this explains why you are interested in the private lives of politicians?"

"It explains why I bother to come here at all."

They were getting nearer home. She said; "Are you married?"

"Not now."

"In America it is always 'yes, just' or 'not now'."

"And you?" he said quietly.

"No. I've told you."

"I didn't know it necessarily followed."

"In my case it does."

"Tell me more about it."

"There's nothing to tell."

After waiting a few seconds Gene said: "Talking of my business, I shall be going to see Michael Michaelis on Sunday. Would you be interested to come?"

"Where—to Delphi?"

"Yes. I shall not be more than an hour with Michael is and there'll be nothing private to discuss. I'd like to see the place afterwards in the company of a kindred spirit."

"What makes you think I'm a kindred spirit?"

"I think you could be."

She said: "You must have plucked that impression out of the air."

"I'm assuming only that the experience of visiting one of the great Greek monuments for the first time would be enlarged if it was shared with somebody who feels the way you do about it."

She took her attention off the road for rather longer than was safe to look at him with her great dark eyes.

"I shall be engaged on Sunday," she said.

"A pity. I can't change the day now."

Chapter Ten

After dropping Gene she did not drive to her flat but went straight on to Constitution Square and left the car to be picked up by the chauffeur. Then she walked across to George Lascou's flat, which was in the penthouse or seventh floor of Heracles House, a large block put up since the war by a Greek syndicate of which Lascou was the chairman.

As it happened his secretary saw Anya come into the building, so she was met at the door and brought at once into the huge salon, which was decorated and furnished in French style with fleur-de-lis wallpaper and handsome statuary set in rounded alcoves indirectly lit from below.

She found George saying good-bye to General Telechos. George looked moody and pale as if virtue had gone out of him, his black brilliantined hair veeing up at the temples rather untidily, though still showing the lines of the comb. Telechos breathed raki and garlic over her as he explained rather unnecessarily that he had called on business to do with the National Museum.

When Otho had shown the soldier out George took her face between his fingers like a goblet to be admired before it was drunk from. Then he kissed her with all the appreciation of a connoisseur.

"So?"

"Darling, I need a drink."

"Of course." He released her quietly and went to a side table. "A martini?"

She nodded and walked to the window, pulling off her gloves and looked out on the crowds below.

She said: "Receiving compliments from General Telechos is like being caressed by a steam shovel. Does he think I am quite ignorant of all the negotiations that are going on between you?"

"Telechos thinks women have no part in these things."

"Does it go well?"

"It goes well. But he has all the cunning of the slightly stupid man, and all the obstinacy."

"Is that why your hair is ruffled?"

"Is it?" He smoothed it down. "It dislikes opposition. And Vanbrugh?"

"I didn't discover his address."

George carefully measured out the gin, touching the lip of the bottle with a napkin so that it would not drip.

She said: "He asked to be put down at the corner of Hirodou Atticou. I don't know if he thought he was likely to be followed."

"Does he know of your connection with me?"

"I told him because I saw he knew." She took her glass and sipped. "Um. Good. . . . He said he would like to meet you."

"That might be worth while." Lascou guided her towards a chair, but at the last moment she slipped away from him and went across to an almost life-size statue of Hermes, looked at it, her eyebrows contracted.

He said: "Are you seeing him again?"

"Who? Vanbrugh? I hope not. He is dull, if probably harmless."

"He may be the first, but his record doesn't suggest the second."

"His record?"

"Oh, I mean his history in a general sense. He's been in and out of trouble a good deal."

"Well, tell me."

"It's not important." George felt in his pocket and took out a typewritten card with a small photograph clipped to the corner. "This comes partly from Major Kolono's own police files and partly from a contact he has at the American Embassy. But it's incomplete yet."

Anya took the card and after staring at the photograph began to read aloud. " 'Gene Vanbrugh. About thirty-five. Comes of old New York family but educated in Europe. At University of Athens when the Germans invaded Greece—fought against them. Probably was in British Intelligence for some years. In any event was in Athens, underground, until liberation.' Mm—mm." She went on reading to herself; after a moment she spoke again. " 'Concerned in both civil wars against ELAS. In '47 badly wounded and invalided home. In States gave evidence to Senate Committee on Foreign Aid.' "

She paused to sip her drink and to turn the card over. " 'Married in Washington but marriage broke up.' Yes, he told me that today. . . . Oh, this is what you were talking about. 'In Greece in '51 . . .' "

"Yes."

" 'involved in death of Spyros Eliopolis, ship's chandler, of Piraeus. This hushed up.' Why was it hushed up? It doesn't say. Kolono ought to know."

"It didn't come under Kolono's department. Anyway, outside influences were at work. Vanbrugh has friends."

She turned back to the card and read in silence. Then: " 'In trouble in U.S. in '53 . . . cited for contempt of Congress for refusing to give information on Communists to the House Committee on un-American Activities.' I don't know what that means. I thought he was anti-Communist."

George put his arm round her shoulders. "I think it simply means, my sweet, that he is a man who prides himself on taking the unpopular line and because of that is always rather an embarrassment to his friends as well as to his enemies. If his own embassy knew he was here, which they probably don't unless Kolono has told them, they wouldn't be sorry to see him go."

She handed him back the card. "Tell me, why were you so angry when you knew Jon Manos had taken me to the Little Jockey last Monday?"

"I wasn't *angry*. . . . Did Vanbrugh mention it?"

"He mentioned the inquiry on the Spanish dancer's death. He had been to it this morning. The wife thought the accident wasn't an accident."

"Does that concern us?"

"You are the one who knows."

"Or Gene Vanbrugh."

"I didn't say so."

"How are the diggings?"

"We're between strata." She stared at the statue. "I don't think this Hermes is very good, George. His legs are too short for the length of his body. I distrust men with short thigh bones. . . ."

"I'm sorry you've had a boring afternoon."

She said: "Do you *want* me to see him again?"

He fitted his pince-nez. "Have you made any arrangement at all?"

"No. I said he might phone me."

"I hope he hasn't made an impresssion on you."

She had finished her drink and held the stem of the glass in both hands. He put his fingers on the nape of her neck under her hair and quietly stroked it. She said: "Of course he has made an impression on me. So does a headache. So does a pinching shoe. Otherwise one would be as dead as Hermes here. Why is sincerity always so tedious?"

He smiled. "It isn't. But it's a plant that needs careful treatment. You have to bring it out regularly and air it alongside other men's so that it doesn't become bigoted and ingrown."

There was the sound of running feet and a small boy of eight burst in.

"Papa, Nina has not been playing fair with me! She says if I—oh, Anya, Papa didn't tell me you were coming—Papa, Nina says——"

"He didn't know." Anya kissed the boy. "Where's Nina? What have you been playing?"

Michael explained to them both in a breathless voice.

Lascou said: "Fair play, Michael, like sincerity, is a matter of proportion. Anya and I were talking of it when you came in."

Michael stared at them with round black eyes, eyes very different in colour and shape from his father's.

"And you were quarrelling?"

George laughed. "No."

"Ah," said Michael.

"Well, what do you expect us to do, pursue Nina and beat her? Where is she, by the way?"

"Gone to find Mama. But I happen to know Mama's out."

Helen Lascou occupied a suite of rooms on the other side of the seventh floor; the children lived with her but unlike the adults trafficked freely between the two flats. Michael was pacified and went off chewing a piece of Turkish delight.

George said: "I find it difficult not to spoil him."

"Should you try?"

"Well, in some ways it's a disadvantage to be a millionaire's son."

"My heart bleeds for him."

"Oh, yes, you can use your tongue, but there *are* disadvantages. Everyone treats Michael with consideration and respect—already. He'll grow up accustomed to it."

"So he should, a son of yours."

"Oh, no doubt. And that's good as far as it goes. But he'll never know what it is to be cold and hungry and in rags, to be disregarded, to be left to struggle, to know himself to be *nothing*, rubbish that could die off and no one would care." He paused. "It's unpleasant at the time, of course, but it develops the *will* to struggle as nothing else can. It becomes a load upon the ego, an obligation that must be discharged. . . ."

"An obligation to whom?"

He shrugged. "To oneself, I suppose. One goes through phases." He moved the ring on his finger as if it chafed him. "At first one wants to *belong*, one's greatest need is to be accepted as part of a larger part, a necessary unit within a community or an army or a party, a cog serving a greater end than oneself. Then, as one develops and succeeds, one's desire is for the opposite, for non-attachment again, for a withdrawal, away from and above the mass of people. It's a passing through, as it were—from the stage of being disregarded by the crowd to a stage when the crowd is disregarded."

She nodded but did not speak.

"Oh!" He swept the thought away with a hand. "It's not

important. Except that no one who has not felt poverty, extreme poverty, can ever understand the inexpressible luxury of luxury. No one who has not grown up in a wind-swept, arid, treeless, soil-less village in the hills, sunbaked in summer, snow-smothered in winter—no one who has not had to apportion his last fifty drachmae between goat's cheese and maize bread and the corner of a draughty shed to lie in . . ."

She said: "You show so little, it might never have happened to you."

"I don't show it but I have it here." He touched his body. "It's what I was saying, it's the thing Michael will lack. I wouldn't be without it now. It's the dynamo powering everything—it's the source of self-control, caution, courage, perseverance, obstinacy—any creative efforts I may make; it's the source of all the things I do to supply an inescapable need!"

She said quietly: "And will you ever satisfy it?"

"No. . . . But in a few weeks I may be nearer that end. Another drink?"

"No, Helen may be coming in."

"Little fear of that."

"I still must go. To tell the truth, George, the only time I'm ever embarrassed is when Nina or Michael come when I'm here"

"No need to be. They both like you."

"Perhaps soon they'll grow up."

"Nonsense. You're full of strange fancies today. It must be this naive company you've been keeping."

They walked slowly towards the door. She said: "Has it occurred to you, though, that Helen has played fair with me over the children? It would have been easy to have turned them against me."

"I've never denied to you that she's an estimable woman."

"So many women contrive to be estimable without being kind."

"Darling, when is he phoning you again?"

"Who? Gene Vanbrugh?"

"Yes."

"Tomorrow morning."

"What will you say?"

"I shall say nothing. I shall be out."

"Don't do that. Invite him here."

Chapter Eleven

When he rang her she said: "I'm sorry. The roads to Delphi are not good and it is 170 kilometres. Too far for one day—if you are to see your poet and also all that is there—and certainly I cannot spare two."

He said: "You were very kind yesterday."

"That's another of those illusions you suffer from."

"I thought you said you would like to meet Michaelis."

"On the whole I've decided it is better just to know him through his poems."

"Then when could I call and see you today?"

"I shall be out all day."

"With George Lascou?"

"Does it matter?"

"How could it?"

She passed the tip of her tongue over her lips. "My friend, if you would be advised by me, I think you would be a happier man if you confined you interests to your publishing."

"I've always found happiness rather an abstract thing to worry about."

She picked up her cigarette-case and opened it and took out a cigarette, but then she put it down without lighting it and snapped the case shut. On the back of the case were some words George had had engraved when he gave it to her. Ἐκ τοῦ ὁρᾶν γίγνεται τὸ ἐρᾶν.

"Hullo," he said.

"Hullo."

"I thought for a moment you had hung up."

"No."

"I would like to see you again."

"Perhaps sometime we can arrange it."

"There are some things I'd like to say to you."

"Well, I am listening."

"Don't be impossible, please."

Her Italian maid, Edda, came into the room with some red roses in a bowl and put them on the piano. She was going to say something but Anya nodded and dismissed her.

Gene said: "I shall be here probably for another week, and . . ."

"And there are some things you would like to say to me."

"As you remark."

She said: "You still want to meet George Lascou?"

There was a brief pause. "Yes, I do."

"Then come there tonight. He is giving a small dinner party—eight or ten. I can arrange it."

"You can arrange it. . . ."

"Does that surprise you?"

"No. . . ."

"Then you will come?"

"Thank you. I'll come."

"At nine. Heracles House, the seventh floor."

"What will George Lascou say?"

"He'll do what I ask."

"I don't wonder."

"Then will you do what I ask?"

"What do you ask?"

"Stop sending me red roses."

"It's just a simple whim I have."

"If you wish to be a fool I cannot be responsible for that."

"Why should you be?"

"No. I should not be."

"Or why should you care?"

"I don't."

"Neither do I," he agreed.

When she had put back the receiver she got up from her chair and walked across to the window. Sunshine fell diagonally through it and warmed her arm and side. She turned away, frowning, and moved to the bookshelf, putting back two books she had taken out, went to the chair, picked us the daily newspaper. Edda was in the bathroom running her bath water. She lit a cigarette and stood for a few moments motionless with the cigarette case in her hand. George's inscription made a roughness under her thumb. "*From seeing comes loving.*"

Chapter Twelve

The Tower of the Winds, an octagonal building put up in the first century B.C. by Cyrrhestes, was losing its sharp outlines in the quick Athenian twilight when Gene came to it, walking like a mean-natured cat expecting trouble. He was about to make a cautious circuit of the place when a woman broke away from one of the ruined Doric pillars and came to him. A vivid scarf over her hair was like a badge of identity.

"Ah," he said, taking off his hat. "You're alone?"

"Yes. This morning I left the message."

"All this week I've been hoping you'd send word."

She said: "I saw you at the police inquiry. Also Philip tells me you have been trying twice to make his acquaintance."

"He wouldn't play."

"He thinks you are a reporter."

"I doubt if he ever did believe that."

Maria looked at him. "You suspect him of not being fair with me?"

"What have you came to tell me?"

"Something it may be very necessary to tell you if that is true."

"Will you come back to my lodgings?"

"No. It is safe here. I—I don't know how it is to begin." Her thick lips, made for laughter, were pouting and strained. "You know that Juan was trying to—make money?"

"Yes."

"I am not quite so ignorant of it as I pretended. You know. If a man and a woman are in love, as we were, they do not have complete secrets. But it is true that I do not know much. He said it is better that I did not know much. I do not know what Juan had to sell. But I know of the—arrangements. He was crazy to paint; he didn't wish for the life of a cabaret artist; he loved Spain and wished to settle in comfort in a small fishing village in Andalusia and spend the rest of his life there. You know. That was why he did this thing. I told him often in the last weeks, go carefully; it is better to work for one's living in honour than to go to prison for a dishonourable thing. But he would not listen. He would say, this is my one chance; if I miss this one chance I shall be dancing until I am old."

"So you came to Greece?"

Maria Tolosa untied the knot of her scarf and pulled it off. Then she shook out her hair, scowling at the sculptured reliefs below the cornice of the tower, which were becoming harder to distinguish against the whitening evening sky. "He had made arrangements. These papers he had deposited in the Banca d'Espagna in Madrid. In the bank he has a cousin. Juan was to ask from this person in Greece that a large sum of money shall be paid into his account in Madrid. As soon as that was paid in, his cousin had agreed to send these documents to him here."

"Your husband was expecting the other side to trust him?"

"I don't know. It is that he may have had some surety which he could give them. You know. I told him; I warned him; I said, you are playing a risk."

"Was Philip Tolosa in this?"

"He knows the attempt to get this money is to be made. He does not know who is the man or what it is that Juan has to sell."

"Has something else happened now?"

"Yes."

Her bracelets jangled as she sat down on a piece of fallen masonry, and after a minute he squatted beside her. The noise and glitter of the city was not far away but seemed as remote as the sea on a frosty day.

"On Wednesday I have talked this over with Philip. We have agreed that now no question of money comes in. We are no longer wanting to sell the papers, we wish to *use* them. You know. That way we can get some revenge. We are agreed on that. And the only way to use them is while we are here."

"So what have you done?"

"I have sent for the papers."

"To be posted here?"

"Yes."

Gene bit his lip. She was watching him closely. "Was this your idea or your brother-in-law's?"

"Philip's."

"And why have you come to me now?"

"Because, now I have done it, I am not happy about it."

"You think Philip wants the papers to sell himself?"

"I am not sure if my suspicion of him is my own or whether you have planted it. But there is something very wrong with him. He is—going to pieces while I watch. Always he has been the high-strung kind; but now . . . While he was persuading me to do this I thought he was upset because he was burning for revenge. Now I do not know what to think. He lies on his bed smoking all day. He has fits of trembling, trying to keep still. You know. He will not even touch his harp. At night I hear him walking about."

"And so?"

"It may be grief for his brother that is destroying him, but if so it is not the sort of grief that is mine. What use will he be when the letter comes, if such is his condition? I am worried and don't know how to turn. That is why I have come to you."

"You think I'm worth trusting now?"

"You have sad eyes, M. Vanbrugh—as if they have seen many things they would like to forget. But I think you are a man of honour."

Darkness had come like a curtain drawn. Bats were circling over the tower.

"When do you expect the papers?"

"Not until early next week. I cannot cable for them, for it is certain our cousin will not send them without a signature in writing which he can recognise. But in my letter I ask him to cable back.

I have that cable tonight." She clasped and unclasped her fat strong hands; they seemed to need something to take hold of. "The cable says he receives my letter yesterday afternoon, that is Friday. The cable says sending today."

"Saturday. . . . They might be here Monday. No, that's barely possible. Tuesday at the earliest."

"That is what I thought."

"Philip knows of the cable?"

"Yes."

"But the letter will come addressed to you—if it is not tampered with."

"Yes."

"Can you be sure of getting it first?"

"The letters are usually put just inside the front door of the house where we live. I can do my best to be about in the hall when the postman comes."

"Do that."

"And then?"

"Can you bring them straight to me?"

She hesitated. In a two-storeyed house nearby someone had switched on a light in an un-shuttered upper room, and Gene's face showed clearly. This time it had no expression.

"And you?"

"If they are what I suppose they may be, then I can help you to make use of them in the most effective way."

"What do you suppose they may be?"

"There's no point in guessing when we shall be sure so soon."

The light went out and they were left in a greater darkness.

'*What* was the name of the man my husband mentioned in Paris?"

"Avra."

"Why are you interested in him?"

"I think when you get these papers it may explain that to."

"I *have* to trust you," she said. "If you let me down . . ."

"I'll not let you down."

Chapter Thirteen

It was just on nine when he got to Heracles House. He knew he was taking a risk in going, but a 'must' within himself made the risk necessary.

There was no one about when he stepped into the self-operating lift and pressed the button for the seventh floor; lights winked and the lift sighed and took him up with a carefully graded acceleration; after a very few seconds it sighed again and let him out. The lobby upstairs was empty and he pressed the bell at the door at the end and a manservant showed him into a small ante-room where half a dozen people were talking.

Some he already knew; Maurice Taksim, the Turk; General Telechos; Gallanova, the Yugo-Slav ballerina; others he knew by sight, like Jon Manos. George Lascou came towards him, grey waistcoated, gold glinting like a welcoming smile from the bridge of the pince-nez. For a short moment their hands touched and eyes met; conventional gestures of welcome and the empty words—good-of-you-to-come, kind-of-you-to-have-me. Almost at once Anya appeared through another door, in a dress that glittered as she walked across the room.

It was a small dinner-party, candle-lit at table, in a handsome high-windowed dining-room; two menservants, black-clad and silent, hovered like benevolent ghosts. On Gene's right was Mme Telechos; on his left was Gallanova, a fine-boned Slav with an imperious chin, in a Molyneux gown of slashed crimson. Beyond her was a stout moustached little man called Major Kolono whom Gene felt he had seen somewhere before and who stared fixedly at him. Mme Lascou was not present. Anya sat on George's right, some distance from Gene. They had only spoken a few words in private, when Gene had said: "I've hired a car for tomorrow."

"What to do?"

"To take you to Delphi, if you will come."

"Thank you, no."

. . . They fed on caviare, coq au vin, fresh woodland strawberries flown in from Corfu; and the conversation was as cultured as the meal. There were three or four very good talkers present; but Gene, speaking Greek now, rose to the mood and held his own. Perhaps only Anya, withdrawn tonight and communing more with herself than other people, perceived the paradox, saw the off-hand wit stemming from the eastern seaboard of the New World, expressing itself in the tongue of Aristophanes.

And George watched them both. George watched everyone with his soft fluid movements and sharp astigmatic eyes. No one could ignore that he was master of the evening: he led the talk, fed it, conducted it down safe and popular avenues, the perfect chairman you'd say, perhaps that was how be had come to lead his party, and then perhaps not, the velvet glove was not empty.

The number was small for splinter groups; when Maurice Taksim asked Gallanova about her early years as a ballerina, everyone listened to her story of the Yugo-Slav ballet after the war. She spoke of her own poverty and early struggles, and Mme Telechos said: "Ah, d'you remember the inflation here? When I sent my son to school he went with his pockets crammed with bank-notes to pay his tram fare. Do you remember when a newspaper cost ten thousand million drachmae?"

"That time must never come again," said Jon Manos, but conventionally as if he didn't believe it ever could, for him.

"We had our troubles in Istanbul," said Taksim, "but of course they do not compare. Were you here, George?"

"It is always interesting to hear how a rich man became rich," said Gallanova, turning her much photographed profile to the candle-light. "Would it bore you to tell us how it happened to you, M. Lascou? Or have you always been wealthy?"

"Happened is the correct word. It happened to me. After the

war I borrowed money and invested it in real estate. Regrettable though it may seem, the successive inflations helped me, and I built more and more flats and offices. Then I was able to buy factories in Piraeus and Salonika. It was all very easy once the start was made."

Everyone murmured in polite disbelief.

"I don't ever quite understand," said Taksim, "why you have bothered to enter politics. Why grub in the gutter now you have money to live on the heights?"

George shrugged. "After a white, when you have enough of it, money becomes unimportant. Then you seek something else—an outlet possibly for idealism."

"And you find it—you find idealism in politics? You must sift the dregs closely."

"I don't find idealism in politicians, but I can find it in political thought. I find scope for it in the situation in Greece today. We do not lack brains in the *Vouli* but we lack reflective brains. Not one in twenty of my fellow deputies attempts to understand Greece outside Athens or the mission of Greece in the world today."

A man at the end of the table said: "I don't see what you personally hope to do."

George sipped his claret. "It is not what one personally hopes to do, it is what one must attempt if one has any vision of the future at all. A nation is not divisible. We share the common lot."

"We need another Metaxas," said General Telechos. "There was a man."

Everyone looked at him. Lascou said: "Metaxas tried to do too much too quickly. No one knows now whether the end would have justified his means."

"The end appears to be justifying Tito's means," said Gallanova.

George smiled gently. "The trouble I see with all these leaders up to now is that ruthlessness and reflectiveness seldom grow on the same stem. Whether a dictator is wholly bad, like Hitler, or partly good, like Metaxas, he is always too much a man of action to be also a man of thought. He has no background of ideas deep enough to maintain him on his way. Plato pointed the solution, but no one has yet followed it."

George was at his most effective in small groups. His persuasive voice did not have to be raised to betray its lack of tone.

"Do men like to be autocratically governed?" cried Mme Telechos. "They are all too fond of equality these days."

"I am all for equality," said Lascou, "but equality on different levels. There can't be complete equality of reward where there isn't equality of service. The intellectuals, the philosophers, the governing élite—they are the brains of a nation and should have equality among themselves; so should the black-coated workers, the heart and the viscera; so should the manual workers, the limbs of the state. But these classes are not the equal of each other. Let each man be equal with his *neighbour* and let every man be judged according to his service to the community."

"Mankind has always been rather unoriginal in his forms of government," said Galianova yawning. "Perhaps that's because womankind has had so little to do with it."

Everyone laughed. George said: "The finest example of the art of government was in this city as it existed two thousand five hundred years ago. The reward of energy, resource, intellect, reached its highest peak. I think you found there love of life, admiration for strength and beauty, the constant exercise of reason, the acceptance of responsibility ... and with it went a self-governing genius never since equalled in the world."

There was a murmur of approval.

"I'm not at all sure," said Gene, "that it was quite as good as that."

Silence fell. Servants moved dishes discreetly in the background.

"Oh," said Jon Manos, "what did your night school say?"

"No one," said Gene ignoring him and addressing Lascou, "is a greater admirer than I am of the city state as it existed in Athens in those days. But I think in honesty you have to admit that distance lends a certain glamour to the view. Surely the whole thing, good as it was, was rather a contradiction within itself. Wasn't it? It was a state where one man in four lived the ideal life—at the expense of the other three. It was therefore at most 25 per cent of ideal. Then it was a military state constantly at war with one of its neighbouring states, and I've seen enough fighting to feel that that was not ideal. Thirdly, for all its excellence it was in a continual state of revolution within itself, and that too isn't a particular recommendation. Given those provisos, I'd agree it was a thousand times better than anything that had gone before and a hundred times better than what came after. I'm only trying to see it in its perspective."

"Perfection of course isn't possible," said George. "I wasn't claiming perfection for the system but giving it as an example to be admired and studied. It's not impossible that it could be improved upon."

"As Plato suggested it could be improved upon?" said Gene.

"Athens was the practical state, in operation. Plato's was the contemplative ideal, never properly attempted. I beheve that Greece is the one country, right as to size, malleability and temperament, where it might be possible, given the right men at the top, to fuse the ideal and the practical and set up an example of government for the world to copy."

Somebody spoke at the end of the table and talk broke out here and there for a moment or two, but Lascou kept his eyes on Gene and when the talk died again he said: "Isn't that to your liking, Vanbrugh?"

Gene made a face of slight embarrassment and sipped his own wine. "Expressed as you express it, it sounds wonderful. I only have one uncomfortable thought. If you put Plato's idealism into practice, with its all-important duties to the state, its sharing of all property below a certain level, its small élite governing class, its belief that no one should be left alone to live as they choose, that children belong primarily to the state, etc—if you have all that and amend it to meet modern conditions, you're going to produce something that will be hard to distinguish from Communism."

Into another silence Gallanova said: "That word does not terrify me as it used to."

"It does most of us in Greece," observed the man at the end of the table.

"Plato in a sense was the first Communist," Gene said. "I should have thought that was generally accepted."

"Communism as Plato conceived it has very little relationship with the world of Marx and Lenin," said George quickly. "The whole conception has changed. As soon as one harks back one finds a purer doctrine."

The talk went on for a while. But as it went on so it became more and more a duologue, a sort of intellectual clash of arms between Gene and Lascou. Others joined in now and then but their interventions were temporary. They didn't measure up. And Anya said nothing at all. She sat quite still, for the most part looking down at her hand on the table.

At last a move was made. Coffee and brandy were served in the main salon. After his talk Gene was preoccupied, as if he hadn't yet got it out of his system, and Lascou seemed to be gathering about himself the robes of the Greek classic past. Very little was said until the ladies rejoined them.

Presently Gene found himself beside Anya. "Who is Major Kolono?" he asked.

"He's—a business acquaintance of George's. I have not seen him at dinner before."

"I know his face but can't place him. What is his job?"

Before she could reply General Telechos came up and began to pay her compliments. Ignored, Gene stood his ground. Telechos looked a man hardened out of ordinary feeling by fifty years of service in arid mountains; the sap had dried in him. One fancied that he no longer saw people primarily as people but as cadres, units, platoons, to be moved, commended, defeated, deployed on the chess-board of a political and military ethos. He was the exact opposite of Lascou, who was all flexibility, all finesse, who would never neglect the human angle in anything, and who would be far more dangerous either in victory or defeat.

Lascou and Major Kolono were quietly conferring together, their brandy glasses like great soap bubbles nodding at each other as they talked. Then Kolono left the room and Lascou joined the trio by the window.

He said to Gene: "I congratulate you, Mr. Vanbrugh, on your knowledge of our language and of ancient Greece. It is quite unusual."

"In the happy seclusion of my night school," Gene said, "I have long been a Graecophile."

Jon Manos, who was near, turned quickly and took a couple of little side-steps: "Of course I can understand your opposition as an American to the word Communism. In the States nowadays I understand it ranks as an obscenity to use the word at all."

Although the room was large, the party was at present clustered round the coffee-table and within earshot. Nobody seemed to want to move away.

"I would have said we were inclined to use it too often," Gene replied. "I'm dead against raising anything as a bogy, however much I may personally dislike it."

Lascou said: "You know, monsieur, you say the old city states of Greece were contradictions within themselves. I wonder sometimes about the new United States of America."

"You do right to wonder," said Gene, "but I wouldn't lose any sleep about it."

"Surely the equality of opportunity that you boast of is really equality of opportunism—isn't that so?—a chance to get rich quick at the expense of your neighbour? And what is this freedom of religion? Freedom to worship money as the only criterion of success? And freedom from fear? I have never yet met an American who is not afraid—afraid of not making enough money, afraid of being cheated, afraid of not being thought superior, afraid of being down-graded in a social scale as rigid as any that has ever existed in the world before. And freedom from want. No race has ever 'wanted' more."

Gene said: "Man always falls far short of his ideal. It happens everywhere. No state has ever existed on earth which has not laid itself wide open to being shot at from one quarter or another. I think if you read Thucydides you'll find descriptions of the Athenian city state that make your criticisms of America read like the Garden of Eden before the snake got in. I might even quote you some. But why bother? One tries to see the best and not judge by the worst. One likes a country or one doesn't like it for better reasons, I hope, than the existence of a few scabs on the surface. The only proviso is that, if one loves a country sufficiently, one may make efforts and even sacrifices to remove a few of the scabs."

The room became suddenly very quiet indeed. Not a coffee-spoon clinked. People's expressions had become frozen. It was clear that the last remark had been taken in its most personal way, as a deliberate and ugly affront. Anya stretched out a hand to tap the ash off her cigarette, but she did it quietly and she did not raise her eyes. Then in the silence Major Kolono came across the room.

"You are Mr. Eugene Robert Vanbrugh?"

"I am."

"The police have been trying to trace you. They called at the address you gave, the Hotel Astoria, but you were not there."

"I was invited to stay with friends."

"They are anxious to ask you some questions about an accident that took place in Galatea Street last Tuesday morning in which a man, a Spaniard, was run over and killed."

Gene looked at him. It was as if the whole room was ranged against him now. "A Spaniard?"

"Yes, a man called Tolosa. We understand that you were seen driving a car away from Galatea Street shortly afterwards."

"Then you understand wrong. I have not driven a car in Athens at all."

Kolono raised his stubby eyebrows in disbelief. "Where are you staying now?"

"In Benaki Street. Number six."

"Perhaps if I called to see you tomorrow morning at nine?"

"You're connected with the police?"

"I am."

"You don't know yet who ran this man down?"

"I think we have a very good idea."

"Have you questioned Mandraki?"

71

Kolono stopped rubbing his moustache. "Who?"

"A gunman. You must know him."

"I know a man of that name. A silversmith. He has not a very good record, but he has nothing to do with this. He was in his shop at the time."

"He always is in his shop at the time. One wonders what protection he has."

"That doesn't happen in Greece," said Manos. "You're thinking of America."

"Shady politicians are not peculiar to any one country."

"Who was talking of politicians?" said George Lascou. "It was an association of ideas."

Kolono said: "May I ask you, Vanbrugh, what you were doing in a hired car on Tuesday morning last?"

Gene glanced at the hostile faces of the men around him. "Your dinner-party, M. Lascou, seems to be turning into a court of inquiry."

"I assure you it is none of my seeking. Perhaps——"

"May I ask—" Kolono began but Gene cut him short. There was a sudden glint in his uneven grey eyes.

"We're meeting tomorrow. I suggest you keep the muzzle on till then. The world won't end if you wait a few hours." He turned his back on Kolono and Manos and said to Lascou: "I'm sorry if I've said anything to give you offence. I was talking in general terms as I imagined you were. However, I think probably your dinner-party will be a greater success without me."

Lascou's pince-nez gave off equivocal glints as he looked at Anya. But she was sipping her coffee and made no sign.

"The matter's of absolutely no importance to me, M. Vanbrugh, and I'm sure my friends will be willing to accept your assurances if I am. But one thing I would certainly advise—and that is, get in touch with your embassy tomorrow morning. It's a common-sense precaution if you have charges to answer."

"I didn't know I had any charges to answer, but no doubt Major Kolono has an inventive brain."

Lascou shrugged. "I only wished to advise you, to help you. I think it would be your advice to me if our positions were reversed.

Wouldn't it? But no matter; let's forget it; let's change the subject; it is all very boring anyway. .."

Anya stayed behind after the others had left. Gene had gone early, and the rest went away in ones and twos during the next hour. A certain constraint had remained till the end; impoliteness from whatever source is not popular with the cultured Greek.

Last to go were General and Mme. Telechos, and while George wanted with them to the door Anya strolled back into the great salon and took a cigarette from an ebony box. She found a lighter and stood a moment, head forward until the smoke came. Then she walked across to a big gilt mirror and began to smooth one of her eyebrows with a middle finger. She heard George come into the room but she didn't turn.

He said: "I shall not see Telechos again publicly before the election. It would not take long for some scurrilous sheet to link our names and smell out a plot."

"And privately?"

"Privately I must. He's not an old campaigner for nothing."

She said: "George, why did you ask me to ask Gene Vanbrugh here tonight?"

He paused to pour himself a brandy. "I wanted to look at him for myself and see what there was about him. One has heard enough."

"And now you have seen him, what do you think of him?"

He warmed the brandy glass with his hands, gently swilling the liquid round. "He has a brain."

"It amused me that you had invited Kolono here so that Gene Vanbrugh could be practically arrested in your own drawing-room."

He considered her. "That was an afterthought. Kolono, the fool, had been looking for Vanbrugh for four days. He traced him to a house in the Plaka and then lost him again. It amused *me* to face him up with his man tonight."

"Sometimes, George, it is as if you were two people. One minute you argue with Gene Vanbrugh as a guest and an intellectual equal—that is a raising of the level of life. Then the next you show you have planned to trick him and cheat him because he is a political opponent—that is where one comes down to earth with a bump."

He caught an unfamiliar inflexion in her voice. He said: "The conflict between theory and expediency can't be a new one even to you."

She began to touch her hair here and there with a comb, but he could not see her eyes in the mirror. "How seriously do you intend to try to involve him in this street accident?"

"That's Kolono's business. It's nothing to do with me."

"Oh, come. Kolono, like John Manos, jumps when you pull the string."

"Well, then, I imagine we shall all be guided by the amount of difficulty Vanbrugh gives. The chief thing is to make him feel when he leaves Greece that he was lucky to get out."

She turned now, but her eyes were not to be fathomed. They smiled at him without apparent emotion.

He said: "You're not seriously interested in him?"

"Interested? My dear, what do you think?"

He shrugged. "One never knows. Men like that with their rather hungry looks and modest-arrogant manners—they can have their peculiar appeal."

"You underrrate yourself."

"Anyway," he said, "you'll not be troubled again. Kolono will see to that."

"If he finds him. I very much doubt if Gene Vanbrugh will be waiting for him when he calls in the morning."

"Oh, we attended to that," said Lascou. "After dinner Kolono telephoned across the square for a couple of his men. They would be waiting for Vanbrugh when he left."

Chapter Fourteen

Soon after seven the next morning Anya was wakened by the telephone at the side of her bed. The blinds were drawn and she stretched out a sleepy arm for the receiver in the sun-shot darkness.

"Hullo?"

"Mlle Stonaris?"

"Yes?"

"This is Gene Vanbrugh."

She fumbled the receiver into a better position. "Where are you speaking from?"

"A call box. I want to know if you've decided to come with me."

"Come with you?"

"Don't you remember?"

"Of course I remember."

"Perhaps you didn't expect to hear from me again."

"No, I didn't expect it. Certainly not this early. You have wakened me."

"Sorry."

She said: "Perhaps it is I who should apologise for last night. I didn't know that that was going to happen."

"I'm sure you didn't. But it was partly my own fault."

"We are not all so ill-mannered."

There was a moment's hesitation at both ends.

He said: "If you did come today I'd have to ask a favour. For reasons you may be able to guess I'd prefer not to come round to your flat. But I shall be outside the Kotopouli in Ommonia Square at eight."

After a moment she said: "I couldn't be ready by eight."

"Name your time." There was a new note in his voice.

She looked at her watch and then at the mouthpiece. "Eight-thirty?"

"Eight-thirty it is. And thank you."

"Don't thank me," she said. "I have always had a sympathy for the stray dog."

He was waiting for her at the cinema, standing beside an old Buick, looking casual and unemployed like a car salesman not too interested in his job. She was wearing flat-heeled shoes and almost got to the door of the car before he heard her. Then she was sorry she hadn't spoken earlier when she saw the suddenly tensed muscles before he turned.

They looked at each other, and his eyes gave him away before he dropped them.

"Welcome to the kennels," he said.

She got in and he took the driving-seat beside her, and there was silence. His banter had rather quickly run out. They had reached the end of a phase. A new one that they both understood was about to begin. But it was like coming to the banks of a deep-flowing river.

She put her bag carefully into the pocket of the car. "What happened after you left last night?"

"I went home."

"You were not stopped?"

"Did you suppose I would be?"

"From something that was said after you left—yes."

"It occurred to me I might be."

"So?"

"I took the lift to the first floor and looked out of the passage window above the front door. There were two men standing there who looked as if they were waiting for somebody, so I thought I'd let them wait. It's always easy to get out of a big business block."

She said after a moment: "And how did you know I – wouldn't bring the police with me this morning?"

"Just a rash belief."

"Someone may even have followed me."

"Oh, I'm safe enough while I'm with you. George won't run the risk of having your name mixed up in a police matter, however trivial."

She stared out at the city as it slid past, but didn't comment.

"I'd given you up," he said.

"I didn't know you ever gave up."

"One cuts one's losses."

"And now?"

"One counts one's gains."

"There is no gain. My coming today is only from a wish to stand aside from last night and say, 'I was not a party to it'."

"Commendable sympathy for the stray dog."

"But since I am here, perhaps you can explain one or two things for me. I have not led a sheltered life. I am a grown person. I now have a vote. My intelligence is normal. But I live in a fog of ignorance."

"I wish I could believe that."

"There is no one to compel you to believe it."

"What is it you want to know?"

"First can you tell me a single thing: why it is that a respectable publisher should come to Greece and stay at a third-rate hotel like the Astoria, and then, if he has nothing to hide, that he should move on from one dingy apartment to another so fast that the police cannot catch up with him?"

"The same respectable publisher came to Athens a couple of years ago and stayed at the Grande Bretagne. From the second day he was a marked man. Obstacles were even put in the way of his meeting some of his old friends. So this time he thought he would be less conspicuous and keep out of the public eye. That's all."

"Because he was up to no good?"

"It depends whose good you're thinking of."

She made a little gesture. "Just good. The public good if you like."

"At any rate, he isn't here to make trouble that doesn't already exist."

"And what sort of trouble do you suppose already exists?"

He let out a slow breath. "We've got all day. Maybe during the day I'll tell you everything I can. But first . . ."

"Ah, I thought there would be a first."

". . . First I wish you'd tell me more about yourself."

They had left the town now. She slipped out of her short coat and leaned back in the seat. She had never looked so young to him as she did today in her yellow turtle-necked jumper and wide-belted skirt. A different person from last night; she wore that brittle sophistication with her clothes. Indeed, looking at her, one could see her entirely afresh, cut free from all association, untouched, beautiful as a renaissance angel. (Or maybe, he thought, this new innocence is something I'm creating with my own eyes; the astigmatism of desire.)

'He said: "I came to Athens with certain purposes in mind. It may seem odd to you, but although I knew a lot about some of your friends I'd never heard of Anya Stonaris. Well, now I have—and getting to know more has already come to mean as much to me as doing what I came to Greece to do. That may not surprise you, but I assure you it surprises me."

She said: "Isn't it quite usual for a stray dog to start looking for a new mistress?"

After a minute he laughed and said: "Yes, I was wrong."

"About what?"

"Just now I thought you looked young and innocent."

"I think it is you who are young and innocent."

"Give me time."

He had to brake as two mule carts laden with vegetables came out of a field in front of them.

Anya said: "And what do you know about my friends?"

"Oh. . . . I know that General Telechos owes the bank of Greece a million drachmae and I know why the bank hasn't yet put the screw on him. Maurice Taksim's wife is divorcing him and he is fixing up a crooked deal in oil. Jon Manos has a big reputation in law—of the wrong sort—and is trying to needle Stavrides out of second place in EMO. I know about George Lascou, his finances and his plans, but nothing about you. . . . Turn right here?"

"Yes. We follow the sea and fork off at Eleusis."

The sun had not quite soaked up the night mists, but the water of the gulf was a rich cobalt with coppery rocks at its brim. In the distance and behind rose the ghosts of the Peloponnesian mountains.

She said: "My father and mother came from Smyrna. Is that what you want to know?"

"It's a beginning."

"But already you know so much. You know that I am—what is it?—innocent-looking but hard-boiled. What more is there necessary to understand about any woman?"

He said: "Isn't it the Greeks of Smyrna who consider their blood purer than the Greeks of the mother country?"

". . . My father's family had been there for over four hundred years, if that is what you mean."

"When did he come to Greece?"

"In 1922."

"The exchange of populations?"

"Yes."

He waited. "Go on."

"Oh, you will know the background."

"I can hear it again."

"My father and mother were of that number of hundreds of thousands forcibly transferred after the defeat of Greece by Turkey. My father had not then finished his training as a doctor, but with what he was able to save from the catastrophe he finished his studies here, and in 1929 he married my mother. I was born three years later. My father was foolish enough to practise for many years among the refugees and dispossessed, his countrymen; and so we too were quite poor. When the Germans came he continued his work in Athens. Twice he was in prison for short periods for helping the Resistance, but the Germans soon let him go because they had need of doctors. Then when the Germans left, the Communists occupied our part of the city."

He waited. "Is that the end?"

"Yes, so far as they were concerned, it is. Because my father had influence in all his district ELAS told him he must publicly join the party. When he said he had no party, but only disease to fight, they shot him and stigmatised him as a collaborator. My mother they took away a month later as a hostage and I never saw her again. She is buried in the north. A priest hid me at that time, in the altar of his church—you know in Greece there are doors to the altar—and he kept me there and fed me for three weeks."

"... I'm very sorry."

"It is stale history now. All it has left me with is a dislike of the smell of incense."

They passed Eleusis and took the main road to the north, crossing the great plain with its ancient distorted olive trees and red-brown earth.

He said: "I was in Greece all that time, and in Athens too."

"What time? During the occupation?"

"Yes. The war against the Germans became my war very early."

"Because of Greece?"

"In the main, yes. I was here when the Germans came but got out in time. Then I came back and stayed around."

"Doing what?"

"I just stayed around. And noted how the various resistance groups were trending."

"ELAS?"

"Well, there were dozens of different groups to begin with. But after a time ELAS became much the biggest and it was soon pretty clear that they were more interested in making an eventual Communist state in Greece than in wasting their ammunition on the Germans. At least it was. clear to a few people but not to those outside. .... Perhaps you know all this as well as I do?"

"I was ten or eleven at the time. It is not always easy to remember."

"ELAS tactics were unvarying. By 1943 they were far the best equipped force in the field. They were the only one with any outside propaganda system, the only one with a proper organisation, because it had been in existence before the war. In addition to doing a little sparring with the Germans to satisfy the British and the Americans, they took on one by one the other resistance movements and wiped them out. It was the same technique as they applied to your father. Each resistance group, each leader of a resistance group was given the alternative—be absorbed by us, toe the party line, or else. The 'else' was to be denounced as collaborating with the Germans and then liquidated. I can give you the names of eight or ten such groups—with their leaders—who went that way. Not three or four killed but hundreds massacred. Some of them were my oldest friends. Only Zervas with EDES survived because he was too big and tough to be destroyed."

"You were in Athens at the end?"

"Yes, and I didn't like that either."

She shrugged. "Perhaps my father was lucky to be shot by a firing squad. At least he was luckier than my mother and some of the others."

For a while they had met on neutral ground. He had tried deliberately to slacken the tautness between them and had succeded better than he'd hoped. They reached Levadia soon after eleven and here swung off the main road on to the loose and uneven surface of the mountain road. A few clouds had blown up, but through them the snow-headed peaks watched them as they passed.

"That's Parnassus," Anya said.

Gene stared ahead.

"I used not to think it existed in fact. I thought it was part of a legend, like Zeus and Aphrodite."

"Nobody knows now what is legend and what is history," she said. "Perhaps there is not all that difference."

"Have you ever been to the summit?"

"No. August is the time."

"It doesn't look difficult. How high?"

"Oh—three thousand metres perhaps. The snow's treacherous of course."

"Next time we come, let's arrange to go."

"Are you very sure of yourself? Or very unsure? Deep down. I'd like to know."

"Physically I'm sure," he said. "The way a rat's sure. Once you've lived in holes, you come to know your own muscles, your own teeth, your own sense of smell. Being wanted by a few tired policemen doesn't worry me. But about you I was never more unsure in my life. Anything you detect to the contrary is purely coincidental."

"It's bad to be on the run," she said, after the minute she had taken to digest what he said. "Even from a few—tired policemen. Bad for something inside oneself. It is like driving on one's brakes too much. I know—though I had it for only a few weeks."

They began to climb by hairpin bends. At one point three ragged children stood by the way offering to sell them bunches of anemones. When Gene did not stop they leapt across the rough moorland like goats and were waiting patiently at the next corner above. When he still went on they got to the third corner before the car, and here Anya made him stop and buy the flowers. Afterwards they went on again between walls of rock and skirting dark and tangled forests. Arakhova was reached clinging uncertainly to the side of the gorge. Then the mountains drew right in upon the pass, they skirted the face of the precipice and began to fall gently into Delphi, which came in view with the clustered tiles and huddled streets of the modern village standing athwart the road and the white skeletal remains of the sacred shrines climbing in tiers to the foot of the great Phocian wall.

Gene found Michael Miehaelis's house just short of the village, and the poet, white moustache gleaming like a scar on his old brown face, limped down the steps to meet them.

They had lunch out of doors on the terrace behind the house, while eagles swooped and circled overhead. Everything here was dwarfed by the great precipice behind them, which both protected and threatened from three sides. But on the fourth the ground fell away in an avalanche of forest and olive groves stretching five miles and dropping two thousand feet to the shining rim of the sea.

Over luncheon Michaelis was talkative, Gene as conversational as was necessary, Anya silent. But it was not a bored or a disdainful silence. For all her assumptions of arrogance Gene saw perfectly well that she would look with the same contempt upon herself as upon anyone else who pretended to knowledge they didn't have. The old man wore an embroidered smock like an artist's coat, with buttons to the neck and a white linen collar. On his head was a little black cap shaped like a beret and worn on the slant. He had no family and his wife had been dead some years, but the three small children of his housekeeper kept popping on and off the verandah like puppies for tit-bits that he took from his own plate to give them.

He said: "I never go down into Athens. The skies of the mind so quickly become overcast. Here in Delphi I think perhaps we can still see. . . .

"Of course I am not a poet. I write songs. They are songs which I hope people sing, and some day may even dance to. Because they deal with elemental things it does not make them great; only truth is great—and for that one digs for ever in one's own soul. Perhaps enlightenment comes in death—the supreme moment of all-knowing—or is there just a blank end and candles burning and the thud of a spade? More grapes, Aristide! Man's mind works always to conceive a unity, and enlightenment would complete it, but that alas does not prove the epiphenomenalists wrong. . . .

"How beautiful you are, Miss Stonaris. Beauty I think is so much more than skin deep: on that most poets are wrong, deriving from a puritan tradition which fortunately never rooted deep in Greece; beauty's an outward expression of an inner grace. I think of Apuleius's description of Isis: 'her nod governs the shining heights of Heaven, the wholesome sea-breezes, the lamentable silences of the world below.' It is pleasant to be an old man because one can express oneself without fear of misunderstanding. . . .

"Yes, from 600 B.C. and before, the pilgrims used to come here, by sea chiefly, disembarking down there in Itea and making the long climb up to the Oracle. The people of Delphi had a bad reputation in those days—they lived off the pilgrims and often robbed them. They murdered Aesop, you know."

"I didn't know," said Gene. "More names."

"Well, yes, we are full of them. Croesus sent money for rebuilding the temple when it was destroyed by an earthquake. Nero robbed it. Domitian restored it. Plutarch was a priest here. So it goes on."

"So it no longer goes on."

"No. . . . Nowadays our temporary Hitlers call and stare but learn nothing from their visits."

After lunch Gene had a few minutes' business talk with Michaelis and then they took their leave and walked up to explore the ruins.

"Well?" Gene said.

She stopped to finger a stone out of the side of her shoe. "I think he understands women."

They were climbing towards the temple of Apollo, and for a few steps they went on in silence. He said: "If I can believe my own eyes, you were as impressed by him as I was."

"Well, so if I was impressed by him? What then?"

"Oh, nothing."

She said: "Perhaps I would rather marry Michaelis than any man I have ever met. Does that satisfy you?"

"At sixty-nine?"

She shrugged. "It would solve some problems. Life would be less complex."

"If one could live and think like Michaelis, life might be less complex any way up."

They climbed into the temple.

She said: "All right. Most of us are children fumbling with the keys of a piano and producing only discords—talking with Michaelis is suddenly finding a harmony. But what of it? As soon as Michaelis is gone the child fumbles again. Bang, bang go the discords. So what of it? What good will it do to burst into tears because we cannot play?"

He put a hand on one of the great ruined pillars and looked down over the torrent of rocks and ruins and trees.

He said: "Whatever else, the old men had a superb sense of fitness for the places they chose to live their epics. Nowhere could be better than Mycenae for Agamemnon to ride out of with his chariots of war to the sack of Troy. Here it's as if they have climbed half-way to heaven to build their holy place."

She came to stand beside him, but she didn't speak.

He added: "I wasn't brought up credulous but I could believe one or two things here. Maybe it's the influence of that man, maybe of the place."

Her great dark eyes slid over him coolly, assessingly, and then went past him to stare again at the scene. "These gods didn't ask much. 'Know Thyself.' 'Do Nothing in Excess.' You saw the inscriptions."

"I saw them."

"That's about all."

"It's too much for today," he said. "Most people would prefer: 'Know Excess' and 'Do Nothing for Thyself.' "

She burst out suddenly laughing.

"What's so funny?" he asked.

"I don't know. It just seems to me very witty."

He hadn't seen her laugh like this before. After a while they went on up to the theatre, and then higher still to the flower-grown stadium where the Pythic Games had been held. They sat on one of the moss-grown stone benches and smoked a reflective cigarette and stared out again over the gulf.

He said: "D'you know what I'd like to do now?"

"No?"

"Climb Parnassus."

Her lips parted as if to smile, and then she didn't.

"When do we start?"

"Any time you say."

"Why not now?"

"Better to stop at one of the hotels and go off first thing in the morning."

She raised an eyebrow. "You're not serious?"

"Why not?"

"How do you suggest we should go—by air?"

"No, the normal way."

"Wonderful."

85

"Well, it can't be more than five or six thousand feet from here and I don't suppose there's snow below the top thousand."

"I've always wanted to climb a mountain in suede shoes."

"That's a difficulty, I admit. But maybe we could hire some."

"In Delphi? But of course. One of the big departmental stores."

"Well, it was an idea."

"You stay on and go up tomorrow."

They sat for a while in silence. The air was like wine, sun glinted on the grass and on all bright things: her wrist-watch, the clasp in her hair.

He said: "I suppose it *is* too much to ask of you. When one lives all one's life in a city, in a constant round of cocktail-parties and fashion shows . . . Aside from anything else, it's a question of not having the stamina."

She said quietly: "I will climb as far as you when I please; but only when I please. Let us go back to Delphi."

They picked their way over the boulder-strewn path and began to descend. As they got down a guide was moving with two other people across the theatre; Anya went across to him. He knew her and greeted her effusively and they talked for a couple of minutes while Gene walked slowly round the amphitheatre. When she came back to Gene it was with a flicker in her eyes.

"A friend?" he said.

"A friend. He has a brother called Menelaus. Menelaus is a good climber. If you are staying tomorrow he would know the practical difficulties."

"And what are they?"

"He advised against it, said the snow was treacherous at this time of year. But for your future information the best place to start from is Arakhova. From there it takes about seven hours. But he said never to go alone because of the dogs."

"The dogs?"

"The sheep-dogs. They are very fierce."

They went on down. Gene said: "Menelaus would be a good guide?"

"The best."

"I'll engage him next time I come."

"You'll not stay?"

"No, I may have business in Athens tomorrow too."

"To do with your publishing firm?"

"To do with something that might be published."

"Isn't that the same thing?"

"Not quite."

They skirted the temple ruins and began to come in sight of the road.

Gene said: "Can it be done in one day?"

"Not really at this time of the year." She stopped and peered down at a piece of inscribed stone. "The best way is to spend a night in a hut about fifteen hundred feet from the summit. Then you start out the next morning before daybreak and watch the dawn from the summit."

"My God," he said.

"So it will be something to look forward to if you are here in the summer."

He stopped, and after a couple of paces she stopped and turned and looked up at him from a lower step. "Anya,"

She shook her head. "Oh, no."

"There must be women in this village. Some may have suitable boots."

"Women here don't climb. They toil in the fields all day."

"Are you afraid of trying it?"

"I've told you. I could climb just as far as you—and as fast——"

"It would be a new experience."

Her eyes were fronded as they looked into the sun. "I don't care to be away from Athens two nights."

"Nor do I. But you don't need to be. It could be done tonight. The new moon's up. We could be back in Athens by noon tomorrow."

"If we have not fallen into a crevasse or been eaten by dogs or caught pneumonia sitting in the hut or altogether worn our feet away in other men's shoes. Yes, that way we should be in Athens tomorrow. But I prefer to be in Athens tonight."

He said: "What were those lines Michaelis quoted? 'Her nod

governs the shining heights of Heaven . . . The lamentable silences of the world below.' Why Athens tonight? An appointment for a manicure?"

She thought about that for a minute. "I am waiting to see how offensive you can really be."

"I'm sorry. . . . You know the old saying. All's fair in war."

Her expression was hidden from him now; he didn't know if he was gaining ground or losing it.

He said: "I'll make a bargain with you. If you come up the mountain I'll tell you why I came to Greece and why George Lascou considers me his enemy—that's if you don't know already. I'll tell you why the Spaniard came to be killed. And also perhaps what he came here to do."

"First it was sarcasm and now it is bribery. And all so very unsubtle: that's the most depressing thing. Have you no threats?"

He said: "I only want you to come. I think it is important, for us both. It seems to me that it's more than the summit of a mountain."

She said: "Ah, symbolism, I hadn't thought of that. I'm always a little allergic to symbolism. It is like false money at the best of times."

"Come, Anya," he said. "You must come."

Chapter Fifteen

They took the car back as far as Arakhova. With them went Menelaus, a man in early middle age, gaunt and bearded and one-eyed, the blind eye slanting across his nose in a treacherous squint. It gave him a look of sneering brutality. With them also went blankets, ropes, two thermoses of coffee and some sandwiches that one of the small hotels had made up. Anya had borrowed the climbing boots of Menelaus's thirteen-year-old brother. In these and her yellow jumper and a pair of shabby ski-ing trousers she said she was ludicrous; in fact they had that provocative effect which ungainly clothing can sometimes have on a beautiful woman.

They left Arakhova at half past four, and there was nothing in the climb while daylight lasted. The sun was still very hot and they made their way without haste up the wooded slopes. After about two hours the going became harder because it was largely over loose stones. Menelaus had needed some pressing to undertake the climb, it being, he said, a bad time of year both because of the treacherous snow and because of the risk of sudden storms. Parnassus, he said, was noted for them; the old mountain was temperamental; like God; you never knew who or where he was going to strike next. He talked almost without a break on the way up, and with the going hard and steep the other two were content to let him.

Once they heard dogs baying in the distance and he said: "Be not afraid: they know me; but they are as fierce as wolves."

As they climbed level with the other mountains snow began to appear—earlier than Gene had calculated, at first only in patches where the sun did not reach, then in long ridges like zebra stripes.

They sat on a high mound of stones to watch the sun wink his red eye over the side of the world. The ravine beside them looked like a great hairy armpit which, as the sun sank, perceptibly darkened and seemed to quicken as if the arm had stirred. The breeze had dropped, and all about them was a great silence. But far away in the distance, far below them, a shepherd was playing his pipe to his sheep. The thin sweet notes came up to them out of the darkening void like the last sounds of a drowning world.

She said in English: "I am waiting."

"What for?"

"For you to tell me why you came to Greece."

"Oh, that."

"Yes, that."

"Can Menelaus speak English?"

"No."

Gene said: "I've first got to ask you one question. Only one, I promise. What's your feeling about Communists?"

"I like them like poverty, like disease, like pain, like dirt under the nails."

In the brief over-coloured after-glow the eccentric planes of his face moved in fleeting symmetries of determination and disillusion.

"I think I started life without political prejudices. I came back to Greece during the war with only one idea, which was getting the Germans out. ELAS has made me feel the way I do. Even now I'm dead against witch-hunts—all the paraphernalia of persecuting people because they have liberal ideas and carried a red flag at a meeting. In western countries Communists haven't a hope. Here it's different. Twice they've nearly made it: first in 1944 when the British stopped them, second in 1947 when the Greeks themselves, with American aid, stopped them. But it's never been a knock-out. Remember the spy ring of a few years ago?"

"Which?"

"The Vavoudis thing."

"Oh, yes. Secret radios and the rest. Very boring."

"Not for Vavoudis. He committed suicide. But there were others who stood trial. Twenty-nine."

"I remember."

"Secret radios, as you say; tentacles everywhere covering labour troubles, military espionage, penetration of the political parties, spreading unrest at crucial times, smuggling in of gold to pay and bribe. I got involved in it some months before it broke."

"You did? How?"

"Military counter espionage had been trying to uncover the ring for eighteen months or more; but they couldn't. Quite by chance, I happened on a sensitive spot. There was a sharp reaction and I ran into trouble and a man was killed. There was a police inquiry, and from that—what came out not in court but in private—a new scent started. From there on it led to the uncovering of the Vavoudis spy ring."

"And what happened to you?"

Menelaus was fidgeting. "Let us go, please. We have less than twenty minutes of the day left."

They made the two stone huts about ten-thirty. The quarter moon, following the sun down, had been very bright except for the last fifteen minutes when they had walked into a cloud. Menelaus lit a fire of sticks in one of the huts and filled the lamp with paraffin, and they had their coffee and sandwiches on the bare woooden table in the centre of the hut. Menelaus ate *keftedes* with maize bread and drank a whole bottle of *retsina*.

Gene said: "How are your boots?"

"Wonderful. Only they were not made for my feet." She sat sideways on a bench in her stockinged feet, her knees drawn up and her hands around them.

"Are you blistered?"

"So far there is very little blood."

"Let me see."

"No, I'm unhurt."

He said in Greek: "It's going to be cold here tonight. I think we should make up the fire."

"Don't worry, I will see to that," said Menelaus. "There is some chopped wood in the next hut. We have always kept chopped wood and paraffin here, even during the war."

"You were here during the war?"

"Around and about. Twice I made journeys to Athens, but I don't like Athens. It's unhealthy. All those people crowded together and toilets indoors. I prefer the open fields, like the animals. One becomes half animal up here." He touched his thick goatskin cape and squinted hideously. "So one cares little for heat or cold."

Gene said: "It was ELAS country?"

Menelaus nodded. "It was. But Greek country before and after."

"That's what we should all have remembered."

"Oh, some were in ELAS but many wished to work alone. That first winter in '41, I was a boy of twenty and I had romantic notions. There were six English soldiers hiding up here, in this hut, and we fed them. One was from Adelaide, two from Christhouse, New Zealand, and three from Manchester. That is England? We sent them off to Cairo. And later we got a message back. I have the message ... No, it's in my drawer at home."

"How did you get them out?" Anya asked.

"We took them by night down to a cave near Kirphi. Then the next night there was a rowing-boat made ready for them on the sea-shore near Itea. All that winter we did that, because stray ones kept coming in. Twice instead I guided men to Athens; but that was in '43; and the second time the Germans caught me and beat me and something went wrong with my eye. But I had the laugh of them in the end because I helped to blow up a bridge across a road when they were retreating and many of them were on it. That was very comical. I will get you some wood."

He heaved himself up, and a great shadow flung itself round the hut as he went to the door and out.

Anya swung her legs down and put her hands in her pockets.

"There are nine children in the family, all living off the same farm and what they can pick up from casual earnings. Yet you would insult this man tomorrow if you gave him more than his agreed fee."

Gene said: "This is the Greece that I care about—that I sometimes care about so much that it hurts—not the shoddy-smart, phoney glitter of fashionable Athens."

"My world."

"By choice?"

"By choice."

"It isn't the only one there is."

She shrugged and there was silence. He studied her two profiles, the lamp-lit one and the shadow on the wall behind it. It was like the other self, the *ka* as the Egyptians called it. Which was the one he was addressing himself to, and what were the risks he was running?

Rather sulkily she said: "You were telling me on the way up about the spy ring and how you were expelled from Greece."

"Not expelled, invited to leave. Trouble was my own embassy thought the same and I couldn't rely on their backing. So I left just as the Vavoudis thing was coming to the boil. I think I could still have been useful, but somebody had pulled strings. The next time I visited Greece all sorts of road blocks were put in my way, as I've told you, almost as soon as I landed. I even had difficulty in getting to talk with the chief army intelligence officer who'd handled the case. When I asked him why, he shrugged and said the Vavoudis arrests had only taken the froth off the barrel: the fermenting was still going on deeper down."

"And why are you here now?"

"Just before an election is a likely time for the froth to begin to rise again. And this time one might see deeper into the barrel."

"And what has all this to do with the Little Jockey or the accident to the Spaniard or your feud with George Lascou?"

He gave her a long considering stare. Up to now he had been taking a reasonable risk; at this point the risk became unreasonable.

"Ever hear of Anton Avra?"

"No."

"He was half Roumanian, half Macedonian, trained in Russia. He was Vavoudis's chief, the organising brain. But he saw the red light and got out of the country just in time. Nobody knew what had happened to him, but it was generally thought he'd gone back behind the Iron Curtain. Then a few months ago it was announced that he'd died in Spain."

"In Spain . . ."

"I suppose he was sent there to improve the organisation of the party. He was brilliant at that sort of thing, especially in places where the party was underground. D'you remember the details of Vavoudis's suicide?"

"Wasn't he surrounded?"

"Yes, in a house in Lycurgus Street. They'd built a big cellar under the washhouse that you could only get into by a sliding concrete door hidden under the sink. Although the military knew there was a transmitter in the house when they surrounded it, it took them a day and a half to find it, and Vavoudis was down there all the time. In addition to the transmitter were all the party papers and records, which he couldn't burn before he was discovered because the smoke would betray him. When he *was* discovered he set fire to them but there wasn't enough draught in the cellar for the stuff to bum quickly. So most of it was saved. Only a few of the most important books and letters were gone. It was generally assumed that Avra had taken them with him when he left."

"So?"

She was sitting now with her back against the wall, her hands round one knee which was drawn up, her lips resting on it; the other leg was stretched out and showed through the thick material the rounded movement of her thigh as her grey-stockinged foot gently tapped the end of the table.

"So these things were lost. But something I believe has recently been found. Did you know that Juan Tolosa was—or used to be—a Communist?"

"How could I?"

"I thought he had brought something back with him to Greece."

"And hadn't he?"

"He didn't have it with him. Otherwise the police would have found it."

"How do you know what they have found?"

"I know that."

"So you are agreeing with his wife—that the accident was no accident?"

94

"I think he was putting pressure on someone here—for private gain; and they didn't like it."

After a minute she said: "What are you saying?"

"That's all I have to say."

"You've said too little or too much."

"Too much, maybe."

Menelaus came back beaming hideously, his arms piled with small faggots. "We have four hours to rest. I will make the fire up and then it will last a time. There is an old straw bed in the other hut and I will sleep there."

Gene looked up. "But the fire's here."

"And only two places to lie." His smile vanished. "That is how you would wish it? I will lie on the floor here if you prefer."

Gene looked at the girl inquiringly.

"It's of indifference to me," she said. "We shall not undress, I suppose? Do whatever you wish, Menelaus."

"I'll go with him if you like," said Gene.

"No, I do not like."

Menelaus said: "Don't be afraid, I shall not oversleep. I'll wake you at half past three."

There was silence while he went about the hut, building up the fire, putting away the remains of the meal. Anya got up and walked across to the window. Gene's eyes followed her as she rubbed the window clear with on old rag and then leaned with her hand against the wall, bending to peer out. She turned suddenly and found him watching her; her eyes glinted and then moved on as if he were part of the furniture.

"Good night, sir. Good night, Miss Stonaris."

When they were alone Gene got up and took a few faggots off the fire. "I think it will get too hot if we have such blaze. I'll put more on in an hour."

"How lovely, the snow looks."

"Have the clouds gone?"

"Yes."

He unfastened his own boots. "Do you want to lie down?"

She came back slowly from the window. "When I first met you, dear Gene, I thought you were foolish. Then I thought you were very clever in disguise. Now I know that you are really a fool after all."

"Thank you at least for the dear Gene. It makes one's demolition more cosy."

She sat on the edge of the table. "From what you have told me so far about this Spaniard, and this Anton Avra, you are suggesting that George is in some way involved in it."

"I'm not saying anything."

"But you are. You're implying that."

"Anya, you wanted to know what I was doing here. I've told you what I'm doing here. Often I grope in the dark myself. I've only told you what has happened."

"And left me to make my own conclusions."

"It's all anyone can do, yet."

"I can tell you that your conclusions are utterly wrong."

"Perhaps you don't know what my conclusions are."

"Apart altogether from George, I know all the chief leaders of EMO. I meet them and mix with them more closely than any other woman does."

"Yes, I believe you."

"Well, I know that none of them could have any connection with this thing."

"How can you be sure?"

"Well, are you suggesting that I don't even know George Lascou?"

"I've said, I'm suggesting nothing. I don't know how much George Lascou confides in you or how much you confide in him. But I know that he's a clever, subtle and complex man."

"Perhaps that is why you do not understand him."

"It could be."

She slid off the table to re-fix the clasp that bound her hair. "The trouble with you is you have too literal a mind. George puts forward some philisophical argument and you think he's talking practical politics. You're too ingenuous to understand the mind of a Greek."

"Even yours?"

"Mine you do not even begin to know at all."

Chapter Sixteen

There had been silence in the hut for some time. The first blaze of the fire had gone down but there was still some heat from it. She had been sitting quite still on her bunk staring at the fire. He squatted on the floor on the opposite side of the fireplace. About half an hour had passed.

He said at length: "How did you first meet George Lascou? Won't you tell me that?"

"Oh, there's nothing more to say."

"Well, say it."

She stretched. "He saw me first at a concert given for Greek and English troops. Because I was young and knew both languages they asked me to sing. The next day he called to see me and asked where were my parents. I said *kaput*, so he went to see the priest who had sheltered me. Soon after that I was sent back to school, and then on to the university. He paid for everything. I was nearly fifteen when it began. When I was nineteen he came to see me one day and asked me to be his mistress."

"Just like that."

"Why not? We had seen a lot of each other during the previous two years. We'd read and walked together and knew each other well."

"Was he married then?"

"Yes."

"So you said yes."

She yawned. "I don't know why I talk to you."

"Go to sleep then."

"No, I will tell you because it may help you to understand him better. He was married but not happy with his wife, but with young children to think of. He said he'd watched me grow, ever since that first night. He said he'd watched and waited patiently. Which is true. It *had* been four years. Since you will wish to know all about it, he put it to me that there was nothing cheap or sordid about the classic women of Ancient Greece—like Phryne, who modelled for Praxiteles, or Aspasia, the mistress of Pericles: they were highly educated, intelligent women living a fuller and more balanced life than any married woman, moving in true society, which was not the society of aristocracy but the society of brains and art."

"I can hear him saying that."

"Well, it was true!"

"Yes, certainly. And has it been true for you?"

"Dear Gene, even you could not expect me to come up to the standard of women like those, or expect the people I've associated with to have the quality of the people they knew. That is a fault of the times, not of the arrangement. I am very happy."

"And you love George Lascou?"

She laughed. "Of course. I've told you."

He leaned forward to put another couple of branches on the fire. One of them left a circle of damp in the hearth where the snow had melted. "I've been through all the conventional motions myself, on all the usual occasions. So as a generalisation I'm all for the ha-ha-don't-tell-me-fairy-tales attitude."

She said: "Love's like gambling. People always play for too high stakes. They overbid their luck and never know when to cut their losses."

He watched her lips as she spoke. "True enough."

"But?" she said, noting the inflexion in his voice.

"But once in a while, you have to admit, the bank is beaten. There's evidence for it."

"In books?"

"Sometimes in books but not only there. Trouble is, as you say, every man thinks his chick is a swan, every man believes in gambler's luck. It isn't till you're broke once again, bankrupt, on your uppers, that you realise another vision splendid has fallen apart and become a shower of rusty tinsel."

"I'm glad at least we agree on that."

"I'm not sure we do."

"No?"

"No, I'm still half inclined to believe the big show exists, even though it hasn't existed for me."

"And so if it did?"

"If it did I think it might make our present knowing talk sound like bright teenagers' prattle. I think it might make even a war-worn type like me, who'd always taken pride in being on the outside even of his own affairs, feel as if he was shooting the rapids in a leaky canoe. I think it might stop him from ever being patronising or superior about it again because he'd know it was something that was bigger and more important than he could ever personally hope to be or begin to be."

She looked at him then. "Are you employing the same technique as you used to get me to climb this mountain?"

"There's no technique that I know of that could make the difference. Either it is or it isn't, that's all."

"I distrust you and your arguments—profoundly," she said. "But I take it back that you are unsubtle. That was a mistake that I made."

"Well, it's, healthy to revise one's judgments. I've recently revised a lot of mine."

The fire had gone down. It was cold in the hut, and he got cautiously up and began to replace the faggots. Outside a wind was stirring, moving through the mountains, lightly playing over the snow. They had turned the lamp down, but as the fire began to crackle a fresh light flickered about the room, and by it he went cautiously to look at her.

She was asleep. Her lips were slightly parted, her hair had curled round and was covering one ear; lashes black on cheeks; breathing hardly to be seen. She looked absurdly innocent; she had that faculty that children have of sloughing off the day's sins. An altar piece, an Andrea del Sarto madonna.

He stayed a long time watching her, content and able to study at his leisure a face that held magic for him either in movement or repose. When he had talked to her just now he had talked half to convince himself. Common sense told him that there could be, for him, only the rusty tinsel here over again.

The blanket had slipped and he lifted it to cover her shoulder. Then, thinking she would probably lose body heat in sleep, he took up his own blanket and put it over the other. She didn't stir. He squatted down before the fire, about three or four feet from her, shook a cigarette out of a packet and lit it from a flickering splinter of wood.

The wind was getting up. It was howling now like a distant wolf, out there among the crevasses and the lonely peaks. Perhaps tomorrow it would be too rough to go on. Perhaps it would be all they could do to get down. Down to Athens. What waited in Athens? The letter from Madrid? Not yet. But all the problems of the things he had set himself to do. They seemed to belong to a world that hadn't a great deal of relevance up here in the snow. He moved his head again and found that she was watching him.

She said: "What time is it?"

"Twelve thirty."

"Only that?"

"D'you want the night to go so quickly?"

"Don't you?"

"Not specially."

"Why don't you lie down?"

"I like it like this."

There was silence for a time, and he thought she had gone off. Then she moved to put the palm of her hand behind her neck.

"I don't need your blanket."

"It's better there than not being used."

"Were you standing over me just now?"

"Yes."

Silence again. He flicked his cigarette into the heart of the fire.

She said: "Your face is like a ship's prow pushing forward all the time into choppy seas."

"Thanks."

"Your nature's like that too, isn't it. Pushing on, never letting up. Why do you not accept life as it is instead of trying to worry it with your teeth all the time, like a terrier with a bone."

"Is that how you see it?"

"I wish I could tell you something about George. It would prove you wrong about him, but alas it is secret."

"Something about General Telechos?"

She looked at him quickly. "Why do you say that?"

"I know about the possible link-up politically."

She said: "You know too much."

"Maybe."

"I think perhaps after tonight we shall both know too much of each other."

"Except the vital thing."

"What is that?"

"You tell me," he said.

Just before two he again built up the fire. It was the last of the wood, and when this went they would have to shiver for a while. He lit another cigarette.

She said: "Can I have one?"

"I thought you were asleep."

"I have been. Light it for me, will you?"

He lit it and passed it to here and for a bit they smoked without speaking.

"Have your blanket."

"No."

"Lean back on something."

He looked around and then moved back against her trestle, so that he was sitting with his shoulders near to her waist. He said: "I detect a mother instinct."

"You are the worst detector I have ever met."

Her hand was lying beside him and he took it. The fingers curved round his and then relaxed. They finished their cigarettes and threw them away. But he continued to hold her hand. So Menelaus found them when he came in at three-thirty. Only this time Gene was asleep and Anya was awake, staring with rather terrible eyes at the dying embers of the fire.

Chapter Seventeen

They drank the rest of the coffee and swallowed a few mouthfuls of bread and honey. The wind was still blowing but the night was clear. When they opened the door of the hut it was bitterly cold, but by the time they had been on the move for half an hour, the bite had gone out of the air. The going was dangerous because the snow was loose and treacherous and much of the ground underneath was rubble and loose stones. Then after a time they went down into a declivity between the two humps of the mountain which stood out on each side of them against the starlit sky. "That is Old Man Rock," muttered Menelaus, as if afraid of being overheard. "This is Wolf Mountain. It is a bad place to be caught in a storm."

They stopped for a few minutes and then attacked the Wolf, climbing round its side and up to its great white head.

When they got to the top after another hour the sky was paling slightly but it was still dark. Menelaus switched off his torch and ploughed across to where a wooden cross was half hidden in the snow. "This is the place to be. If you stand here you are out of the wind. . . ."

For a few minutes he stayed with them, talking at a great rate, then he went off and stood by himself staring out over the mountains, his tall, gaunt, short-coated figure outlined like an Evzone against the lightening sky.

Since they woke they had hardly talked together at all; Menelaus had been with them all the time and they had been strangers. They stood together now, staring and unspeaking. Then Anya said harshly:

"Without enmity—without bitterness—I think this is the last time we can ever meet."

He didn't look at her. "If you give me your reasons I shall probably agree with them."

"We are on opposite sides in all this. I am not a traitor to the people I care for. You are against them and therefore I am against you. Nothing we can do can alter that—even if we wished to do it."

"Is that your reason?"

"We come from different civilisations—what is the word?—irreconcilable. Everything we do and think is referred back to different principles, different sets of values. You cannot build a bridge across two thousand years."

"Is that your reason?"

She didn't say any more. The wind was dropping, as it so often does at dawn. The light came very quickly. One moment day was over the horizon, then it was in the sky, then suddenly it had fallen on them. One moment the land all about them was secret and unknown, then it was suddenly all in place, assembled, a crag here, a heap of boulders there, a ravine, a waste of snow.

And as the light came the view fled away from them for endless distances through the crystal air. Mountains and forests, land-locked bays, arid plains, tiny villages. Sea beyond land and land beyond the sea and sea beyond the land again; and then the sun came up a wild cadmium colour and the yellow feathers in the sky crimsoned and preened themselves and the washed green streaks faded and disappeared.

"You are lucky," said Menelaus, coming back to them and baring his broken teeth. "It is good today. It is very good. See over there Mount Timfristos. That is seventy kilometres away. Could you believe it! And over there to the north—see, that way and much further—is Pelion; and beyond and behind it—to the left—is Ossa. And more to the right, far beyond the sea, that grey mass, I don't know what it is but they say that is still Greece. Imagine it! And that, looking right into the sun, that is an island, I have forgotten its name. South, those are the mountains where you came from.

And here, here in front of us is the Gulf of Corinth. And behind that the mountains of the Peloponnesus, see the peaks like teeth. It is good after all that we came this morning."

"It is good," said Gene. Anya didn't speak.

They stood in silence for a time. Menelaus went over and began energetically to kick away the snow from round the cross.

She said: "To find that cross on the top of a mountain dedicated to the Old Gods . . . One would say it would have been better to have left at least *this* little part of the earth to them."

"It could be that the old and the new gods are not so different."

She shook back her head as if there was a wisp of hair in her eyes. "Could that be Mount Athos—that Menelaus said was 'still Greece'? It is surely too far."

"Anyway, it's going. It's not as clear as five minutes ago. The miracle's nearly over."

She said: "Miracle? Yes, it is almost that. A pity, when the eyes can see so far . . ." She didn't finish.

He said: "Were those your real reasons why you felt we should not meet again?"

"Would they be yours?"

"Not altogether."

". . . But you agree that this should be the end?"

"Yes." After a minute he added: "We're running on rocks—at least, I am—so quickly that to miss total shipwreck . . ."

She said: "You want me?"

"It goes without saying, doesn't it?"

"But it is much more than that?"

"Much more."

"If it was only that."

"It can never be only that."

The sun was gaining warmth, but the day and the moment seemed very cold for them both.

She said: "Then go, Gene, go. Leave me as soon as we get down. Leave Greece and never come back. Promise you will go—at once—so that I shall never have the fear of meeting you again."

"I'll go," he said. "Write it out of your life. I'll go."

Chapter Eighteen

She got back to her flat about six on the Monday. When she put her key in the door she found it unlocked. It was late for Edda. Then she could smell his cigar smoke.

He was sitting turning the pages of a French novel, a glass with brandy in it by his side. His pince-nez glinted as he turned and nodded and half smiled. "You're late, Anya."

She went over and after a barely noticeable hesitation kissed him. "Late for what, darling?"

"I said I'd drop in for a drink about five today."

"Did you?" she said flatly. "Of course it's Monday! Have you been waiting long?"

"An hour. I'm usually punctual."

She went across and unstoppered the sherry decanter and took up a glass. "What a day! I need a drink."

He added: "But it appears I shall be unpunctual now. My next meeting is just due to start."

"I'm so sorry. I was quite mixed in the days of the week."

"Have you been out of town?"

"Yes. I'm dirty and lame. Can I fill your glass?"

"Have you been with Gene Vanbrugh?"

She sipped her drink before replying. "Yes."

"Where did you spend last night?"

"Why do you suppose I wasn't here?"

"I rang. But there are other reasons. Go on."

"I spent it in a hut in the mountains near Delphi."

"With Gene Vanbrugh?"

"Yes."

With his tidy fingers he put a book-mark in the pages of the novel and closed it.

"Did he make love to you?"

"He was not invited to."

"I shouldn't have thought a man of his type necessarily needed the invitation."

She said slowly: "For once it is not your place to think. Six years ago I made a bargain with you, George. When I break it I'll no longer take your money or your fiat."

Lascou's ductile sensitive mind seemed to accept the statement and close around it and absorb it undigested, moving on all the time into prepared country. "Darling, it's strange, this sudden feeling for this man. I think you have even tried to disguise it from yourself. Perhaps it is the unfamiliarity of such a person as Vanbrugh. Please, I am not trying to blame you, I am interested, inquiring. I am on your side—though frankly I don't think he is worth it."

"Worth what?" she said, still with a queer tense politeness. "Three days of my time? I have given longer to the Earthquake Relief Fund."

He watched her attentively while she finished her drink. Then she sat down and began undoing one of her stockings through her skirt.

He said: "Where is he now?"

"I don't know."

"Did you go by car?"

"Yes. He hired one, but asked me to return it to the garage for him."

"Where did he leave you?"

"At Daphni."

"What are his plans?"

She slipped down her stocking and took off her shoe. "D'you suppose he discussed them with me, his enemy?"

"I imagine you had some conversation in thirty-six hours."

She flexed her ankle. "I borrowed shoes up there; but I see there's no blister after all. I shall not be lame for life. Talk? Oh, yes, we talked: God, what a bore it all was! What a silly little man he is!

I shall take a bath and then go out to dinner somewhere and on to a night-club. The Little Jockey, probably."

He watched her foot for a moment, then his eyes travelled up her leg to her thigh and to the peculiar twisted angry grace of the way she was sitting.

"Anya."

"Yes?"

"Look at me."

She raised her head and gave him a smile as taut as a wire.

"In the last ten years I have lavished a great deal of money and attention on you."

"Yes, George. One of your less profitable investments."

"Far from it. Working admittedly on the finest material, I have turned you from a long-legged underfed waif into one of the most beautiful and sought-after women in Greece."

She slipped on her shoe and got up. "Dear me."

"And it's been worth it. Don't think you owe me anything. If it ended tomorrow I should regret nothing. But there may be one drawback from your point of view: I am not willing that it should end tomorrow."

"Don't forget your other audience is waiting."

"Anya!"

She turned on him like a flash. "Well, *what* do you want me to say? What do you want me to do? D'you want me to tell you that I've separated from this man and will never see him again? Well, I have! Today. This afternoon. Before coming here. When I left him that was good-bye! And d'you think I *care*!"

His eyes flickered. In the last year he had become much less tolerant of opposition from any quarter. "Yes, I think you care—in some rather perverse, unformulated way. Men like that appeal to something in women. If——"

"At this moment, George, you do not appeal to me! In my perverse unformulated way I find you very offensive."

They stared at each other. Like brother and sister quarrelling, they showed their tensions in the same way. Suddenly supple and pliant he said: "Don't let's fight over this, darling. I say that not because it's not important enough; but because it is too important. I'll go now."

"Whatever you say."

"But I put this to you to think over—if it ever came to the point, I should not be willing to lose you—to anyone. I put it to you both as an entreaty and as a threat."

"A threat? Oh, come. Isn't that a little heavy in the hand?"

"Life frequently is. It's only we would-be sophisticated ones who try to take the sting out of it with a laugh and a shrug and a few cigarette stubs and a cocktail shaker. Scratch the sophisticate and you will find the polish goes barely skin deep."

"You terrify me."

"No, my dear Anya, I don't terrify you. You lived too long in terror to be able to feel it any more. But you are a very honest person, within your limitations, as, within my limitations, I try to be. I was not trying to offend you when I said what I did—only honest. But I do hope if I threaten you—or him—or anyone else—you'll not think I'm merely bluffing."

She said: "I could never accuse you of that."

He picked up his white pigskin gloves. "Remember, preferably, that I have loved you since I first saw you. Nothing has happened since then to make me change my mind."

"Does your mind direct your love?" she asked desolately. "That must be very convenient. Or better still perhaps, can one direct oneself not to feel at all?"

Chapter Nineteen

The letter came at one o'clock on the Tuesday. Maria had been on the look-out all day. Several times she had been in to Philip, who lay on his back on his bed in a litter of cigarette ends, but he wouldn't speak to her. For two days he had spoken to nobody. Once each day he had been out of the house to buy more cigarettes, but each time when he came back he seemed worse. He was getting through nearly a hundred and fifty a day.

Often there was no one in the shabby office-reception-desk when the post came and it was slapped down on the shelf which topped the half door into the office. Anyone was then free to paw over the letters and maybe take what didn't belong to them. She was down before eight and hung about until the morning delivery came, but there was nothing for her. Then just after twelve she went down again and stolidly read the cinema advertisements for an hour. Mme Nicolou, who ran the boarding house, was frying some fish, and the smell and crackle of it came through to the lobby, but Maria had no sensations of hunger or thirst. All normal feeling had gone on the day of Juan's death, leaving nothing but the one desire. She carried it with her like an ikon, in her breast. For a week she had fasted like a saint before some time of trial.

It was a strong envelope when it came but not very big, being about seven inches by five, and not even registered. But she knew her cousin's handwriting. She crept with it up to her bedroom. Philip was useless. One person only she could be sure of, and that was herself.

She slit the envelope up the side and took out a flat stained waterproof wallet about the size of a tobacco pouch. With it was a brief letter from her cousin which told her nothing fresh. She opened the wallet. Inside this, behind a mica screen, was a man's photograph and some details of his age, appearance, profession. In the pocket of the wallet were about ten letters. She opened the first letter.

Maria Tolosa's father had been a night club dancer too, and before something went wrong with his kidneys that killed him off prematurely they had travelled Europe together. So she had a smattering of all the western languages, Greek among them. But reading Greek was a different matter from speaking it, and to her anger she found she could not read these letters at all. Five of them were, badly stained, but they were all quite clear. The dates ranged from 1947 to 1950.

She bit her thumb nail. Sufficient to see the pieces of the jig-saw? But she wanted the pattern. She had a belief in her own memory. A thing in her own mind was more indelible than any paper.

And although she trusted Gene Vanbrugh she knew she had nothing as yet stronger than instinct to go on. Here was one way of putting him to the test. Get the letters read by somebody else and then ask Gene Vanbrugh to read them. If he didn't know she knew what the letters contained and the two accounts tallied. . . .

But who? . . . Mme Nicolou? Mme Nicolou had not always kept a B-category lodging house. Before the war she had been an actress of promise, until the starvation of the German occupation had jogged her mind one groove out of true. She would be able to read the letters and, what was better, would soon forget them.

Maria slid the letters into their wallet. Afterwards, after they had been read, they would go next to her body in the top of her girdle, where temporarily they would be safe. . . .

She unlocked the door and found herself facing her brother-in-law.

In thirty-nine Spanish summers Philip Tolosa had never sweated so much as he had done in this one week of cool Athenian spring. He was sweating now.

"So it has come."

Caught with the thing in her hand she could not deny it.

"The letter? Yes. There are some papers. I am taking them to get them read."

"I shouldn't do that." He made a move to take the wallet but she held it away.

"Why not?"

"Let me see what it is."

"You wouldn't understand. You know less Greek than I do."

"Where are you taking them?"

"To Mme Nicolou."

"Don't do that. Give it to me. Let me see."

"No. See it later."

"Maria!"

She said: "I was his wife. What was his is now legally mine."

"You don't know what you're talking about! You don't know the danger we're in."

"Do you think I care for danger!"

"Well, *I* do. If this——"

"*You*," she said with contempt. "It is nothing to do with you if you don't want it to be. I can handle this quite alone."

"You young fool!" He grasped her arm, but feverishly, almost without strength. "Don't you know this house has been watched every minute since Juan died! What chance have you of doing anything on your own? What chance has *either* of us——"

"Then why did you press me to send for this, if you thought——"

"Because it was the only *hope*! Maria, I tell you I'd no choice! If Juan had taken heed of my warnings! I tried to persuade him. I threatened not to come to Greece. I wish to God I had broken up the act before we came."

"Get out of my way!"

"If you do anything with those letters except hand them over they'll kill us both!"

"They? They? Who are they?"

"Do you think I would choose this? Do you think I wanted it that way——"

"You—*betrayed* him," she said suddenly.

He stood with his back to the door, his face the colour of wet linen. He showed his teeth slightly each time he drew in his breath.

"You call it that. Of course you call it that. But d'you think I wanted to do it? D'you think I cared nothing for him? He was my brother as well as your husband. I tell you I tried to stop him—I quarrelled with him! I knew what he was up against. Besides, it was a betrayal on *his* part. When one ceases to be a Communist one does not cease to have some honour, some loyalty. . . . I do not know how they knew it was Juan, that he was responsible for the attempt to get money; for that was due to no move of mine. All I heard, all I got, was notice to report to the Party. I am still a member, you know. What was I to do? It was right to go from all points of view, to divert suspicion. But when I got to the meeting place, it was no party meeting at all—only thugs waiting for me. . . ."

She stared at him, but she said nothing at all.

"They beat me up—d'you remember I said I'd fallen in the street. . . . It was Juan's life or ours; they put it to me, one life or three. . . . When he was dead they came again—get the papers, they said, or it will be the end next for you. . . . Well, I've got the papers. Now they're going to have them!"

She moved carefully an inch or two forward and spat in his face.

Brushing the insult away as an irrelevance, he wiped his hand across his cheek. "What chance have you got? You couldn't even get out of the house. I tell you you're fighting the world."

She said: "You are an Andalusian. I am from Castile. When a man from Castile does what you have done there is only one thing left. He *destroys* himself."

"Maria——"

She thrust at him with both hands, thrust him aside and took the handle of the door, got it half open. He clutched her arm, tried to snatch the letter, and she swung round with her clenched fist and all the weight of her body behind it. It took him off balance and he fell down. She pulled the door and was out.

Half down the stairs she stopped to gulp for breath and listened, but he wasn't yet following. She slid into the office, which as usual was empty, but the door beyond was open and she heard the clatter of plate and fork. Mme Nicolou was just finishing lunching alone, in a pink artificial-silk kimono and scarlet mules. She had dyed blonde hair, heavy and straight and drawn back in streaks so that the white tips of her ears showed through it. The two sides of her face didn't quite match; one side was wide-awake and confident, the other eye drooped as if it had just seen a sly joke.

"The laundry's been back an hour, dear. I specially asked them to be quick; it's two sisters who work for me; and they haven't charged extra for the bloodstains on the shirt; help yourself to it if you want it; over there; my, how I hate cooking for myself; one stinks of the food before one can put a knive to it." She picked up a piece of dark-coloured bread in her long pointed finger-nails and began to rub it round and round on her plate mopping up the grease.

Maria shut the door behind her and stood breathing thickly. "Can you read these letters for me, Mme Nicolou? They belonged to my husband and I can't read this Greek. You know."

Mme Nicolou twisted the crumbling bread into a ball and pushed it into her mouth. The grease smeared her lip-stick and ran down her chin. She wiped it off on the arm of her kimono, which was already black just there. "Men are always writing. Why I don't know. Why were they ever taught to write? It only leads to trouble, and don't we have enough trouble without that. I knew a man who——"

"Mme Nicolou, it is urgent."

The other woman stared. With her tongue she carefully explored her teeth. "That was what the man said. It's urgent, he said." Her drooping lid closed, showing more of the blue eye-shadow. "But you can't fool me. Urgency, I said, is for Germans and the other vandals, not for Greeks who know how to live. ... Well, where are my glasses? Let me see."

She fumbled a pair of black evening spectacles out of her pocket and put them on. Maria thrust the first letter into the woman's long, thin hand. She stared at it.

"These are old letters? Was your husband in Greece in 1947?" she asked after a minute, fixing Maria with her wide-awake eye.

"Can you read it?"

"Of course. But it is not the official, it is the literary script. *Demotiki*, they call it. Mm-mm, people pretend to prefer one or the other. As if it mattered!"

As she was speaking Maria saw someone crossing the street towards the house. A stout man in a black alpaca coat who walked with a slightly anthropoid roll. He had a beard growing like a bonnet string under his chin. She heard his footsteps come into the hall but they did not go up the stairs.

"Not to *yourself*," said Maria sharply. "*Aloud* for me to hear!"

Mme Nicolou had been mouthing what she read. "But, dear, this doesn't sound like a love letter. Mm-mm. . . . Was your husband called Anton or George? I can't recollect."

"*Read.*"

"It says," began Mme Nicolou. "Mm-mm, it says, 'Dear Anton, the usual stuff is here. A purser from the Italian ship brought it. Five thousand. Via Paris. I can add to this one for one, but not in gold. With prices soaring that's too precious to me and I regret I can make what I consider better use of it. Well, it all comes to the same thing in the end. Don't tell your masters.' " Mme Nicolou raised her head. "Was that someone ringing the bell?"

"No. Go on."

"Where was I? 'Your masters. Mm-mm. . . . They expect a man to have not thought of self-advancement. Do you too? I believe no creed is above criticism or dogma too sacred to be submitted occasionally to the lights of common sense. I have too high a regard for your intellect to suppose you think otherwise. Regards.' And it is signed, 'George.' Does that mean anything to you? Was he your lover? It doesn't sound so to me."

"Is there a key to this door?"

Mme Nicolou put her hand inside her kimono and scratched with great concentration and satisfaction. She scratched like a bitch after a flea. "No, dear. My husband lost both keys before he died.

He was careless. But then nothing mattered to him but sex. It was his religion, his meat and drink. So I had a bolt fitted."

"A bolt? *Where?*"

"At the top there. Men have always followed me. At one tune my dressing room was never less than two deep. Never less. In Sofia. I remember once in Sofia——But why have you bolted it now? I sleep lightly in the afternoon."

Maria stood with her back to the door. Her heart was beating. She knew now the extent of Philip's cowardice and betrayal. "There's—a man outside. He has been trying to make up to me and I don't want anything to do with him. Go on."

"Go on? What with? Oh, the letters. You look upset. Has this man been annoying you?"

"No. Go on."

"And your husband only dead a week. They have no decency, men. You may not believe it, Mme Tolosa, but I was brought up very strictly. My mother warned me when I was thirteen——"

"*This* is the second letter. *Read* it."

There was a gentle knock on the door.

"Shouldn't we open it?"

"No."

"Well. . . . This begins like the last. 'Dear Anton, Mm-mm. . . . I hope you got everything as promised. Your rebuke might have come straight out of the party ink-pot. Oh, I know and agree with most of your arguments, but I claim the right to an independent voice now and again. Anyway, I'm sure you won't wish to dispense with my valuable assistance. D'you realise it amounted to eighteen thousand pounds sterling last year? Incidentally have a care how you receive Mlle d'A. She may be all we wish her to be, but she's also a famous actress and expects to be treated as such. Let Manos meet her. He has the approach that women like. All that she brought is now delivered into your hands——' "

There was another, louder knock on the door.

" '—into your hands.' Mme Tolosa, do you think this man will soon go away? Perhaps I could speak to him? I shall have to go upstairs in a few minutes. It's a trouble I suffer from."

"I want you," said Maria, "to call the police."

Mme Nicolou put down the letter as if it was hot. Her face seemed to try to break up. "The *police?* What are you talking about? They were here last week! I couldn't stand another visit like last week: it reminded me of when the Germans were here. I can't *stand* it! Tramp, tramp, I can't stand the sound of the *boots.*"

She put her hands up to her face and began to cry.

Maria gripped her shoulder. "Tell me, where is the telephone? You have one in here?"

"No . . . There—there is only the one in the hall."

"Is there another way out?"

"There's a back door. But I don't want to be left a-alone. This man might rob me."

"He wants only me. Don't open the door to him until I'm gone."

She grabbed up the two letters and put them back in the wallet. Then she slid through into the little scullery with its bubbling stove and copper pans. Coffee was steaming in a pot on the side.

She opened the door to the street. A tall young man stood there. He had a long narrow nose, smiling eyes, and a pert girlish mouth.

He said: "Hullo, sweetheart," and smiled and put up a hand to her face and pushed her violently back into the scullery. He followed her as she fell and shut the door behind him.

Chapter Twenty

Gene was there ten minutes before her, and as soon as he saw her he knew what her phone call had meant. She came stumbling into the cellar, half blind after the brilliant light outside, lurched against the stove, making the tin chimney sway and rattle, came up against a chair and clutched the back with both hands.

"I've lost it!" she said in a sobbing voice. "They took it from me! Philip had sold us to save his own skin! Now there's nothing left!"

He tried to make her sit down, and poured her a brandy, but she swept the glass off the table and it tinkled to pieces on the flag floor. Tears began to run down her face, over the bruises on her cheek and the cuts on her mouth and chin. But even now, though she had recently fought two men and been knocked down and kicked by them, they were not tears of weakness but of anger. She cried like a man, harshly and coughingly.

He heard the story through, while men brought in and arranged the furniture overhead ready for the evening auction. When she had finished he said:

"The letters were all signed?"

"I've told you. I saw only two. They were both written to Anton and signed George. I know no more than you about the last eight."

"There was also this identity card?"

"It is not an ordinary identity card but I think a Communist Party membership card. I am not sure; I turned at once to the letters."

"You saw the name on the card?"

"Yes, it was George Lascou."

Something was scratching among the waste paper in the cellar. The movements upstairs had stopped.

Gene said: "I hope nobody knows that you know that."

"I don't care what happens to me now. I have been cheated, robbed in every way. There is nothing more to lose!"

"Were you followed here?"

"I don't know."

He went across the cellar and slid a grating aside.

"Yes. Zachari is outside."

"Zachari?"

"The young man with the nose. You've torn his suit. No wonder he kicked you."

"So I have led them to you."

"It doesn't matter. There are six ways out of this cellar."

He came back and lit a cigarette. "Maria, do you know who Lascou is?"

"Yes. I have not played quite fair with you. I think I have almost known that all along."

"How?"

"Juan mentioned Lascou's name twice in front of me. But it was then only a name. When he died I suspected but could not be sure. Then you put me off by saying Avra. But gradually this week-end I had come to the conclusion. Lascou was in the news. I have not wasted this week-end."

"What have you done?"

"That does not matter. What is there to do now?"

He frowned down at his cigarette. He was not a man who took defeat easily, but to go on now would be the act of a fool. For her sake as well as for his own, the right way was to cut losses and go.

But would *she* go? Even if he told her to, would she go? He looked at her and knew she would not; and a worm of satisfaction moved in him that he could find an excuse for not letting up.

He blew away a spiral of smoke. "The letters won't be destroyed yet. Lascou has been out of town all day. He's addressing a public meeting in Piraeus at six, so he's not likely to be home before eight.

As these things you had are dangerous to him, he must want to see them and destroy them with his own hands. Otherwise he would never have any peace of mind."

She threw back her mane of hair: "Well?"

"He's likely to have them delivered to his flat, which is on the top floor of——"

"Yes, I know where it is. Well?"

"I think I could take a chance on getting them there."

"He has a secretary and others about him."

"The advantage is they'd not be expecting me."

"You would have a bullet in your back."

"Not in his flat, I think. For the next month at least he must be above scandal. If I failed I should be arrested. But that may happen anyhow."

She stared at him sombrely. "If you got these papers, now that you know what they are, what would you do with them?"

"Hand them to the Army Intelligence."

"Would he be shot?"

"I don't know. But it would finish him in the way that matters."

Her eyes hadn't moved from him. "It is very unlikely you could do this."

"But worth a try."

"Did you know that Lascou's wife lives in a separate flat on the opposite side of the top floor?"

"How do you?"

"I have not wasted my week. Between the flats there are communicating doors. It would be easier if you called on Mme Lascou first."

"It might be." He had been watching her. "Maria, don't take a hand in this yourself."

She said: "I went up on Sunday, carrying laundry. I got right to the door of her flat without being stopped and could have gone in. I did not go in. But I think you could get in that way."

Chapter Twenty One

Gene did not take Maria's advice. While a woman looking like a laundress might get into Mme Lascou's part of the building during the day, a man at night would need a better excuse. And his quarrel was with Lascou.

He left the cellars before Maria and slipped into the cinema next door. When his watch told him it would be dark he came out and took a devious back-street route for Constitution Square. He blamed himself bitterly for not having been more active in saving the letters, but his self-critical faculties, always alert, hadn't even the satisfaction of being wise after the event.

The Square was crowded. People were taking advantage of the first pleasant evening to sit out of doors, drinking coffee and gossiping. The tobacco and newspaper kiosks were doing good trade. The moon, shining between the trees, was only another streeet light hung too high for the best effect. The Parthenon was flood-lit. The windows of the penthouse of Heracles House were in semi-darkness.

Gene turned in at the swing doors past the concierge, walking like a man with a purpose. The lift was in use and he had to wait until the *libre* sign flashed on in green at the side. He opened the door and stepped in, noting that the concierge had not turned. He chose the sixth floor. The lift wafted him up.

Three concerns shared the sixth floor, a lawyer, a ships' broker, a tobacco exporter. The business day was over and there was no one about. At the end of the passage was the door leading to the fire escape. He looked about as he came up to it but there was no one to see him push it open and step out on the steel platform.

He wedged the door with a bit of cardboard so that it would not lock behind him.

Up here the moon had more say in things. Midgets moved irrationally about the chequered floor of the square, their lights hung at a uniform level a few feet above their heads. The gardens and the palaces beyond bloomed in the soft night air, and fashionable Athens twinkled discreetly as it climbed the slopes of Lycabettus.

Moving under the shadow of the platform above, he quietly climbed the fire-escape steps up to it. A smooth concrete ledge a foot or so wide ran a complete circuit of the building at this floor level. Gene didn't know whether there was any architectural reason for it or whether it merely existed to satisfy the architect's latent and otherwise carefully suppressed urge for decoration; but when one came level with it one found it had the disadvantage of a slight slope downwards and outwards so as not to provide a lodgment for rain.

He lowered himself on to the ledge and his rubber soles landed comfortingly on solid concrete. Though it was a secure foothold, no handholds were provided, and it meant edging one's way along, face and hands pressed to the wall and body thrusting against the building to counteract the slope of the ledge and the subtle gravitational or psychological pull of empty space and a seven-storey drop.

The building was a great rectangular block of ferroconcrete and the angle of the corner he must get round to reach the balconies and the french windows of the penthouse was an exact right angle. To do it there had to be some moments when a man was delicately balanced. He leaned his face against the concrete and carefully wiped his hands down – the sides of his trousers. Then he put one hand firmly on the wall he was leaving and stretched the other to lay it flat round the corner. Having gripped the angle so far as he could, he put out a foot and groped until he had a firm footing on the other side. Then he began to transfer his weight.

As he got his body half way round a button of his jacket caught on the edge of the corner. It seemed to upset his balance, and just for a few seconds the whole weight of the building appeared to lean forward upon the angle of concrete that bisected him. Then he withdrew an inch the way he had come and deflated his chest and curved it inward and the button got past. Soon he was round to the other side.

From here to the first balcony was about fifty feet, and this side he was less exposed to the lights from below. A sudden police whistle startled him once, but it was not blowing at him.

The balconies did not project but were recessed into the main structure, and the stone balustrade was within his reach, so he was able to pull himself up. This was one of the balconies attached to the large salon, and had a fountain in its courtyard. The windows were wide open. The room was lighted now, but in a subdued way. Two shaded lamps burned beside the fireplace, that was all. There was no one to be seen. He stepped in.

Considering its size, the room wasn't an easy one to hide in. There were places enough for a casual moment or two, behind a Louis XV settee or in the shadow of one of the statues, but nothing for a long wait.

Up here the sound of voices from the square was like the murmur of the sea. Four doors to the room. A light was burning under the door to the entrance lobby, but the others were in darkness. He chose the nearest, the one he had seen Lascou and Major Kolono come out of on Saturday night.

The door creaked noisily as it opened on a study. By the light coming in from the salon he could see a filing cabinet, beside it a cupboard, a telephone on a desk, a tape recorder. A black jacket was hanging over the back of a swivel chair. As he hesitated on the threshold, voices and footsteps came from the entrance lobby.

It happened so quickly that he had only seconds to make a choice. He stepped inside the study as the other door opened and more lights suddenly lit the big room.

Wisely he didn't try to shut the door behind him; there was no time; Lascou's voice and another, probably his secretary's. Gene slid behind the door, there was nowhere else; the bright lights from the salon showed a plain square room, oddly workmanlike after the decorations of the others; some bookshelves, a safe, a radio.

"... disposed of right away," George was saying. "How long has Mandraki been here?"

"Over an hour, sir."

"Well, I'll not keep him waiting any longer. Shut the windows, will you."

The light clicked on in the study and George came in.

He had not even waited to take off his coat. If he shut the door after him Gene would be standing like a dummy. But he didn't shut the door. He dropped his brief case and a package on the desk and then moved out of sight. Presently there was the noise of the opening of a heavy metal door, and he came into view again with two clips of new banknotes in his hands. They were 1000-drachma notes. He opened a drawer and took out a long thick envelope and put the notes in. They crackled as they disappeared and he licked the flap and sealed the envelope.

All this was done with his back half turned to the other half of the room.

"Otho."

"Sir?"

"Give this to him."

"Yes, sir."

The oiled head of his secretary came half into the room and a hand accepted the envelope. Lascou followed him out of the room as he withdrew, but then suddenly turned back and picked up the package he had put on the desk. He went out again but did not switch off the light.

"See that he leaves by the side entrance."

"I take it you don't want to give him any further instructions?"

"I don't want to see him again. And Otho."

"Sir?"

"I don't want to be disturbed for a quarter of an hour."

"Dinner is ordered for nine, sir."

"Then let it wait."

Gene did not hear the secretary go out, but after a while he concluded he had gone. For some minutes he waited for Lascou's return to the study. But it didn't come. Then he heard the clink of a glass.

The French clock in the salon began to strike nine.

When it had finished Gene moved. As he did so he touched the door and it gave a loud creak. That finished it. He stepped into the salon.

George Lascou was rising from a chair to face him. In the empty fireplace ashes smouldered, and on a small occasional table were some faded letters a waterproof wallet and a glass of marc: Lascou had one hand in his pocket. When he saw Gene he withdrew it holding the smallest gun Gene had ever seen. It was about the size of a cigarette case.

Gene said: "I guess your doors need oiling."

Lascou's surprise drew at the corners of his mouth and eyes: the years of comfort and good-living had slipped away, he looked hungry and alert.

Gene said: "I came about those letters."

"How did you get in?"

"Through the window."

Another clock was striking nine. The little crow's feet on Lascou's face softened and smoothed themselves out as the normal secretions began to work again, the reassurances of thought and position; he sat back in his chair.

"What are you doing here?"

"I told you. I came about those letters."

"What letters?"

"The ones you wrote years ago to Anton Avra."

"These?" said George, pointing with his revolver to the faded papers on the table. "I was just reading them as I destroyed them. I didn't write badly in those days."

"They've caused a lot of trouble."

"Yes, I suppose they have. None that I looked for, I assure you, Vanbrugh."

"You should teach your subordinates not to keep such dangerous evidence."

"He wasn't my subordinate," Lascou said. "He was my brother."

125

Gene came slowly forward. "That's something I didn't know."

"Even the omniscient find gaps in their knowledge."

"I'm not omniscient and I'm not armed. D'you mind if I sit down?"

"I was going to suggest it."

Gene took a corner of a seat about ten feet from the Greek. The table was between them. They stared at each other, men from different worlds. Although violence was implicit in their meeting, the moment they confronted each other it was as if combat had to be on a rational plane.

"Which was the right name, yours or his?"

"Avra means nothing. Many Communists have pseudonyms. . . . Anton was fifteen years older, was trained and indoctrinated in Russia. Mine was a local culture."

"Which differs from the party line?"

"A little."

"Was that why Avra kept the letters?"

"For him they became the big stick which would keep me faithful. Seriously, how did you get in here?"

"Through the windows. I've told you."

Lascou shrugged. "You can read these letters when you want, but of course I shall burn them in a few minutes."

"Well, you might as well put your gun away. You wouldn't use it in here."

"I wouldn't *wish* to."

"Mind if I smoke?"

"Get one from the table, not out of your pocket."

Gene did as he was told. He offered one to Lascou but the Greek shook his head. They were still studying each other.

Lascou said: "I wish you'd be honest with me. What do you want out of all this? Is it just money?"

"No."

"Then what?"

Gene said: "You pretend to hope for some sort of a majority at this election, but you know the only way it could happen would be if you came to power with the help of the ten or more splinter parties you're at present tied up with. That would be like driving a car with ten men holding the wheel. So either way, win or lose at the election, you need General Telechos and the army."

"Telechos is right wing, Vanbrugh. If you knew the slightest thing about him——"

"I know that he owes the Bank of Greece a million drachmae and that you're guaranteeing the loan. Not that Telechos, even to save his wife and family, would co-operate with a Communist. But I think it will persuade him to play along with a man he doesn't trust."

Gene lit his cigarette. He knew that time was on Lascou's side, but he was taking the chance.

"Telechos," he said, "is one of the last of the old guard. They're thrown up, his type, all over the world from time to time: the senior officer who has always been above politics, the man the army can trust, and the nation too. He's immensely popular just now with the army—you'd call him the last of the Papagos line."

"And in what way do you suppose he is going to cooperate with me?"

"A *coup d'état* after the elections. There hasn't been one since the war and it's time Greece was true to her traditions. You haven't the power to do it on your own, and if Telechos did it on his own he'd split NATO and lose the American loans. But you can give just the right democratic flavour to it all. You have the tongue, the easy diplomatic explanation, a parliamentary party which will have more seats by then if not a majority; you'll make the reassuring pronouncements, you'll go and see the ambassadors and the sentimental Grecophiles and explain apologetically how it is. *Then*, when you and Telechos are firmly settled in there'll be a gradual shifting of power. Once you get your fingers on things, Telechos will be squeezed out with the other officers who've helped him, and the right centre will edge further and further left."

Gene stopped. During his last words he thought he had caught a glimpse of something moving, reflected in the polished wood of a table halfway down the room. He carefully hadn't turned his head; but now he shifted his position to put a leg over the arm of his chair and allowed his eyes to wander idly. There was nothing.

Lascou had not spoken. He had only moved once, to sip his glass of marc.

Gene said: "Were you ever a true Communist? I don't reconcile it. It seems to me that you covet power for its own sake."

"I covet power for the use I can make of it, as any honest man does. The fact that I want to build something on more ideal lines doesn't make it a worse undertaking."

"Can you ever build something good on murder and bloodshed and lies? Can you found an ideal state by seizing it and ruling it against the wishes of the majority?"

George's pince-nez suddenly caught the light: contact was cut off by a series of glints and refractions.

He said: "The majority often doesn't know what it wants—certainly it hasn't an idea in the world what is good for it;—and I mean *truly* good for it, economically, socially, culturally. Violence as an instrument of policy I dislike: it should always be the *last* and not the *first* resort. But when it has to be used, then I agree with Thrasymachus, that it can help to win all the power and the glory of the world."

"How many will die in the coup? And how many before and after? Tolosa was one. Am I next? And then, when he's served his purpose, General Telechos?"

"I assure you that in the end there will be far less bloodshed and corruption in my state than in Washington D.C. You accuse me of egoism. What of yours? You remind me of a Christian missionary who goes abroad to convert the natives to a creed nine tenths of his own parishioners don't practise. Why don't you clean out your own stables? There's plenty of room for proselytising in Washington D.C."

Something moved again in the reflection of the table. Perhaps it was Mandraki re-summoned by the pressing of a secret bell.

Gene said: "I've no particular creed. I'm not here to spread any gospel. But you forget I was here in 1944 and 1945. That's why I've come back now. I've seen Communism at work. I've seen the cold mass slaughter, the children dying, the brutality to women, the absolute ruthless callousness in gaining one set objective. Above all I've seen the lies—so that no words have *any* meaning any more. *Nothing* that's worth living for has any meaning any more." He stopped and said quietly: "You asked me what I wanted out of all this. That's what I want. Just to stop you. Just to stop that ever happening in Greece again."

"Does it occur to you that that is my aim too?"

"You go a queer way——"

"Has it ever occurred to you that by trying to stop me you are trying to arrest the course of history?"

"Is that how you consider yourself?"

"I'm swimming with the stream. Face up to the facts, Vanbrugh; look at the truth. The present Greek state is a house of cards, kept in being by money from the West. Everyone who knows *anything* admits that. It can't go on for ever. Already the Americans are getting tired, as the English got tired. When the money stops, Greece will slip into its proper place in the new pattern of the Balkans, which is a Communist pattern. The *only* way to save it from the pogrom, the mass starvation, the kind of imposed brutality which has happened farther east is that before then it should possess its *own native* Communism well established and rooted in its own ancient traditions. As Jugo-Slavia has, but *much* better, more subtle in its workings. Only a man like myself who understands the *mystique* through and through can see how to wed the individualism of the Greek with the collectiveness of the modern state."

It was a hand and it had moved for a moment round the base of the Hermes statue.

Gene said: "You're being frank tonight."

"With a reason."

"Oh, I'm sure of that."

Lascou picked up one of the letters and crumpled it into a ball, nicked it into the fireplace. "That's where they're all going; but now that you're here, now that you've given yourself up of your own free will, I want to tell you *my* point of view. . . ."

In a mirror Gene saw a woman move behind the statue, a peasant woman in a black shapeless dress and with a black doth covering her head. But you could not mistake her build or her eyes. It was Maria Tolosa.

"... You presume to think that you're the only patriot," Lascou was saying. "You protest you love Greece. Well, so do I; I want to serve her too, and who's to say which of us knows best? You say Communism is bad. I know, good or bad, that it's inevitable in his part of the world. So did Tito. Stop me now and you lay up a far worse fate for Greece in the future."

"I can't stop you, it seems."

"Happily not."

Maria Tolosa had moved, was about as far from the Greek as Lascou was from Gene. Something glinted in the light. Gene's eyes, caught in a sort of magnetic field, could not stay on the Greek. On his last visit he had seen and admired the thing she held. The blade was of bronze, very ancient, with a lion hunt inlaid on it.

He fumbled with words, they knotted on his tongue. "N-now that I've—that I've failed—what d'you propose to do about it?"

"It must all wait until after the election—even later than that. There's no other way I can shut your mouth——"

"Drop it!" Gene said, the words spilling now, as if he had swallowed too many. "You—won't get anywhere . . . Revenge isn't . . . Maria! understand, you——"

"Sit down," George said. "If this is——"

"Maria!" shouted Gene, starting up.

Lascou didn't shoot him because he heard the movement behind him and half got up as the knife slid in. It went in as easily and as undramatically as a knife into a cake. It encountered no bone, no opposition. The small gun wavered away from Gene as he stretched up, but it still didn't fire. The trigger finger had slipped out of its hold. Lascou looked up in surprise at Maria, a strange woman he had never seen before.

Maria screamed: "*That* is for Juan!"

He was standing now, the knife handle sticking out of his back like a Christmas joke. There was a dreadful sense of unreality. He put the tiny gun on the table and fixed his pince-nez. Then he wobbled slightly, steadied himself with the back of his chair, straightened. "Get a doctor," he said to Gene.

"For Juan!" panted Maria, her hair and lips suddenly loose as if blowing in a wind. "For Juan! For Juan! For Juan!"

"Where's the phone?"

"No, not phone. A doctor—ground floor. Get Otho. *Bell*!"

Gene made a move and then stopped. Lascou had put a hand to his mouth and to his obvious surprise it came away slightly stained. Always neat, he fumbled to take out the folded handkerchief from his breast pocket, and while he did so a trickle of blood suddenly ran down his chin, leapt from chin to floor. His eyes flickered upwards as if reaching for something they couldn't find; he snatched at the table with the letters on. Gene jumped to hold him but the table went over and he slithered down dragging Gene with him. A new sign was written on his face. He said with terrible incredulity: "I mustn't *die*. . . ." And while he spoke he was already going, sliding over the edge of life, clinging and slipping at the same time while the world tilted against him.

He choked the blood out of his throat and said: "Burn the letters."

Gene nodded.

The pince-nez slipped. "Tell Anya . . ."

And then he was no longer with them. Only one finger flexed as if still groping for the trigger it would never find.

Chapter Twenty Two

They were alone together in the great salon while the French clocks ticked and the traffic mumbled far below. The room had become very still: and thought had stopped with movement. Time went round them, passed them by.

Then Maria Tolosa fell on her knees. "*Santa Maria*, Mother of God, Holy Mary, Queen of Heaven, *Santa Maria*, Mother of God, Holy Mary, Queen of Heaven," and a jumble of Latin words slurred together, over and over again, like beads told in terror without thought or meaning, just a talisman to hold on to in the void her own act had created.

Some of Lascou's own incredulity still lingered after him: it couldn't happen so quickly. No noise; no blood; the human envelope, punctured in a single vulnerable spot, had deflated like a tyre. Gene bent over him; but during the civil war he had seen too many such. He straightened up, wiped his hands on his coat to quiet them. He went to the outer door. No sound outside. Another door, open, led into a sort of butler's pantry—this way Maria had come. He shut it, came back.

He scraped together the scattered letters, the membership card—a phrase caught his eye: '*so don't upset yourself; one stays, however reluctantly, faithful to the general scheme of things.*' The miniature revolver. That in his pocket too. It was ten past nine. They had three or four minutes. Maybe.

Lascou had stayed faithful to the general scheme of things. Gene went to the praying woman.

"Maria, where did you get in?"

"Holy Mary, Queen of Heaven, *Santa Maria*, Mother of God——"

"Maria, listen to me!"

She stopped, stared at him without recognition.

"*Maria!*"

Her eyes weren't even seeing him. He caught her shoulders and shook her.

"*Maria!*"

"Yes?"

"Where did you get in?"

"Through her flat. She was out."

"Did anyone see you?"

"There was a little boy."

"Did he see you?"

"No."

"Why not?"

"When I ring the bell he runs out into the passage and I am able to slip in without—without him seeing me.'

"Listen," he said. "Can you listen?"

She wiped the back of her arm across her face. "Yes."

"There is a way out—not going back that way. No one must see you. Understand?"

"I saw the dagger as I came in. God gave it into my hand. Then I heard this man talking. I have to destroy him. . . . It is God's will."

"We must leave separately. Can you walk?"

". . .Yes."

"See that door? Go through the vestibule beyond it, to a passage outside this flat. Go past the lift to the end of the passage: at the end there's a door behind curtains. Understand?"

"I think so."

"It will be locked on *your* side. It leads to the fire escape. Go down that. The last flight, to the street level is weighted so that you have to stand on it to swing it down. Understand?"

"Yes." Her balance, her possession was returning. She kept filling her lungs with trembling air and blowing it out through her thick pouted lips.

"It will land you in a yard. The door into the street will be bolted on the inside. It's on the left of the fire-escape. Now then this is more difficult. You have to remember a street."

He paused and waited. He could not go too fast.

"Yes?" she said.

"Go to the kiosk at the end of the square—remember it?—Papa André. Ask for number 12, Eleuthera Street. Got that? Then do what you're told. Do exactly what you're told and ask no questions."

She was still on her knees. "You think I am wrong to do what I have done. I know you do! But it was God's will! God put it into my hand!"

"Leave that now. Do you want to get back to Spain?"

"What does it matter?"

"I can't help you unless you'll help yourself."

She tried to get up, swayed, stood with his help. "I will do what you say."

He took her firmly by the arm, led her to the door. She said: "It was he who killed Juan. He——"

"Yes. Now then. . . ."

He opened the door into the vestibule. There was no one about. They crossed to the further door. As they did so, a boy's voice came, calling. "That is the boy," she said. "If he——"

"Now." He pushed her out.

She swayed across to the other wall of the corridor, glanced at him out of pain-dulled eyes. Then she put out her hands against the wall, set her jaw, stiffened and began to walk down the corridor, swaying as if she was drunk.

He could not wait to see if she remembered; he shut the door and slid back through the vestibule into the salon.

Quieter than ever now. The clocks said fourteen minutes past nine. Out with his handkerchief. Handle of the knife first. Sounded easy, but in practice not so: blood had oozed out round the hilt; a spot or two got on his handkerchief. Now the table he'd grasped. There was brandy spilt on it; he picked up the fallen glass, then had to wipe that. More haste etc. His own cigarette end. How many handles had she touched? The boy calling again. The door of the study. Up and down it. Difficult to be sure where one had had one's hands.

"Papa! Papa!" said a boy. "Are you there?"

The door from the pantry was opening. Gene flew across to it, got to it as a small dark boy came in.

"Otho said you were back—" He broke off. "Oh, I thought . . . Who are you?"

Gene said: "Your father isn't here. He's gone out again. Have you a——"

"But Otho said he was back. I want to show him——"

He made a move to go round but Gene barred his way. "Where is Otho now?"

"Back there. Do you want him? I'll fetch him. What if——"

"*No.*" Gene caught the boy's arm. "Is dinner ready?"

"Dinner?"

"Yes. Your father said he wanted it when he came back. Will you go and see."

The boy's suspicious dark eyes were fixed on Gene. He was seeking and sensing something wrong. There was a contagion of tension.

"Why can't I go in?"

"You can, when you've seen about dinner."

"It's nothing to do with me—I had my supper an hour ago. Where has Papa gone?"

"I don't know. Hurry up, now." He gave the boy a push.

Michael turned to go; and then with the speed of a fish in a net, darted under Gene's hand into the room. Gene whirled round and grabbed his coat but could not hold him. He caught him in the centre of the room staring across at a man's body which lay islanded in a sea of white carpet.

Gene caught his arms as he began to scream. Kicking and wriggling he was dragged back towards the pantry door. His teeth nipped like a badger's as Gene tried to stop him shouting. Into the pantry he went, half fell as Gene released him, turned back to the attack, eyes glazing with fear and fight. Gene had opened his mouth to try and reason, to reassure, to smooth over the truth with gentle lies, but he saw it was no good. He slammed the pantry door in the boy's face. No key. He dragged across a chair and wedged it under the handle. The screaming stopped, and a kicking and a rattling and an animal panting took its place.

Gene flattened his hair, tried to get his breath, pushed up his tie into a tighter knot. She would be clear of the building now. Time to go.

The inner vestibule door now, one glance back. Forgotten anything? Anyway it was too late. A silent man speared like a dolphin. Otherwise the room was just as he had entered it half an hour age. Only the pattern of life had changed. The elaborate salon had become a pantheon for the man who had created it.

As he reached the outer door the assault on the pantry door suddenly changed, the kicking stopped and the door creaked and bulged under a sudden weight. Otho had come.

No one in the hall—yet. Out you go. Along the passage to the fire escape. As he neared the lift it suddenly glowed with light, and he slid rapidly past and gained the heavy curtains at the end which hid the escape door. The lift hissed and the door opened and Manos stepped out. He went straight to the door of Lascou's flat and pressed the bell. After a second he saw that it was ajar and pushed it and went in. Gene came quickly from behind the curtains and went to the lift. As he got in he heard shouting. He pressed a button; with agonising slowness the lift door closed; he began to go down.

Telephone messages travel faster than lifts. Might be someone at the bottom waiting. But he hadn't yet been seen, been recognised; the boy would hardly give a coherent description.

The lift stopped at the first floor. He got out, wedged the inner door with a packet of Gauloise cigarettes. To the curtained door on this floor: push the bar and go out on to the iron platform above the fire escape. Crowds, lights, traffic, people, noise were suddenly full size again, telescoped up to him. This was the way he had left the building on Saturday. He stood on the steps of the last flight, and as they swung down ran down them into the darkness of the yard.

The walls of the yard stood up all around him. It was deeply shadowed in here, a pool out of the sun. Only one light showed on the first floor; soon there would be others. As he moved towards the door of the yard someone tapped his arm.

Maria stood there in the dark. She looked dreadful. The brief shot of energy he had been able to pump into her had dissipated itself like adrenalin. She said: "The door is locked."

"I told you. But it will unlock."

"Not. I could not."

She swayed and he grasped her arm, pulled her across the yard. On Saturday there had been a bolt at the bottom of the wooden door, but when he bent to this he found it already pulled back. He tugged at the latch but it wouldn't move. He felt along the door with his fingers.

Someone had found it unbolted from the inside on Sunday morning. At the top there was another bolt. He could reach it with his fingers but couldn't get grasp enough to shift it. He looked at Maria but she was too far gone to help. Back across the yard, casting about, nose down like a rat, he grabbed up a bucket, ran back with it, stood on it, tugged at the rusty bolt. The bolt grunted and screeched back.

He took Maria by the arm and guided her out into the street. One or two people stared at them as they came out; Maria needed his support. Since Saturday the outer wall of the yard had been plastered with election slogans. They began to walk towards the square.

She said: "And I do not remember the name of the street."

"Maria, an eye for an eye isn't much of a philosophy these days."

"It was a repayment. He had got the letters. Look at my face from this afternoon. What else could I have done?"

They reached the busy rim of the square, crossed to the great space given over to cafés and promenading and talk. He stopped and looked back. Heracles House without its founder showed no distinguishable change. The top floor was lighted but no distress flares blazed. Nothing in nature's aspect intimated. . . .

She said: "And now the scores are even."

"Not if you're caught; they won't be even then."

"I don't care what happens to me now."

"There are other things to live for besides revenge."

"At least I can live with myself."

Circulation, you could tell, was coming back to her brain.

"Eleuthera Street you must ask for. Number twelve. But if you take this way out, you must promise me two things."

"Yes?"

"Do what you're told, no questions asked. No breaking down or breaking out. And if you're caught, no talk about the people who are helping you. Got that?"

"Yes, I understand."

"There is the kiosk. I am coming no further with you."

"I am not such a fool as I seem, but—I am shaken. You know? I have never killed a man before. God, it is much – worse than I ever thought!"

Gene smiled wryly: "It usually is."

Chapter Twenty Three

He pressed the button, the coins tinkled and he said: "This is Vanbrugh."

The tired voice of the old man at the other end said: "Well, my son?"

"I need your help. The way we once talked of it—remember—the last time I was here."

"Of course. When will you come?"

"It is not for me, it is for a woman. I want you to get her out. She's on her way now."

"A Greek? What has she done?"

"No, a Spaniard. Name, Maria Tolosa. You'll find her very upset, stunned, but she'll do as she's told. She must go."

"By the way we talked of? Yes. It may take a little time——"

"Get her as far as some port—Bari or Istanbul, where she can take a ship for Spain. If she needs money, give it her; see she has enough for her passage."

"And you? You are all right—safe?"

"If she's clear, when she's clear, I'll maybe take you up that promise myself."

"She is wanted for something?"

"No. It's unlikely she ever will be. But there's the risk. You feel like taking the risk?"

"Of course. She will not talk?"

"She'll not talk. I'll phone you this time each night, if I can."

"You will like me to make arrangements for you? In two, three days? It's as you feel."

"In two or three days, maybe. But it wouldn't be safe—us travelling together. First things first."

"So long as you are sure, my son, that you are putting it the right way round."

He glanced through the glass at the crowded taverna half fogged in steam and smoke. A radio was blaring a local dance hit. Near the phone a fat man with a napkin tucked under his ear was gulping up dripping spoonfuls of *avgolemoui*. Two girls were drinking retsina out of blue mugs and shouting a conversation at the proprietor who stood behind a marble slab cooking something on a charcoal fire and working the bellows with his foot. Gene tried another number.

The ringing went on and on.

"*Pronto*," said a voice at last.

"Mlle Stonaris, please."

"Mlle Stonaris is out. Who is that who wants her?"

"Can you tell me where I can get in touch with her? It's a private matter and urgent."

"She has gone out for the evening but she did not say where. Can I leave a message?"

"Thank you, no," he said, and rang off.

It was not yet eleven. He pushed his way out of the taverna and then through the interwoven crowds in the street. He jumped on a trolley bus crawling up Venizelou Street but got off it again about a quarter of a mile beyond Ommonia Square and made in the direction of the main station. He turned into a mean street lined with stalls and the remnants of a market. Faded vegetable leaves and stalks crunched and slid under his feet; a boy with a tray of sweet almond cakes cried his wares. Someone caught Gene's arm.

"*Oktopadi*," said an old man. "Fat shrimps. A bargain price for these I have left. Don't go in. The police are there."

Gene stared at a wizened face. "Where?"

"They came this morning an hour after you left. They have questioned the old woman but she will tell them nothing. Can I be permitted to sell you half a kilo?"

Gene felt in his pocket and began to count out some dirty notes. "They have found my things?"

"That is so. I did not see them but that is the message."

"Old Agnes?"

"They can do nothing to her for taking a lodger in all innocence. She asked me to be on the watch for you. Thank you, *koubare*. Eighty drachmae change."

"Keep it. Was there any other message?"

"No, sir. Your health, sir. And *thank* you." The old man turned away.

After a moment Gene went along the street as far as the next turning, ducked into a narrow alley and walked quickly down it. At the corner was another small taverna; he went in and ordered beer.

It was quieter here and the proprietor, a lowering Boeotian with Slav cheek bones, did not encourage custom. Gene smoked a cigarette while he thought it out.

Agnes could tell the police nothing even if she would. Nor would his belongings: a change of clothes, some money, shaving tackle, letters of introduction to two Greek publishers. He had latitude, time to breathe, time to get out. But sooner or later—and it might not be more than a matter of hours—someone would bring his photograph to the little boy, and the boy would point and say '*yes!*' Then it would no longer be a little game, side-stepping a few policemen egged on by Kolono to question him about an accident he had not even witnessed or to harass him on some technical infringement of regulations.

He watched a lizard inching its way up the wall beside him. It paused now undecided and flicked an experimental tongue. He must get out of the city, if possible out of the country, before the real hunt began. Every hour counted.

But one thing counted more than hours, even if it meant missing the night plane out.

A customer's shadow touched the wall as he moved to a table and the lizard darted suddenly into a crack. By the time the shadow was gone the lizard had gone.

One other call had to be made now for different reasons.

He finished his drink and left. He walked back the way he had come, moving easily through the strident crowds, cutting across the main streets until he was in the quieter residential district. Mme Lindo's house was well lighted, more so than he had expected. He pressed the bell.

Louisa recognised him at once and let him in. "Good evening, sir. The others are all in the drawing-room. They've just finished dinner."

"Mme Lindos has visitors?"

"Oh, yes, sir, I thought . . ." She looked at him. "You—weren't coming to the party?"

"I wanted to see Mme Lindos privately. Is there a chance to do that?"

"Well, sir, I can't . . ."

A door opened on the landing above and Mme Lindos began to come down the stairs; with her was a tall dark woman; they were both in evening dress. Near the bottom Mme Lindos stopped, holding the banister and peering.

"Gene. So you have come after all."

"Yes," he said, making the best of it. "But I'm afraid I can't stay."

"Of course you must stay. I have a surprise for you which may help you to change your mind." She came awkwardly down the rest of the stairs, looking at him keenly. His was a difficult face to read, but there was a casual-seeming alertness about it that reminded her of the first time they had met. "Gene, allow me to introduce you to Lady Camwell. She and Sir Giles are visiting this country and are naturally intesested in our press. Mr. Vanbrugh is an American with a profound knowledge of Greece."

Gene bowed and murmured the usual things. His memory had come to him; Vyro and his fiftieth anniversary; he *had* been invited here tonight; a week ago only; a week ago he had come here in innocence, or it seemed like innocence now. He said in Greek to Mme Lindos: "Sophia, I'm in trouble."

142

Mme Lindos had been moving them towards the drawing-room. "Trouble? What sort?"

"I want to talk to you alone."

"Come in, then. How can I help?"

"Money. And some advice."

Mme Lindos said to Lady Camwell: "Forgive us, my friend likes to practise his Greek. It is a joke we have." To Gene: "Of course. Anything I have. Are you in a hurry?"

"I can stay a little while."

"I told you I have a surprise for you. Mlle Stonaris is here."

Gene stepped back as if he'd moved on to an unbolted trap-door. "I thought you didn't know her."

"She phoned and asked if she might come. She came before the others and asked me questions about you. I persuaded her to stay on. What is wrong, Gene? Tell me now."

"I'm on my way out. But it's not a thing to involve my friends in." He smiled at Lady Camwell. "Excuse me."

"Of course," said Lady Camwell vaguely. She was a tall absent-minded-looking woman in a long greenish dress that didn't fit her and didn't suit her.

They went into the warmth and chatter of the drawing-room. Coffee cups clicked and a dozen faces turned to look at him. Only *she* did not look up.

Leon de Trieste; two Americans called Regent, proprietors of a Chicago magazine; Sir Giles Camwell looking like and elderly schoolmaster; the Greek Ambassador to Turkey, who was on home leave, had his sister with him; there was a scattering of other distinguished Greeks; Angelos Vyro, of course, and in a far corner his younger son, Paul Vyro, talking to Anya.

One or two of them looked at Gene's clothes. Anya's eyes at last came up to his. They were as cold and as hostile as he had ever seen them. All the same, for ten seconds he forgot murder and the people round him, and she didn't go on with what she was saying. Then she looked away and the thing was gone like a momentary shiver. The boy beside her was all eyes; to re-claim her attention he got up and brought her more coffee. She said something in her soft voice and he laughed.

"I keep the squares on the walls to remind me," said Mme Lindos. "In one's mind's eye one can still see ... Left was the Utrillo; that went first and paid for wood and coal. Right was a Toulouse-Lautrec, the Moulin Rouge from the balcony, it was considered one of his best; above was an unfinished Cézanne. . . ."

"I don't know how you could bear to part with them, really I don't," said Mrs. Regent.

"When one has had no food for two days it is quite astonishing how weak one's artistic sensibilities become."

"The installation of modern printing presses," Regent was saying to Vyro, "is the aspect of modern journalism most frequently neglected. Nobody, I say, can carry up-to-the-moment ideas if he's using yesterday's tools. . . ."

Gene stood obstinately over them until Anya was forced to say: "You don't know M. Paul Vyro? Mr. Vanbrugh."

"I rang your flat," Gene said.

She looked at him again, blindly now, deliberately dropping a blankness between them. "Oh?"

"Your maid said she didn't know where you'd gone. Was that a diplomatic ignorance?"

"Does it matter?"

"In this instance, yes."

"Well, she didn't. I came here—quite on impulse."

So she would not be telephoned here.

"Maybe I can see you home? If——"

"Mlle Stonaris is coming to see over my father's newspaper," Paul Vyro said stiffly. "We shall be leaving in a few moments now."

Gene was given coffee and a glass of *raki*. On the tray also were cubes of Turkish delight and a dish of apricot jam.

"... Istanbul," the Ambassador's sister was saying to Sir Giles Camwell in perfect over-precise English. "In those days one had lovely times. . . . And every summer swimming and boating on the Bosphorous. But it was difficult for a girl. One dared not venture out alone or some Turk would come up behind one and pinch one's bottom. . . ."

Cigars were being lighted, but there was a general movement as if people were ready to go.

"You are in *Aegis* yourself?" Gene asked the young Greek, since he could not get rid of him.

"No, in law. It is my elder brother who is editor. No doubt she will meet us at the paper."

A hand touched Gene's. Mme Lindos said: "Come and talk to me for a moment." As they moved off she said: "I have only about two thousand drachmae, and some of that is upstairs. As much as you want tomorrow."

"Thanks, what you have will be plenty."

"Why are you leaving Greece like this?"

"I can't explain here."

"I wonder if—Dear Count, thank you, but I never drink now. Alcohol, I think, is bad for one at either of the extreme ends of life. . . . You are coming to the newspaper with us, Gene?"

"You're going?"

"I don't want to, but fifty years of friendship demands it. Why don't you spend the night here? Perhaps I can help you in other ways."

"I can't. From now on the less you have to do with me the better."

She was spoken to by M. Vyro. Gene glanced back at Anya and Paul Vyro. He was bending towards her deferentially, she was smiling at him brilliantly, destroying him with her look.

Gene said to Mme Lindos: "I must come with you to the *Aegis* offices. I must see Anya alone."

"I'll get you the money. Go in the third taxi."

"Thanks."

"You look tired. What have you been doing?"

"What you told me not to."

Her wise eyes went over him again. "I was afraid you might."

"Lascou is dead."

Her expression did not change. "So. . . . When?"

"This evening."

"She does not know?"

"Not yet. I must be the first to tell her."

"I'll arrange it. Wait for me."

The company began to file out, Sir Giles bending his benign head to the confidences of the Ambassador's sister; Lady Camwell trailing tall and vague with the Comte de Trieste; Anya with Paul Vyro in close attendance; in the hall Gene waited with M. Vyro and Mrs. Regent. Temporarily a sense of inanition had come on him; he was a puppet caught up in these elderly formalities; for him it was a period of quiescence which he must make the most of, resting within himself while still on his feet. What news *Aegis* would have for its evening editions tomorrow!

Mme Lindos came down the stairs. "I'm sorry to have kept you, Angelos. I had forgotten my bag."

They went out to the taxi. M. Vyro handed Mme Lindos in with old world courtesy. Gene shared a seat with Mrs. Regent. They drove rapidly through the bright streets, which were still busy at midnight.

Mrs. Regent said: "Sam and I are making a comprehensive tour of the Balkans and the Near East—with our movie-camera. Our 16 mm. goes with us everywhere and later, properly edited, the film has nation-wide distribution in the States. My husband speaks the commentary."

Gene shifted in his seat.

"We have two days more in Athens, then we go on to Rome. Our Ambassador is planning a big programme for us there. We shall make no more than a whistle stop in Vienna, but shall study Istanbul extensively and then go through to the Arab countries. We plan to have three weeks over here altogether. I guess we felt this was too important a commission to entrust to anyone but ourselves. Do you know Greece well, Mr. Vanbrugh?"

"Pretty well," said Gene.

"Maybe you're not interested in the political scene. Sam and I have visited fifty-seven countries in the last two years with our 16mm. movie-camera. We have very efficient sub-editors who carry on in our absence. I may say we're very pleased indeed with the situation as we find it in Greece. We're very impressed with the way the political parties are presently handling the situation. When we return to the States we'll be able to interpret election events over here to our readers over there with up-to-the-minute freshness and understanding."

Gene didn't speak. The car had turned off the main streets. Mrs. Regent said: "Are you one of these Europeanised Americans, Mr. Vanbrugh?"

"Why?"

"You don't seem to me to have an American way of speaking."

"Oh, I have."

She looked at him. "To tell the truth I haven't much room for Europeanised Americans. Some of them talk like Englishmen, and in that case I say it's better to *be* English and the hell with it. Besides that, most of them live over here and by their behaviour are no credit to their country or their countrymen. They live loosely in Paris or London and pay no heed to world trends."

"Here is the letter you wanted," said Mme Lindos, opening her bag and handing him an envelope. "I will give it you before I forget."

They were slowing up. She said to Vyro: "I hope this visit will not entail a lot of walking, Angelos."

"Ten minutes will see us through. Then we will meet my son in his office and drink champagne. It is merely a little formality; but you may go straight to the office if you wish."

He spoke stiffly and she patted his hand. "No, no, I would like to come."

They drew up outside the offices of the *Aegis*, a squat white building with a polished mahogany hall. The rest of the party were in the hall waiting, and a number of others had joined. Among them were the French ambassador—the Vyro family had strong ties with Paris—several members of the Greek press, an Egyptian official, an American Gene didn't know.

At this point each member of the party was presented with a souvenir of the occasion. Each woman was given a silver propelling pencil, each man a penknife. They were all dated and inscribed: *'Presented with the proud compliments of Aegis on the 50th Anniversary of its foundation.'*

Gene edged away from Mrs. Regent, who was talking to the new American, and towards Anya, who was still being cavaliered by Paul Vyro.

"Anya, I have to see you. I'm sorry—after yesterday—but it's vitally important."

Gene glanced at young Vyro but he did not give way.

Anya said angrily: "What is it?"

"Come, mademoiselle," said young Vyro, "the others are moving off."

They went up in lifts and walked through a large editorial room. Gene found himself next to Lady Camwell, who looked at him vaguely as if she was not sure whether she had seen him before and then said: "Is this a daily paper?"

In a room full of Linotype machines, at which men sat setting up their columns, M. Vyro halted the party and began to explain.

"... trouble?" said Lady Camwell.

"What? I'm sorry, I didn't hear."

"Are you in trouble?"

He stared at her. "Why?"

"I heard you saying so to Mme—what's her name."

"You speak Greek?"

"In my parents' house we all had to read and write it before we were ten. The modern is a little difficult at first. Can I help you?"

"Thank you. Thanks a lot. No. . . ."

They went downstairs. A member of the staff began to tell how a raised surface was etched for printing. The Greek-ambassador to Turkey and the French ambassador to Greece had their heads together in a corner, but the subject was clearly nothing to do with fish-glue emulsion.

Mme Lindos said to Gene: "If it is true, what you told me before we left. . . ."

"It's true."

"How did it happen?"

"Not naturally."

"Oh. . . ." After a minute she said: "You want to tell Anya Stonaris that?"

"I want to tell her it was not my doing."

"Is it likely it will be thought so?"

"Possibly—later on."

"You must leave at once. I have a cousin in Piraeus. I think he could help."

Gene patted her arm. "This is none of your business."

Vyro stepped forward beaming. "You are not too tired yet, Sophia?"

"Not too tired but tiring."

"A few more steps, that is all."

The group moved on to the foundry hall. Here moulds were coming in and being thrust into the giant casting box. Beside this the great metal-pot was bubbling with molten metal; and at a signal the metal ran down the pipe into the casting box, where it spread over the mould. An impression of fatality began to take hold of Gene, as if he was in the grip of foreseeable circumstances which left him no hope of escape. He saw a predictable end as one might if caught on a conveyor belt and moving towards the cogs of a great machine. The sweat kept starting from his body.

The casting box was open, and men with leather gloves picked out the semi-circular metal plates and carried them still warm towards a further door. At this door M. Vyro stopped and stood on a stool and made a short speech. Gene edged towards Anya.

As he did so Lady Camwell got in his way and he felt something pressed into his hand. It was a roll of 50-drachma notes. "You may need them," she said. "I've always believed in backing my fancy." She looked across absent-mindedly at her husband. "I'm not often wrong in a man."

M. Vyro was talking about the two new printing presses in the room beyond, how much they had cost and what they would do, and how they were now going to be set in motion for the first time. It was fitting that they should first come into use on the fiftieth anniversary of the paper's founding and still more that they should be switched on for the first time by his oldest and dearest friend Sophia Lindos. . . .

Gene said: "Thank you. But I . . ."

Lady Camwell had moved on, leaving him with the notes. He thrust them into his pocket as absent-mindedly as she had given them; money was for a future which now might never arise.

He looked for Anya and saw that she had moved with young Vyro towards the door and away from him. He changed his direction and edged nearer. He could not shirk the compulsion of the nightmare, but he bore like a load of guilt all the dreamer's anxiety to avert catastrophe.

Somebody led a little applause as Vyro stepped down and Mme Lindos limped forward to press down the switch. As she did so a low pitched hum began in the room beyond; it increased second by second as the party moved towards the little door, soon it over-rode the noises in the foundry.

Some had already passed in. Gene caught Anya's arm as she reached the door. "Anya, I *must* tell you. . . ."

She stopped and looked at him, her eyes wide and hurt. Then she shook her arm free. "*What* have you to tell me? Nothing that I don't know. It was a weakness on my part, coming here; I know; but I'll get over it. I'll get over it. Leave me alone."

She turned and rejoined Paul Vyro who was waiting at the door. Gene followed them in.

The roar of the screaming machines inside was like the obverse side of sound. One had broken a new kind of barrier beyond which noise was the basic medium instead of silence.

There was not much room in the hall; the visitors grouped in casual spaces here and there to watch. Four men tended the presses, ant-brains ministering to the monsters, tiny dwarfs reaching a hand into the vitals with oil can or rag. Gene was right beside Anya again, but all communication was reduced to gesture. Once he shouted at her but she did not even turn her head.

Mme Lindos had drawn as far away as possible from the machinery, her quizzical eyebrows a sufficient expression of her views—tolerating and condoning her old friend's pride but disclaiming enthusiasm. By gestures Vyro himself was indicating exactly how the machines did their job, explaining how the paper raced round the plates at lightning speed, snatching at the print and whirring through the folders and cutters, to be magically transformed into a completed newspaper and flipped down upon the delivery platforms in quires.

After a time the noise took not only one's ears but one's breath. It was something for which one's body had only a limited absorption. As the first newspapers were delivered, men lifted them upon a moving platform which carried them away to the packing room, and Mme Lindos had already taken a step or two in this direction. As the party began to move M. Vyro took one of the papers out of the quire and opened it to demonstrate the completeness of the modern miracle.

It was there. The headline took up nearly half the front page. In black print of enormous size at the top of the page were the words LASCOU ASSASSINATED. Below them was a photo of George Lascou. What caught Gene entirely by surprise was another word WANTED, and under it a quarter page photograph of himself.

Chapter Twenty Four

The robots went on their screaming way, swallowing up bales of blank paper and spewing out an endless repetition of the same sensation, the same news, the same shock. The ant-brains were busy at their tending and took no notice; the papers were flopped endlessly upon the delivery platform and borne away. It went on without purpose and without sense, an automaton grinding uselessly through its routine.

Not all had seen the news. But enough to take in the first part. Vyro himself stared at the paper and then held it for others to see. Mme Lindos saw, and it was her first glance at Gene that gave Vyro the hint of recognition.

But none could speak. They were puppets jerked by invisible wires of surprise; gestures, expressions, became larger than life, grotesque and slightly inhuman. Vyro dropped the newspaper back upon the others, but the Greek ambassador to Turkey picked up another, and then Leon de Trieste. They mouthed at each other. Someone tugged at Gene's arm. It was Lady Camwell. She gave a jerk of her head towards the door they'd come in by. Gene looked at Anya; she had gone grey in the face.

Gene moved back towards the door. A hand caught him. Paul Vyro shouted something in his face, making his meaning clear; Gene shoved him hard and he went back against a bale of paper.

At the door two others were moving towards him. Through the door and slam.

In the foundry room deafness was beset by indistinct ordinary noises trying to come in. No lock on the door. A man came towards him carrying a newly-cast cylinder for presses. He said something to Gene, can you get away from the door.

"Way out?" said Gene.

The man answered but Gene was still deaf; he leaned forward and the second time heard; "Over there. The green door."

Gene began to run down the foundry room. The others were out before he got to the green baize, but he was through it. A long dark passage dusty and cold ended in a small office with several time registers, but no one in charge. A door faced him in the semi-darkness; he fumbled for the handle, scraping fingers on the woodwork. Double back and push open the office door; voices and shouts down the passage.

Rough coats and heavy boots. Two doors. Wash-basins. If this was a dead end he was caught. But there was another door, a door with a push bar. He pushed.

Someone was coming through the office as the door opened and he fell down the two steps into a narrow alley. He ran along it, came to the end and an empty street. Down the street at full speed, the opposite direction from the main doors of the building; a wider street. But he'd gone wrong: it wasn't a street but a square for unloading lorries. It was ill-lit; two lorries were there backed against a wall, abandoned for the night.

No way out. Buildings cast rectangular moon-made shadows. He shinned up into the van of one of the lorries, but the ignition key was missing. Then through the rear window he saw that the lorries were backed against an alley which ran into the yard of a factory. As he slid round and down and disappeared behind the back wheels he heard footsteps running in the square.

The yard of the factory seemed just another cul-de-sac. Doors locked and bolted from the inside; empty packing ceases from which two cats stared their disapproval, broken bottles, corrugated iron, steps. He took the steps four at a time. At the top was a locked door but beside it a concrete path ran round the corner. He stopped a few seconds for breath. All pursuit was a delicate balance between coolness and speed. As bad to be too hasty as too slow. But not many yards away from him someone had opened one of the doors of the lorry.

He went round the corner hardly hoping, found that the raised path went along the side of the building, and beyond the wall were steps leading down into the street at the factory entrance. This street was not empty but he got down and wriggled unobtrusively over the small gate at the bottom of the steps. Then he began to walk briskly but not too briskly away from the scene.

Lucky about the taverna; from it you could just see the steps leading up to her flat. An old yellow house, bland and bleached; two great palms stood before it like Corinthian pillars gone to seed; he had been in the taverna half an hour and while there two o'clock had struck. A meal swallowed as an excuse for occupying a table—also he had not eaten for twelve hours, and who knew when next?

This feeling of being hunted, really hunted again, was like a reminiscent pain, forgotten until it returned; not since early '44. A sensation to be dreaded: the beating pulse, the catch of the breath, the loneliness. Yet it carried savours. One had the freedom of the atheist denying God; there was nothing more to lose but one's life.

As a young man his nerves had lain too near the surface he had fought them as well as the Germans, disciplined them so that a triumph over one became a triumph over the other. Contempt of his own nervous and physical stamina had often carried him past the breaking point; beyond it was a no-man's-land few knew and understood.

Tonight after leaving the newspaper offices he had spent half the Lindos-Camwell money on a change of clothing. Behind Pandrossou Street you can buy almost anything at almost any time. A second-hand suit of Greek cut, a pair of spectacles, a wide-brimmed hat, a bottle of dye, an old gladstone bag which now held his own clothes.

The murder of Lascou had been broadcast on the late news. The police, said the proprietor of the taverna, were seeking a noted foreign *agent provocateur* who had been seen committing the murder.

"What nationality?" Gene asked.

"They did not say—Bulgarian I would guess." The proprietor rubbed greasy fingers down his blue striped apron. "They are the trouble makers. Hairy perverts. . . . Oh, well, a politician more or less—but there are those one could spare more easily than Lascou. Not that he's of my party, d'you understand; I could not vote for a man like Manos. And Spintharos—well, I can tell you sometime about him—poo! you wouldn't believe. But Lascou—he was not a bad figure of a fellow."

She came in about half past two, and there was a man with her. Gene thought it was Manos but they were past too quickly to be sure. He dallied in the taverna drinking coffee, but the proprietor was waiting to close so he paid his bill and got up to go. As he did so Manos came down the steps and passed out of sight. Gene went to the door in time to see a pale blue saloon drive away.

Good night to the proprietor, and he pulled his hat over his eyes and stepped into the street. There wasn't anybody about and a light chill wind rustled a newspaper thrown in the gutter. Lights in her rooms now, but cagily he walked first to the end of the street and looked quickly back. Out of the corner of his eye he thought he saw something stir beside the trunk of a palm tree just beyond the house. He waited patiently but there was no other movement except a gently waving frond. The lights in the taverna had gone out. He came back and walked up the steps.

When she saw who it was she tried to slam the door in his face but he got his foot in the door.

"Anya, I must see you."

"I—don't want . . ." There, was a sharp angry struggle and then the door gave. He was in a hall with double doors leading into a large sala, but she had gone from the door and was inside lifting off the telephone. He stopped in the doorway, short of breath.

"Go on," he said. "Ring the police if you want to."

"Why shouldn't I?"

"Go ahead. There'll be time to talk to you before they come."

She had changed into a green jersey and narrow black velvet

trousers. They stared at each other. He said: "D'you really think I killed him?"

"Didn't you?"

"D'you suppose I'd stab him in the back? Is that what you think?"

She put the telephone down. The hard certainties had gone from her eyes. He came into the room.

"You have a maid?"

"She goes home, at night."

"So we're alone?"

She didn't answer but put up her hands to her face. "God, I think I'm going to faint."

He went to a corner cupboard and clattered among the glasses and bottles there, came back with half a glass of brandy. "Sit down. Drink this."

She said: "Michael said you were there."

"Michael?"

"George's son."

"How did he know who I was?"

"He'd seen you on Saturday. He always peeps in at his father's guests."

"I was there. But I didn't do it."

She burst into tears. "I loved him."

He got her to sit down. She tried hard to keep her hands steady to hold the drink, but they were shaking like someone with ague.

She said: "I have b-been holding on tight, tight. One can't go on for ever. . . ."

"Don't try. . . . Finish this."

She took the glass in her own hand again but could not steady it, and he took it back, holding it while she sipped.

He said quietly: "Anya, I had to come and see you. It was the only thing to do. The one absolutely necessary thing in my life now is to get this straight with you."

"I thought—you see what I thought."

"You wouldn't have, if you'd had time."

"But you were *there*. . . ."

"I was there."

After a few minutes she began to steady herself. It was with an anger directed against herself. She blew her nose, tucked the handkerchief into the waistband of her trousers, took the glass a second time, trying to claim self possession, like someone denying illness because it was shameful to be weak.

He said. "I also came to you for another reason. Because I'd promised George."

"You promised *him*?"

"When he was dying he said two things: 'Burn the letters' and 'Tell Anya'. I've come to do what he said."

"I don't understand. What letters?"

"The letters that came from Madrid."

"Some did? Today? . . ."

"That's what I have to tell."

When he'd finished she stared at the pile of letters he'd put on the table before her.

"So what you said, what you implied in the mountains—that was true."

"Yes. . . ."

She took up one of the letters, read a few lines, let it fall.

She said: "As men go I do not think George was a bad man."

She said it half challengingly, as if she expected him to disagree. But he said nothing and got up to re-fill her glass.

She said: "George made his money perhaps to begin with in shady ways, and he increased it tenfold by speculation during the inflation. But the money, once got, he used often in good ways. He was, within limits, kind and generous to his wife, *devoted* to his children, he gave money and time to the arts. He loved his country. He was a *thinker*. I thought, I always believed, that he was working for the future of Greece."

"So he was."

"These letters prove he was a Communist?"

"Communists are not necessarily bad men. They are only working for what we conceive to be a bad thing."

"With my background it is hard to see the difference."

"Yet you say that you loved him."

"When did I?"

"Just now."

She got up, went to the mantelpiece, subtly recovering herself every moment. "D'you suppose that I can take his death without feeling it? He did everything for me. He made me, kept me. I owe everything to him."

"Did you give him nothing in return?"

She made an impatient gesture. "He said so. But when someone who has been very close to you dies, you *feel* that loss here—you don't first weigh everything in a balance and think should I be sorry, should I grieve, should I be upset!'

"No. I know, my dear. I'm sorry."

"And where is this woman that you say did it? Where is she now?"

"Soon out of Greece, I hope. I had to give her the chance to escape."

"*Why?* If she did it, she is responsible, not you! Are you too making a mistake in your feelings?"

"She's nothing to me except that I have to take some of the responsibility."

"Why?"

"Without my help Juan Tolosa's widow would have gone back to Spain. Her brother-in-law would have given up the letters as the price of his freedom and they would never have been heard of again."

"And George would have been free to go on with his plans for a *coup*. Is that what you wanted?"

"*No*," he said, coming up against it hard like a wall. "*No*."

"Well, you've stopped him."

"I've stopped him and I'm glad—even if it meant his death—even if it means mine. But too many other people have got involved for me to have satisfaction out of it. I didn't expect it to lead to a woman committing murder and a child crying for his father and . . . you being hurt——"

"And you are wanted for that murder." She turned on him. "D'you realise what you've done? It's not just a question of getting out of Greece. Wherever you go you'll still be wanted—and when you're caught you'll be extradited wherever you are—and you'll have to stand your trial here in Athens! And who's to believe your story—except those who know and—and perhaps understand?"

He shrugged. "I'll worry when the time comes."

"You have taken such a risk in visiting me. Every minute counts now against you."

"I had to see you."

She would not look at him. "What am I to do with the letters?"

"What you please. He asked me to burn them."

"But you haven't."

"Not yet. I had to bring them to you in case you doubted what I told you."

"I can't now."

Gene said: "In a way, even doing this, I haven't played quite fair with him. 'Burn the letters. Tell Anya.' He didn't mean it this way."

"Does that worry you? You have such strange scruples."

"Well burn them now—now you've seen them. They've caused enough trouble."

And what are *you* going to do?'

"Go," he said. "I can get out all right."

She considered for a second. "I don't believe that."

"Why?"

"It's—a hunch. When you came into Mme Lindos's . . ."

He held up his hand. "What's that?"

"What?"

"A car, I think. It may be nothing. . . ."

He went quickly to the window and moved the blind a fraction of an inch. A car had stopped at the door and men were getting out.

"Police," he said.

Chapter Twenty Five

Gene said: "What way out is there?"

She'd gone that transparent white which sometimes follows fever. "No way but the front. This house stands with its back to another. Everything comes through the front."

He grabbed up his hat and bag. "Then I'll get out of here."

"*No*"

He stopped a second, his movements as high-strung as hers.

She said: "Let me think——"

"There's no time to think——"

"Stop!" She got between him and the door. "It's too late: you know what the staircase is like: they'd see you."

"Perhaps not leaving this flat; I can take care of myself." He tried to get past, she caught his arm, he wrenched it free but she snatched it again.

"Then maybe I can put you in the clear," he said, raising his hand.

"*No, no, no!*" she said. "I can hide you. Let me *think*!"

"The window?" he said.

"Wait."

She fled past him into the bathroom, turned on the bath taps, was back.

"This way."

She led him into a bedroom. It looked like a spare room or a maid's room. He said: "Which way does this window look?"

As he spoke there was a ring at the door. They had lost no time.

"Here. . . ." She beckoned him to a chest of drawers beside the bed. "Help me."

He helped her to lift the chest out. Behind in the wall was a panel about two feet square. She pressed some sort of a spring catch and the panel swung open.

"*In.*"

"If they catch me this will mean——"

"*In.*"

He crawled through into a mass of pipes, which were obviously behind the bathroom. The trap door was for getting at the plumbing, but it was not a man-hole as such because there was no room for a man. He had to force his way in and lie on a tangle of pipes, with his head bent against the sloped roof and his feet cramped at the other end. The panel would just shut and he was in complete darkness. He could hear her struggling to get the chest of drawers back in place. Then the door-bell went again.

For half a minute there were indistinct noises. He heard her calling something. The taps were shut off.

Silence fell, except for slight hurried movements in the bathroom. Something dropped on the floor. Then she must have opened the door to them for he could hear the growl of men's voices.

He could tell she was arguing and indignant; but after a minute she gave way. Heavy footsteps. The hot water pipe was burning his back. It was very close in the confined space and he could hardly move an inch any way. His shoulder was pressed hard against the door. The footsteps moved on.

Suddenly her voice came quite clearly: "Do please look in here if you wish!" They were in the bathroom.

"I'm sorry, madame. You realise it is solely a matter of duty. I personally should not wish to intrude on your grief."

Nevertheless their apologetic manner didn't seem to be preventing the police from having a thorough look round. He heard them moving about. His shoulder was cracking.

She said: "I think it a little strange that you should suppose *I* would conceal this murderer."

"I'm *very* sorry, madame. We thought perhaps he might have got into you flat unknown to you."

"And into my linen basket while I was in the bath?"

"Of course not. That's enough, Cassimi."

They went out, and for a time Gene could only hear movements further away. Then abruptly they were again within hearing. They had come into the spare bedroom.

She said: "But who was this man who reported that he had seen the murderer entering this building?"

"We received the information. We took it to be a reliable source."

"How do you know that this man even knows the murderer? How do you know it is not a hoax?"

"We can't be sure, madame. But it is our duty to check the information we receive."

A cupboard door opened very near Gene.

Any minute the pressure of his shoulder on the panel would make the spring catch fly open. Yet he could not move to take away the strain.

"There are other flats in the house, officer."

"It is what I was thinking myself, madame. This is a spare room?"

"My maid sleeps here when she sleeps in."

"She isn't sleeping in at present?"

"As you see."

There was a creak of the bed.

"If I may advise you, madame, I would suggest that you keep your door locked for the rest of the night."

"It's a custom I often follow."

"Yes—er—I beg your pardon. Is this the last room?"

"There's the kitchen."

"Of course. If you will——"

"It's this way."

A long wait in blackness and in heat. Sounds and movements for a time, and once Gene thought he caught some stirring in the bedroom still, as if perhaps one of the men had stayed behind in the room. Then there was a murmured conversation in the sala. Then silence.

Lack of air in the man-hole. Gradually the pipe, which had nearly burned through his coat, began to cool. The beginnings of cramp in both feet. Mustn't think of cramp. Or suffocation. A door banged somewhere in the distance but no footsteps followed it.

He began to count. It was a way he'd followed for years of getting through high discomfort. He had counted to beyond four hundred when someone turned on the water again in the bath. That went on for two or three minutes and the pipe behind him grew hot again. He began to wriggle his feet, fighting the cramp again and fairly sure that any slight noise he made now would be covered. He was soaked in sweat, and it was running off his forehead, down his face and trickling inside his collar. The water stopped. Then someone came into the room and he heard the chest of drawers being cautiously dragged back.

Light fell into the dark. She said: "I think they're searching the other flats. Are you all right?"

"Yes, fine."

"Can you stick it for a few minutes more until the car goes?"

"Yes, if you leave the panel open."

He watched her feet move away. She was wearing the same green pumps, but above four inches of bare ankle was a scarlet bathrobe. He stuck his head out and gulped at the air. Almost immediately she was back.

"They've just gone. Did you hear the car?"

"All of them?"

"I can't be sure. But it's safe to come out."

He began to wriggle through the opening and got to his feet. There was no feeling in either of them and he collapsed into her arms and thence to the bed.

She said: "I am sorry. I could have come earlier but I was expecting a trap; I thought they would come back."

He began clumsily to massage his feet, and she stood and watched him. Presently she pulled off her bathcap and shook out her hair. He said: "Did you change into all that before they came?"

"Yes. I was terrified of two things. The bathroom was too—unused, too unsteamed. And that mark." She pointed to a scrape on the polished parquet floor. "I made it pushing the chest back. I was in too much haste."

He got up, first testing one leg, then the other. "I'll give them another ten minutes and then go."

"Go where? I was asking you when they came."

He limped back into the living-room, moved over to the blind, peered out. "It wasn't the police who saw me come in. I don't like that. This evening, when I went back to the place where I'd been staying, the police were there. I was warned just in time. I doubt if they would have found me on their own."

She tightened the cord of her bath robe. "There's the paper. The Lieutenant left it for me. Perhaps he thought I would recognise you better."

He picked *Aegis* up and stared at the two photos, at the glaring headline. The paragraph underneath was very brief—later editions would carry more. "No name or nationality."

"That's a government tactic, I should say. If possible they'll hush it up or try to call you British. But it won't stop them bringing you to trial. George had many friends."

"I'll get out."

"Which way can you go?"

"I shall make my way down to Piraeus and smuggle on board a ship, if possible one going to Venice. From there there's all Europe to choose."

"It will be impossible." When he looked at her she added: "Without help."

He offered her a cigarette. She shook her head. "Do you know, there is only one safe place for you, Gene, for the time being."

"Where?"

"Here."

He lit a cigarette for himself, broke the dead match, put it in an ash-tray. "No."

"Yes."

"Well, thanks, but I don't see it."

"It is obvious. Everyone will expect you to be on the run, to be trying to get out of Greece. The last place the police will look is here—*which has already been searched.*"

He thought round it carefully. "Maybe you have something. But even if that was so, I'm not willing to involve you any more."

She said: "Don't you know I am involved?"

"Not if I get out now."

"Whatever you do now—I am still involved."

He looked at her, his eyes going carefully, almost painfully over her face. "Yes ... in that ... but that's not the way I mean."

"I sent you away," she said. "It was your view too. But tonight you have come back. That is—just the way the cards, have fallen. It does not mean I may not be permitted to help you."

"It does if your safety is concerned as well."

She said: "If you stay here tonight I think I can make arrangements. I have money and still some influence. Perhaps you could leave tomorrow night, but that will depend."

"And your maid?"

"I can telephone her. I will tell her not to come."

He shook his head. "If I stay tonight it may mean I'm stuck here for three or four."

"Does that matter?"

"Yes, yes, yes. Every hour increases your risk. D'you realise what being an accessory after the fact means?"

"Do you realise that I don't care?"

He came across slowly and put his hands on her elbows and smiled his crinkly smile at her. "You don't care?"

She looked at him directly for a moment, then glanced beyond him with a sort of removed matter-of-factness, a drawing back as if he were a stranger. "I must hide you here until I can make arrangements to get you out. What chance do you think you would have of slipping through tonight or tomorrow at any Greek port or station or air terminal?"

"I've slid out of difficult corners before."

"But this is not war. You have not got the population on your side. You have no passport except one which will get you instantly arrested. You have no disguise but a pair of spectacles. You admit you will not ask your friends to help you. Therefore it's essential you should stay here."

He released her and walked up and down once, thinking it over, knowing she was watching him.

He said: "Are you proposing I should spend another night with you in—in intimate celibacy?"

"I don't know what that means."

He explained.

"Yes," she said. "Yes. . . ."

He smiled at her again. "You think—that is going to answer with us now?"

"With things as they are, it cannot be any other way."

Chapter Twenty Six

They slept for three hours. She had set a clock to wake them but before it went off he was stirring, moving round the sala, examining the grey empty street through the slats in the Venetian blind. He made coffee, and a few minutes before the clock was due to go off he went into her bedroom with a tray and touched her hand.

She was instantly alert. "Yes?"

"Just before seven and all's well."

She slowly relaxed and yawned against her fingers. Her hair lay thick and black on one bare shoulder. Her face looked strangely naked and unguarded without make-up in the filtered morning light.

She said: "I had horrible dreams."

"Coffee?"

"Thank you."

They drank in silence.

He said: "I wouldn't have waked you so early but for calling your maid."

"Have you looked out?"

"Yes. There's someone watching the house."

"What? Who is it—the police?"

"No. A young man I first saw with Mandraki at The Little Jockey."

"So you were right."

"They may be watching only so they can follow you when you go out."

"I must telephone Edda."

He left her while she got up. Looking for a towel in the bathroom, he opened a drawer and found a razor and a tooth brush and some hair cream. In a small silver box were collar studs and cuff links, and clean handkerchiefs. For a moment they shocked him, and he was startled at being shocked. Sometimes common sense barely goes skin deep. A stain lay suddenly across his mind—like an overturned inkpot.

When he came out she said: "I've given her two days off. She knows about George's death, of course."

"I'll make breakfast while you have your bath."

"There's no new bread. Edda usually brings it."

"If it's old I'll toast it."

Over breakfast they didn't speak for a while. Presently she got up and switched the radio on. They listened to an advertisement and then the news came through.

"Progress is being made in the search for the international spy who is wanted for the murder of George Lascou, ex-minister and leader of the newly formed EMO party. All available police have been allocated to this task, and Major Kolono, who is in charge of the investigation, stated that an arrest could be expected shortly. The assassin is described as of medium height, fluent in Greek, about thirty years of age, brown hair, grey eyes, of thin build but muscular and athletic. All Athens is shocked and horrified by this dastardly crime which robs the political scene of one of its most talented and popular figures.

"M. Stavrides, deputy leader of EMO, stated late last night that the death of George Lascou will not affect his party's plans for contesting the election. 'We shall go on,' he said, 'saddened but inspirited by the example of this good man. And we shall win.'

"In Salonika yesterday dock labourers———"

She switched it off and ran her hands up and down her arms as if to suppress a shiver.

When she sat down at the table again he touched her hand. "That's nothing fresh."

"I don't like to hear it."

"What are you going to do today?"

"Mme Lindos is entirely to be trusted?"

"She's an old woman. She mustn't be caught up in this. She lent me money; that's enough."

"Gene, give up for a little while denying to your friends the privilege of helping you!"

". . . Anya, what made you go to see her yesterday?"

"I thought you had gone. I thought I wanted to know more about you."

Thinking of the things he had found in the drawer, he said: "Perhaps we already know enough."

She looked at him. "What do you mean?"

"It was just a casual remark."

"But what did you mean by it?"

He hesitated and then said: "I was only thinking that for love you must have some degree of innocence. . . . Maybe we both know too much ever to achieve that innocence again."

She got up and went to the mantelpiece. It was a sudden almost defensive movement he had not seen her make before.

He tried to follow up the sentence, but he was struggling with feelings he didn't recognise in himself. Before he could add anything the front door bell rang.

"Oh, good day, Mlle Stonaris, I didn't know if your maid would be in yet. I'm glad to see I haven't disturbed you. I've only been stirring myself some few minutes but I had to come round at once to tell you about the water."

"Water, M. Voss?"

"Yes. I woke about twenty minutes ago and could hear the dripping. *Tap, tap, tap*, it went, and I thought it was raining and dripping on the window sill. Then when I got up I found a pool on my bathroom floor. It appears to be running along the beading of the ceiling and be coming from a corner by the hot water pipes, but the water is only just warm. Have you a leak in you bathroom?"

"No."

"I feel it must come from up here. There's nowhere else, is there. Could you make sure? It's leaking quite fast."

"Of course. Will you wait in here a moment?"

She showed her neighbour into the little vestibule but no further. Then she slipped quickly through the empty living-room into the bathroom. Gene was in there, having decided in the absence of a police car that there was no need to hide.

"You heard?"

"Yes. There's no leak here."

She glanced under the bath. He stayed her with fingers on her arm. "I may have damaged something last night in the man-hole."

She went out. "I'm very sorry, M. Voss. There seems to be nothing, but I'll look round."

"I'd be very glad. My bathroom floor is quite awash. Could I help you at all?"

"No, I'd prefer to do it myself. My maid will help when she comes."

"Well, if you can't find anything I'll have to send for a plumber. But perhaps you'll let me know when you've looked again."

"I'll phone you, M. Voss."

"Thank you. Thank you."

She showed him out and went back to the bathroom. Gene said: "There's nothing to see here."

They went into the maid's bedroom and pulled the chest away. He opened the man-hole and wriggled part way in.

"Yes, it's here."

"Much?"

"There's a split at the joint. I must have done it when I forced a way in."

She crouched beside him, said rather stiffly: "Can you stop it?"

"It's iron. You can't mend it without tools; there's a leak at the joint. I might try wrapping it with cloth."

He tried wrapping it with cloth.

"That's no good," he said. "It'll have to be a plumber."

"Can't you put something underneath it? A basin, a bowl?"

"It's pretty difficult because the water runs down the pipe instead of dripping direct to the floor. But if you get me something I'll try."

She got him a basin. When he'd put it down he said: "Have you a stop-cock?"

"Yes, I think so. Under one of the tiles in the bathroom."

"I thought for today maybe we could do without water. It would save a plumber."

"It won't work. It cuts off the water for the downstairs flat also."

He bit the end of his thumb. "Then a plumber it'll have to be."

"I don't like it." She squatted on her heels and frowned.

"It will be better than having the man downstairs complaining."

"I shall have to wait in until he comes."

"Maybe not. Go out and do what you want to do and phone the plumber when you come back. In the meantime if I can have a good supply of old rags I can keep it under control for an hour or two."

She phoned a soothing message to M. Voss, and changed into a black frock and went out. She said, still distantly: "Don't answer the door. Don't answer the phone. I don't think anyone will come."

"What are you going to do?"

"I don't know. I don't know yet at all."

When she had gone the flat was suddenly foreign and empty. He was not a man to whom inactivity was ever welcome, and inactivity at present was harder than usual to take. So long as Anya was with him he could forget it, but as soon as he was alone he began chafing at his own helplessness. To him movement was not just a means of escape, it was a way of defeating the enemy: the positive choice instead of the negative one.

Before she left Anya had opened the windows and pulled up the blinds. It was necessary to give any watchers the appearance of naturalness; but it restricted his movements to the far side of the rooms and even made these undesirable. When the sun came round this afternoon it would be right to let the jalousies down again.

It was a brilliant day and summer was falling on the city. One or two white clouds hung in the sky but their vapour was being absorbed by the sun. A bee droned lazily in and out of the open windows. People walked on the shady side of the street. A little puff of dust rose every now and then with the wind. In a corner on the opposite side a thin dark sneering young man with a drooping bow tie and a petulant mouth shifted from one elegant leg to the other and spat. Gene saw him and knew that he had not followed Anya.

The leak took most of his time. He tried tea towels and floor cloths to mop the water up, but the result didn't justify the effort. In the end he let it run and devised a series of basins and cups to catch most of the leak.

Once he cast about the flat for the Avra letters he had brought, but in the panic of last night Anya had either hidden them securely or burned them. Once the telephone rang. It went on insistently, and after a minute he crawled to the window and peered out. Zachari was gone. He waited there on his knees till the phone stopped; then presently the watcher opposite came back to his post.

The little Limoges clock with the blue and gilt face struck ten and then half past. With the windows open he did not dare switch on the radio. Opening the escritoire to put away a book he saw a roll of strong sellotape and thought that even yet there might be a chance of saving a plumber. He went back and pushed the basins aside to see if he could bind over the split.

With his head and part of his body inside the hole he had no chance of hearing someone come into the flat and then into the room behind him.

Chapter Twenty Seven

Nerves long trained will show their training in a crisis; like soldiers under ambush they answer by instinct, responding to the conventional call. When someone exclaimed behind him he didn't crack his head on the pipes but slid quickly out and sat up to stare at a short thick-set woman in a linen coat and white shoes.

"What is it you are doing here?"

"He swallowed saliva in his throat and coughed. "I didn't hear you come in."

"Who are you? What is it you are doing there?"

He said: "What business is it of yours?"

Her halting Greek had given him a lead. But he wanted to be quite sure.

"I'm Mlle Stonaris's maid. Where is she?"

"She's just gone out. D'you want her?"

"I come to pick something up. I do not expect . . . What is gone wrong?"

He was in his shirt sleeves, and even the old gladstone bag he had bought was on the floor behind him, lending the right colour to the idea. "There's a leak. The man downstairs called me in. Name of Voss. It's coming through in his bathroom."

"Is it you are from the builders?"

"No, I work on my own." He took out a packet of cigarettes and offered her one. "They're French."

"No, thank you." The surprise was leaving her and she was a little on her dignity. "I come for a dress. It so happens to be in here."

"All right." He lit his own cigarette.

Still sitting on the floor he watched her go to the wardrobe. If you watch someone, someone hasn't the same opportunity to watch you. His chief danger was lack of tools; but it was unlikely she'd stop and peer into the man-hole.

She took a black frock from the wardrobe, and then out of a drawer a few things she didn't let him see.

She said irritably: "What is the matter; can you not mend it?"

"Oh, yes, nearly done. Just taking a breather."

"When is Mlle Stonaris coming back?"

"She said she wouldn't be long. She said if I was finished before she got back I was to let down the catch."

The woman hesitated. Gene knew pretty well what was going on in her mind. He said: "I'll not be more than another hour."

"Another hour! . . . Phoo! Be sure it is good work. Often one hole is stopped and another made."

She folded her frock on the bed and then laid it carefully over her arm. Gene opened his brown bag and pretended to look for something inside.

"Are you going on holiday?" he asked.

"Perhaps." She was on her dignity again. "Where did Mlle Stonaris say she is gone out?"

"She didn't tell me. Why should she?"

The woman moved to the door and went out. But she didn't leave the flat. He thought she was just slightly suspicious and uncertain and was perhaps looking round to see if anything had been disturbed. His mind flickered over the things in the flat. Nothing to tell her he had been here all night. Lucky he'd made this bed. His hat? No, that was in here. Coffee cups? Anya had stacked them in the kitchen. Cigarette ends? Unlikely she'd read anything from that.

He heard her moving about in Anya's bedroom, then in the kitchen. He picked up a piece of old piping left on the floor of the man-hole and began to tap one of the other pipes with it. Silence fell. He knew she had not gone. Was she sitting waiting for *him* to go? Anya might be out till one o'clock.

He picked up his piece of pipe and went out into the sala. She was not there, but the first thing he noticed was this morning's *Aegis* face upwards on the piano with his own photograph staring at the ceiling. He could not touch it, not even to turn it over.

He went into the kitchen but she wasn't there. She came quickly and suspiciously out of the bathroom as he opened the nearest drawer, bending his head over it.

"Yes?"

"Have you a small spanner?"

She hadn't yet recognised him. "Do you not have your own tools?"

"My spanner's too big."

"There are a few things in that cupboard."

He opened the door of it and rummaged about. He took out a pair of pliers. "These may do. Thanks."

She stood aside to let him pass. He wondered if he should make the move, his hand over her mouth, into the spare room. It was the act of despair, the final surrender to panic.

He went past. He went into the sala with the paper staring from the piano and thence to the spare room. As he did so he heard a key in the outer door of the flat.

He couldn't greet her as she came in, to warn her and explain, but he stood just within the door where she could see him as she went past, and clinked the pipe with pliers.

She came through the double doors and began to speak; but stopped in time.

"*Edda!* What are you doing here?"

"Ma'am, I thought already you had left for the hotel and I have the need for my black dress. So I came up for it."

"Oh. . . . Oh, I see." Anya had heard his hammer from the spare room.

"You do not mind? It is my best dress and I have the wish to visit my brother. And then I find this plumber here." The voice was lowered. "I think perhaps it is best. . . ."

"Yes, of course. . . ."

The voices mumbled on. Gene went back to the man-hole,

breathing deeper. Edda had taken it on herself to make the situation clear.

Anya came to the door. "Have you nearly finished?"

He withdrew his head and they looked at each other. There was a glint of irony in his eye. "About ten minutes, I expect, ma'am. I've just to tighten the joint."

"I see. . . ." She put down her shopping basket. "All right, Edda, everything will be all right now."

The Italian woman still wanted to linger; she explained that she'd passed the time tidying up, and would Mlle Stonaris tell her which hotel it was to be? and she was desolated to hear the terrible news, and she hoped . . .

Anya got her to the door and out. When the door was shut she leaned back against it and stared at Gene.

They didn't speak. He slid across to the window watching, Edda came out and down the steps and walked off up the street. But Zachari from his corner, though he may have taken note of her leaving, did not try to intercept her.

". . . You were in there when she came?"

"Yes, I never heard her."

"She has her own key. It never occurred to me. . . ."

Gene watched the Italian until she was out of sight. "It's a chance we'll have to take. There wasn't any other choice except keeping her here by force."

Anya opened the paper she carried and put it beside *Aegis*. "They all have the photo. And you see now, there's a reward. . . ."

It was a copy of *Telmi*, the principal newspaper of the EMO party. Gene's photograph occupied three-quarters of the front page. Under it was a headline in red offering 25,000 drachmae for information which would lead to the discovery of the criminal.

He said: "The most I had on my head during the war was a hundred pounds in gold. Prices are rising everywhere."

"Manos is behind this," she said. "Manos and the party. It is enough to make every man look at his neighbour."

"What have you been doing?" he asked.

"I have seen Mme Lindos. Also I called in and ordered the

plumber. He is coming round at once; that was another reason for getting rid of Edda quickly. I have bought some food. Also I went to Heracles House."

"You've done a lot."

She began to pull off her gloves. "The—funeral is this afternoon. You know of course to be quick like that is the custom in Greece."

"Yes."

"I must go."

"Of course."

"It will be a big one. EMO will try to make capital out of the loss of their leader. If they can bring you into court as a murderer—an American who at one time worked for the British—it would appeal to this—this stranger-hating emotion which has been creeping over Athens of late. . . ."

"And your arrangements?"

"Where will you hide while the plumber is here?"

"In your bedroom? He may want to go in the bathroom."

"Well, go in there now, will you? He may be here any minute."

Gene took his bag and slid along the inner wall to her room. He found her peering slant-wise through her blind.

"There is someone in the flat on the opposite side of the street. . . . Oh, I don't know; it may not be anybody; one comes to suspect. . . ." She lowered the blind a little. "It is reasonable now; the sun is coming round."

"You saw Sophia Lindos?"

"Yes. But I think you will have to stay here another thirty-six hours."

The telephone rang.

She went out, and came back after a minute. "A reporter. They tried to get me to talk at Heracles House. I hope they won't wait outside here. . . . Where was I? Oh, Mme Lindos. There is nothing yet settled. But I said I felt sure I could get you out of Athens if she could get you out of Greece. So for the moment it has been left that way."

"You're being very competent about it all."

She lifted an eyebrow. "Competence can be so dull."

"Where you're concerned?"

"Well, tarnished, then. Perhaps that is the word." She picked up a pair of nylons from the back of a chair and folded them and put them in a drawer. "Isn't it what we've both agreed?"

Before he could reply the door-bell rang.

"It will be the plumber," she said. "While he is here I will do some telephoning and try to get a meal ready. Then I shall be able to keep an eye on him. I'll tell you if he's going to be very long."

The sun was coming round to the bedroom windows, and Gene saw that it would soon be reasonable enough to lower the blinds completely. He heard Anya using the telephone, and a conversation she had with the plumber. At the taverna where he had eaten last night the proprietor was brushing the steps, which led down; he therefore appeared to be brushing all the dust into his room and not out of it. Behind the blinds of the room on the opposite side of the street someone moved; a hand reached through the slats to fumble with the cord and raise the blind a few inches. In the street below Zachari had apparently gone. The plumber began to knock.

Anya slipped into the bedroom and at once went to the jalousies and let them right down.

"Half an hour. I have spoken again to Jon Manos and also to Mme Lascou. It was necessary, you understand. Also I must have your passport when I go out."

"It's here."

"Put it in my bag, will you?"

They were talking in whispers, her face close to his but her expression very distant. Once her breath fanned his cheek.

He said rather quietly: "Anya, I want to talk to you."

"Not now. It is a silly time."

"I think we've both been deceiving ourselves."

"About what?"

"About this." He drew her against him and kissed her quietly on the mouth. She shook her head for a second or so after their lips touched. The plumber continued to hammer. Then she slid away, put the back of her hand up to her mouth and looked at him. "You don't suppose that solves anything?"

"Not on its own. It will in time."

"Don't be a fool."

"We've been deceiving ourselves, because that's the only thing that really matters between us."

"Is that what you think?"

"That's what I think."

"You know we both agreed it was impossible."

"I knew we agreed nothing of the sort. We agreed it was ill-advised, slightly crazy, unrealistic, likely to get right out of hand and so the more sure to come a crash in the end. But now——"

"This morning you said, just after breakfast you said——"

"Just then it was as if for a second Lascou had come between us. It was entirely my fault——"

"Has he ever stepped aside?"

"I don't think he's ever *been* between us. Not in the way that counts. . . . Anya, at least accept what you yourself said last night. We tried to write this off. By chance we haven't been able to. So we can no longer avoid what we tried to avoid. Isn't that it?"

"Is that it?"

"There isn't any escape for either of us." he said. "You know that now."

She turned her darkest glance on him, half smiled, half shrugged, her eyes slipping over him. Perhaps her attitude expressed exactly what she felt, a delicate but sensual disclaimer of responsibility. Her fingers closed round his and then she left the room.

Time passed. Zachari's replacement was Mandraki. Gene felt a prickling of the skin when he saw him. This was something instinctive, something much more fundamental and less cerebral than his antagonism for Lascou. The plumber took longer than he had said, as plumbers always do. Anya did not come back.

Conflicting with his unease, with his impatience in inactivity, was a ripple of excitement coming up as it were against the current, a wave running up a river. The sunlight was broken in pieces on the floor where it came through the blinds. In his mind, in his heart, it was as if all the disparate pieces there had come together, as if all the hesitations and qualifications of experience had solidified and become a knowledge and a unification no less complete than would happen to the sunlight on the raising of the blind. The foreseeable future was short he was content to let it be so.

At last there was more conversation in the sala, and at last Anya came back. She smiled at him with that rare brilliance she seldom gave to him, as if a little afraid of its effects on herself.

"He's gone. And our lunch is ready."

Going down the stairs the plumber fingered the pen-knife he'd found on the floor of the man-hole. He wasn't a thief, but it seemed a handy little thing and he'd lost his own a few weeks ago. He hadn't noticed anybody returning *that* to *him*. Besides there was nothing to prove that it belonged to the wonderful looking girl who had called him in. It might have lain on the floor for months and have belonged to some previous owner.

At least he thought that until he took it out of his pocket in the bright light of the street and read the inscription on it. It ran: *'Presented with the proud compliments of "Aegis" on the 50th Anniversary of its foundation.'* He had to stare twice at the date which followed, because it didn't seem to make sense that it should be today's date. But there it was.

He crossed the street and turned past a man lighting a cigarette. As he did so the man touched his arm.

"Been working in number four, brother?"

"What?" The plumber moved to go on but the hand held him. The man was all in black, fat, with a beard growing only under his several chins.

"You been working in Flat 4? I thought I saw you come to the window up there."

"What's it to you?"

"What was wrong with the plumbing, brother? What did you do in there?"

The plumber said: "A burst pipe. I mended it. That's the way I earn my living—not by standing on street corners."

The bearded man breathed in his face. "Be easy with your answers, brother. I'm not asking you this for love. Remember, I don't love you. What was the man like who let you in? Middle-sized, grey-eyed, bit of a foreigner?

"Look," said the plumber. "You're chasing the wrong hare. There was no man. Only a girl. You've got the places mixed."

"Didn't you see a man in the flat at all?"

"What business is it of yours?"

"None, brother. I just like to know. Did you go in every room?"

"How do I know? I'm a plumber, not an architect. I tell you, I saw no one but the girl, the lady, whatever she is. Now move aside."

Chapter Twenty Eight

The funeral was at four. Anya left at three, in her deepest black and wearing a veil. She was gone until eight, and when she came home he saw at once that the distance was back, the defensive shell. Not only had she truly grieved for George, she had been in contact with the people and the world she understood and had known all her life. It was as if she had been re-injected with a familiar drug.

"You're in the dark. Has anyone called?"

"Someone rang the bell at four. And there were two phone calls."

She dragged off her hat and veil, threw them into a chair, went to the blinds to see that they were properly drawn, then switched on two of the table lamps. "Oh, I am so tired. It is—you know—the emotion."

"Let me get you a drink."

"Thank you. I will change out of these."

When she came back she was wearing the narrow black velvet trousers again and a scarlet tailored shirt with stiff cuffs. She smiled at him but not freely. He took her the drink and she curled up on the settee with her feet under her. He offered her a cigarette but she shook her head. He did not smoke himself but squatted on the piano stool and watched the expressions moving on her face.

"Do you want to hear about it?" she said.

"Only if you want to tell me."

"Then not. I would rather not."

"Did you go back afterwards? To Heracles House, I mean."

"Oh, yes, I had to; it was expected. In a way I wanted to. . . . I wanted to see it for the last time."

"You have come from there now?"

"No, I left at six. There was nothing more for me after that. . . . I have come now from Mme Lindos. And I have seen several other people."

He waited but didn't speak.

"Mme Lindos thinks she can fix it for Friday. Not before because her arrangements, you understand, have to be made at a distance, and she dare not use the phone. My part is easier."

"And what is your part?"

She shrugged deprecatingly. "It is not very clear and it is not very original, but I think it will work when the time comes."

"Friday, you mean?"

"Friday morning."

"I don't want you concerned in it."

"I am not. At seven every morning the milk comes here in a small van. The man leaves his van and delivers the milk outside each flat and then drives away. On Friday morning a milk van will come at fifteen minutes to seven. The man will bring the milk up, and when he reaches this flat he will come in and give you his coat and cap and you will walk out and drive the van away. You will drive the van out of Athens—I don't think you will be stopped—and as far as you can towards the destination that Mme Lindos is arranging for you; all the way if possible."

He looked at her with a little wry smile. "It is in the classic tradition."

She flushed slightly. "It is not very clever but it may do."

"You've found a man to take the risk?"

"I have friends. And I can pay more than the official reward. . . . You know Nafplion?"

"On the Peloponnese? I've been near it."

"It is a small harbour. There are fishing boats. Mme Lindos has a friend there. I shall have to go out again tomorrow morning."

"What for?"

"I have left your passport with a man. He is photographing the photograph. He has promised to make you into a French citizen. There is also the question of getting lire and francs."

Gene said: "If you can do all this for me in a day, I wonder what you could do in a lifetime."

She looked at him as if trying to see deeper than her gaze would penetrate. "I do not see the hope or the prospect of that."

"I think there's the hope."

She looked down abruptly at her glass, and appeared to meditate on that too. She did not reply.

They were about half-way through supper when Jon Manos called.

They had made the same preparations as at midday against a surprise. Nothing of Gene's was in the sala except the plate from which he was eating, his wine glass, a slice of bread.

Manos came in, hair-oiled and plump-cheeked and smelling of Roman hyacinth. "My dear, I hoped you wouldn't have started—it's early yet and I've found a new place in Ekali—very quiet, we could dine privately. What do you say?"

"Thank you, Jon, but I've almost finished. In any case it is more fitting for me . . ."

"I understand how you feel. The formal rites this afternoon. EMO did very well at short notice. Mme Lascou, I thought, did not behave politely to you."

"I thought she was splendid. We met as mourners."

"Of course. Of course." He glanced once round the apartment, summing it up swiftly and in a different way from ever before, like a man suddenly being asked to bid at an auction. Then his eyes came back to the girl as she sat on the arm of the settee and summed her up too, missing absolutely nothing, from the curve of her breast under the scarlet shirt to the hand rubbing itself meditatively along her trousered leg. "Anya, this will make a difference to you."

"And to you, Jon."

"Naturally. Will you smoke?"

"No, thank you. But please smoke yourself."

"We have—a lot in common now, Anya. We both—attached ourselves, in very different ways, to a star. And now the star has fallen!"

"I hadn't looked at it that way."

"Of course I am putting it too bluntly. But many years ago . . . May I?" Manos slipped off his thin white overcoat and dropped it on a chair. ". . . many years ago, when I first met George Lascou, I saw him as a coming man in the biggest way. One had to be with him only a little while to appreciate his penetrating yet subtle mind, the great driving force behind that too quiet manner. I—made my choice. Sometime—I don't know when—you made your choice. That is what I mean by saying we had much in common. Of course, in our different ways, we had much to contribute in return."

"You're too kind."

Manos paced across the room lighting his cigarette. His white foulard tie contrasted with a navy blue shirt and a suit with a just visible pink stripe. He said: "My trained legal mind was of great value to him in his transactions. We helped each other. I learned much from him. I hope—to carry on in his tradition, as it were. All will not be lost, Anya, all will not be lost."

She remained perfectly quiet, holding her knee in her hand now, profile to him, ankle gently swinging.

He said: "It was my ambition to serve George faithfully until he reached the highest eminence. I would have been his second man. Stavrides is a nonentity who would have been swept away after the election. George was agreed on it."

"So?"

"Now that George has gone I serve Stavrides for the time being. He is the only figurehead we can rally behind. But he is too weak to survive permanently." Manos stopped in his pacing and made an expressive gesture with his hands. "He will go and the leadership will devolve on me. That's certain."

"So?"

"I cannot hope to bring to this position the gifts that George Lascou had. But my best will not be inconsiderable. It's not impossible that you're looking at a future Prime Minister of Greece."

Anya got up then and poured herself more wine. "Will the *coup* go on?"

He looked at her quickly. "You knew of it?"

"Of course."

"George did not tell me he had told you."

"George told me many things."

"Well, it cannot. General Telechos has already indicated that he will deal with no one else. I shall see him again in the morning, but I'm afraid the chance is lost."

"Then your chances of being Prime Minister of Greece . . ."

"Will depend—temporarily—on the outcome of the election. But we shall not lose votes through George's death." In his pacing Manos stopped before a mirror and tightened his tie. "Anyway, I'm not sure that it would be a good thing to win this election."

"Why not?"

"The country is too evenly split. With Telechos, yes, we could take over and hold what we took. Without him—and depending on parliament—it is better I think if the Government is returned, but with a very small majority. Then we can exploit their weaknesses, make capital out of the discontent that must come, and carry the day next time."

"Wine?" she said. "Or brandy? It is George's brandy, so you should like it."

He glanced at her, sensing the equivocal, poured himself a drink. She said: "Do you think the Communists have a chance?"

"The Communists?" He took time over putting back the brandy bottle. "They're finished—we could never stand them back in Greece, could we?" It was half a statement, half a question.

"George talked of it sometime. He said that there were many disguised Communist sympathisers."

"Some, I suppose. . . . Do you know any?"

She smiled. "They do not confide in me."

"No." He stepped uneasily away from the mirror. "The immediate point is not that at all—it is that EMO has a chance—and I with it."

"Which you intend to take."

"Which George would wish me to take—in the interests of Greece."

"And in your own."

"He would have wished me well, because, as I repeat, I have always subordinated my own interests to his. Even my interest—my very deep interest to his. Even my interest—my very deep interest in you."

It was out now. If she had not taken the point before, it was here plainly stated. Manos's take-over bid did not stop at political parties.

She sipped her wine and looked at him over the top of her glass.

"Don't you think, Jon, that it would be better to leave talking of that until a little time has gone by?"

"Naturally you're upset. Naturally you want time to adjust yourself. We all do. But I didn't wish you to be in any doubt as to the way I feel. My holding back has been entirely out of loyalty for George. . . ."

"Has anything been seen of the man who—did this thing?"

"Vanbrugh? He hasn't been caught yet, if that's what you mean. But he will be."

"It's twenty-four hours."

Manos's eyes had become smaller and colder. "You knew him well, didn't you?"

Anya shrugged. "I knew him. Because George asked me to, I made a friend of him."

"He regretted that later, didn't he?"

"Who, George? I don't think so."

Manos finished his drink and poured himself another. "I happened to be at Heracles House when he came back from visiting you the day before yesterday. He was very angry. He said little to me, but I gathered that he had quarrelled with you."

Anya leaned her elbow on the mantelshelf. "Dear Jon, between a man and a woman things like that can always happen. It's quite true he thought I'd gone too far in encouraging Gene Vanbrugh. So he was jealous. That did no harm. I should only have had more flowers, more presents when he came to his senses. But alas, that did not happen, cannot now ever happen."

Manos said: "I'm glad to know there was no foundation in it. Glad for myself, of course. And glad for you. I did not see how you could possibly betray all the things we have been working for these last ten years."

Anya said: "What exactly *have* we all been working for these last ten years?"

They stared at each other, and ultimately it was Manos who made the little disclaiming gesture. "Need you ask? For the good of Greece. But this man Vanbrugh will be caught—I've no doubt at all."

"Why?"

He walked across the room, his shoes toeing in. "In politics, money and diplomacy will not always do everything. Political life is rough sometimes. I used to argue with George. He always preferred to exercise his power through money if he could. Sometimes he could not—and then he would leave it to me."

"And you?"

"In my legal career I have made contacts where contacts sometimes are invaluable. Little jobs can be done at a price—and no questions asked."

"You mean the Spaniard?"

"So George told you that. It seems——"

"Why did you take me to the Little Jockey the night before it happened?"

"How can one explain these impulses? Curiosity, bravado, a wish to see these people for myself. . . ." Manos made another of his gestures, dismissing it with his plump hands like a legal technicality. "What is important is that I have not left it entirely to the police to trace this Vanbrugh."

When he talked he moved like a dancer, a slow step here, a quick step there; it was a trait that had always amused her. Now it no longer amused her.

"And when did you—decide not to leave it entirely to the police?"

"Monday evening."

"Did George tell you to?"

"No. Sometimes he would hesitate too long. In this case *I* hesitated too long also."

"Is it without any doubt that this man killed him?"

"He was clever enough to remove his finger prints, but Michael's evidence alone will convict him."

"Michael saw the blow struck?"

"No, but everything else. Have no doubt, my dear. Vanbrugh will be found, alive or dead."

She came back to the supper table, picked up a plate and put it over another, slid her used knife and fork on to them. "Forgive me, Jon, I think I am going to bed soon. All this has greatly upset me. . . ."

"Of course." Smiling with his teeth and talking all the time, he allowed her to see him to the door. He took two little side steps and bent to kiss her hand. "Don't forget what I said, Anya."

"About what?"

"About ourselves."

"No. . . . No, I'll not forget."

His smile encompassed her breasts, her shoulders, her neck and face and eyes, and then slipped politely past her to take in again the handsome room he was leaving. "I suppose you haven't heard—you will not have heard yet how any of the money has been left?"

"To his children, I expect," she said. "In trust for his children."

"And in the meantime?"

"I don't know. I hope none of it has been left to me."

Chapter Twenty Nine

"You heard?"

"A good deal of it." Gene moved away from the blind. "The man outside hasn't spoken to him. They're obviously not sure themselves."

"It was Jon Manos who did this—not George."

In silence they cleared away the things. Then she washed up and he wiped.

He said: "Do you care anything for Manos?"

"How could I? A man like that!"

"He has George's bad qualities without his good."

"He could *never* lead Greece. He can only buy the gangster and the bully."

"Which he appears to have done pretty efficiently of late. I don't think we should under-rate him."

"I don't under-rate him but he has no hopes of ever taking George's place!"

After a minute he said: "Was it true, what you told Manos, that you allowed me to make the running on instructions from George?"

"Not instructions. But he thought it a good thing."

"I see."

She said: "And did you first 'make the running with me,' as you call it, to find out more about him?"

"Yes."

She looked at him thoughtfully.

He put down a plate. "I think we've come rather a long way in a week."

"All your invitations to me were—part of this policy?"

"Of course. As all your acceptances were?"

"I didn't come to Delphi because of what George had told me to do! You heard. We quarrelled because of it."

He took up another plate. "I didn't ask you to Delphi to find out about George. By that time I was in love with you."

"But you—went on helping this Spanish girl?"

"It was something I'd promised her—and myself—before I even met you."

She stopped. "I asked that out of jealousy. It's a feeling I have never had before."

He put his hand on her arm and turned her gently round. Her eyes were warm.

She said against his mouth: "So I think I love you too."

When they separated it was as if they had run up five flights. His fingers were trembling. She leaned against the chromium sink.

She said: "And yet—can you understand it?—in spite of this and in spite of what we have said, I don't want—anything here tonight."

"You mean, this flat?"

"*His* flat. He is—to me he is still here. You said this morning that he had come between us. He cannot *help* but be between us here. *Everything* reminds me. I am still part of his belonging. Are you superstitious?"

"No."

"Neither am I. But there are some things that one . . ."

She stopped and looked at him.

He said: "What's between us is too important to begin wrong. I've confidence enough in my chances of getting clear to let this opportunity by if you think it right we should, for the right reasons. But I make one condition."

"What?"

"That we stop talking as if this was something temporary. Whatever else, it isn't temporary. It's the big thing for me—like no other ever. I don't have to say it again, do I?"

She answered: "I think it is the first time you have ever said it."

The plumber had finished his evening meal, and although his children were still up and making a noise, his wife was out, so he enjoyed his daily paper in more detail than usual. It was the warmest evening of the year, and he was regretting he had not gone out for a glass of mastica with his friends, when something he read took his attention, not solely because it was in blacker type. (*Telmi* was a great paper for bigger and blacker type.)

"The murderer was last seen at a ceremony held to commemorate the 50th Anniversary of the founding of the newspaper *Aegis*, from whose offices he made his escape on being recognised. In the interests of fair play we forbear to comment on a situation in which a man such as this, a notorious criminal long wanted by the police, finds himself in the company of high-placed Government supporters, entertained by them, on the best of terms with them, while the blood is still wet on his hands from the commission of his latest and vilest crime."

The paragraph puzzled the plumber. He took out the penknife he had found and stared at it and then re-read the paragraph twice more. The man with the beard stopping him on the street corner—did that mean anything? And—in spite of his denial—the voice he *had* heard in the flat?

"It's no good," said the constable, next morning. "The sergeant's busy. Tell me what you have to say and I will tell him."

"He is my cousin," said the plumber sadly. "It is a family affair."

"Family affairs can wait until the sergeant is off duty. That he will be at six o'clock. You can see him then."

"Certain family matters," said the plumber, "demand immediate discussion."

Flies hummed in the lazy sunbeams that fell through the shutters of the dusty police station. Nothing else stirred.

The plumber added: "I have come here specially to your station, neglecting my work, in the heat of the day. D'you suppose I would go to that trouble without cause?"

The policeman scratched his shirt sleeve. "What is it all about? Your wife? Your daughter? His? Tell me, then I will judge."

"I'm sorry, it is a private matter. But I will tell you it may be to do with the police also."

The plumber had been skilful in the way he had worded his argument. Affinity and consanguinity meant much.

"At four," the policeman said, but speculatively.

"Now," said the plumber.

The flies buzzed drearily and the policeman irritably flicked one away.

"Someone is dead," said the plumber, playing his last card. "It is a matter I must discuss with the sergeant as man to man. Then it may be for someone higher up still."

"Well, well," said the policeman. "Wait here. I will see."

Major Kolono was just beginning his lunch when the call came through.

"What? What? Who is it? Speak up! What information? Who gave it you? Yes, of course, if it is of value. But is it of value? Very well, I'm listening!"

He listened. He said: "Where was it found? Number what? Flat 4. This plumber found it? What was he doing there? . . . I see. Wait a minute, the address is familiar. I will just make sure about that. Hold the line."

He walked into his office and took up another phone. "Find out who lives at Flat 4, number 11, Baronou Street." He waited until the information came through, then stumped back to the other telephone.

"You fool!" he said with considerable pleasure into the receiver. "Don't you know who lives at that address? It is Mlle Stonaris, M. Lascou's mistress. She was at this Anniversary Reception on Tuesday night at the *Aegis* offices and would naturally receive any gift which was being presented on such an occasion. What does it matter where the plumber found it? In any case her flat has already been searched. What? I say it has already been *searched*! Send your plumbers about his business and attend to your own!"

He slammed the receiver down and poured himself another half glass of wine, to which he added iced water. Then he sat down to his interrupted *pepóni*. But towards the end of the meal certain thoughts began to stir in his mind, like frogs in a pool after the ripples of the stone have settled.

Chapter Thirty

It was by far the hottest day of the year so far in Athens. For the first time the sun was a presence to be reckoned with, an injection into the blood-stream of the city. Pulses beat faster, blood flowed hotter and thinner, shadows developed substantial architectures to be sought before they shrank at noon. So now it would go on each day, iron hot in the morning, punitive almost until dark, changeless through the summer until the parched city was swept with the storms of autumn.

But in Anya's flat, with the windows open and the jalousies down, it was only pleasantly warm. She went out early. He did not like her calling on Mme Lindos again, but there was no escape for it. To pass the time while she was gone he read the morning paper through to see if there was anything fresh relating to Lascou's death or to himself. There was nothing new, but on the back paper his eyes suddenly came on a paragraph headed 'Spaniard's Death.' 'Philip Tolosa, 39 year old Spanish dancer and harpist, was found gravely injured in the street outside his hotel window from which he had apparently jumped or fallen. He died on the way to hospital. Tolosa is the second of a troupe of Spanish dancers and entertainers to meet his death in an accident since the troupe arrived in Greece three weeks ago. His brother was knocked down and killed by a car, which failed to stop, in Galatea Street on the 12th. Mme Nicolou, proprietress of the boarding house, said that Tolosa had brooded a great deal over his brother's death and seemed to be unable to get it off his mind. An inquiry will be held tomorrow."

Gene folded the paper. A contrived accident? It seemed unlikely. No one now had anything to gain by his death. For ten days Philip

Tolosa had been working himself into a frame of mind from which there was no return.

And Maria? Safe by now. She was the only one of the three that mattered.

It was noon when Anya returned, bringing his new passport. It was not a bad copy. He did not think it would satisfy the Deuxième Bureau, but it would pass the casual examination of a frontier officer. The photograph was no worse than the original.

"And Sophia?"

"She has had word from Nafplion that it is all right as far as there."

"So tomorrow morning I leave."

"Yes. I'm afraid so."

"I wish you could come with me."

She said: "When you are free let me know where you are, that you're alive and well. That is the first, all-important thing. When that is so, then—maybe—we can begin to plan."

They had their mid-day meal near one of the shuttered windows. They ate and talked in a filtered, aquarium light, but more yellow, thicker, as if it was a world of sunfish. They ate a cold chicken which she had bought, and zucchinis and a mixed salad, and drank a white Tour la Reine.

They didn't talk much. There was still eighteen hours for planning. Just now it was a warm and friendly companionship that didn't need words. It was an astonishing advance in their relationship—of far greater import than the mere physical act of love would have been.

By the time they finshed, traffic in the street outside was drying up like a trickle of water in sand, pedestrians almost disappeared, more blinds came down, dogs and workmen curled up in the shade and slept.

They sat there exchanging a word or two, in their own quiet country, isolated now. They were protected not so much by indifferent walls and slanting jalousies and locked doors as by the sleeping town. For two hours nothing would stir. He came to sit beside her but made no move to touch her.

She said: "Do you want—now—to make love to me?"

"Only on your terms."

She said: "I know it is strange for me, a woman like me, still to have qualms. ... It is pretentious perhaps a little." She smiled at him, considering her words. "It is very difficult. I am not just an animal desiring to be desired by you, but neither am I just a detached brain existing in a—a vacuum. My reason says to me: the fact that this has come in George's flat at a time when George has hardly gone from you, where everything, everything is reminiscent—and I grieve—you may not believe it but I grieve—for a friend. ... All that is ill-tasting only because of a coincidence of time and place. My reason says, how can that really affect what is so separate from it in thought and feeling that it might be happening to someone else? If you refuse this now it will prove nothing except that you are turning away from what is good, what is true, because you cannot rid your memory of what it tries to forget."

"Your reason has a lot of reason on its side."

"But there is another thing. We are in the very centre of danger. What we feel for each other should not be flawed by fear, by the heart jumping for the wrong causes, by a chance telephone call, by the ring at the door, by the siren down the street. It should not be flawed by being snatched at in haste and in dread."

He was a little while replying. In the centre of his mind was a truth that he now fully recognised but was afraid to grasp at and discipline too soon. It might even escape him in speech, in the effort to be completely honest both with her and with himself.

"Anya, I don't know what is true or not true about tomorrow. I can only be sure of today."

"And today?"

"Today I have absolute certainty. I don't need to say it or to think it any more."

"And you would begin this—now?"

"... You must decide."

"Lift off the telephone," she said. "That way we can be sure it will not ring."

Chapter Thirty One

Major Kolono woke about ten past four. Sometimes baby octopus gave him acute indigestion and he was nervous about his stomach. He knew he should see a doctor but he was terrified of being told that there was something gravely wrong.

He got off his couch and went into the next room for the bismuth tablets, and while he was doing so that other discomfort, of the mind, returned. Memories of Saturday came to trouble him—he had seen the wanted man talking to Anya Stonaris—and *why* had her flat been searched? There'd been some report, that. . . . He swallowed the tablets and blew out his chest to let them go down; he persuaded himself he felt better. Then he sat in his chair and pressed the bell, and when it was not immediately answered he kept his finger on it until it was.

His second in command came bustling into the room fastening the top button of his tunic. "Sir?"

"Have you done anything more to check that plumber's report on Flat 4, Number 11, Baronou Street?"

"No, sir. I thought you were satisfied. You gave no instructions."

Kolono stared his subordinate down. "Everything in this department I have to do myself, it seems. No one has the initiative to stir a finger; I wonder how you live in your own houses; are you spoon-fed, dressed and washed? . . . Telephone to the offices of *Aegis* and ask if the penknives which were presented to guests on Tuesday night were given to everyone, especially if it is remembered whether Mlle Stonaris received one. And I want to see that plumber. Also get me Mr. Manos on the other line."

"Very good, sir."

The man went out, and Kolono rubbed his little black moustache and belched. A routine inquiry; but Manos would be able to tell him whether Mlle Stonaris still retained any power, whether it would be permissible to worry her a second time. It was a good policy while on the subject of Vanbrugh to ring the various branch stations for news. An inquiry would keep them up to scratch.

He had finished with two stations and was lecturing a third when his assistant came into the room. Kolono slapped the phone down and said: "Well?"

"Sir, penknives were given only to the gentlemen at the Anniversary Reception. The ladies received fountain pens."

Major Kolono felt a knot twist in his stomach, and it was not dyspepsia. "So."

His second in command waited patiently.

"Mr. Manos?"

"He is out of town, sir. He is expected back this evening."

Kolono said: "How did it come about that Mlle Stonaris's flat was searched in the first place? An anonymous report, wasn't it?"

"A phone call, sir. Late on Tuesday night."

"Nothing was found?"

"No, sir."

"Who was the lieutenant who searched the flat?"

"Andros, sir."

"Send for him at once."

Mme Lindos was a woman of resource. She had seen more wars through than she cared to remember, more civil upheavals and revolutions than she could count. She had suffered the loss of a husband and a son, weathered the storms, it seemed to her sometimes, of more than one lifetime. She could not have survived without great courage and resource and the constant exercise of them.

When her cousin's son-in-law, who happened to be Kolono's second-in-command, called her on the telephone just as she was about to sit down to tea and gave her an urgent but guarded message, she didn't get flustered or panic. She told Louisa to take the teapot back to the kitchen and to keep it warm, then she picked up the telephone. There was a certain risk attached to the use of the telephone, since the line might be tapped, but it was a risk that did not disturb her. She still had a few friends in exalted quarters.

She also had one or two friends in Athens in a lowlier sphere, people whom she could trust, and she decided that now was a time when she must make use of them. She first telephoned the proprietor of a small garage whom she had helped to start in business ten years ago. Having talked with him she rang Anya. The line was engaged.

This was the first point at which she showed some emotion. She lit a cigarette and got up from the telephone and limped across the room. Then she came back and tried again. Still the engaged note.

It was now a matter of timing and carefully calculated risks. It might be that the line was being deliberately cut; or it might be that in five minutes she would still get through. Either event must be prepared for. She pulled across a pen and a piece of paper and tore off the address. Then she scribbled a few lines and put it in an envelope. She rang the bell.

"I want you to take this round to Baronou Street. Deliver it only to Mlle Stonaris, who you remember came here on Tuesday night. And Louisa. . . ."

"Yes, ma'am?"

"Take a basket with some flowers in. Take these flowers from the vases. Just put them in the basket as if you were delivering them. It is a matter of appearing you are going on ordinary business, not delivering a message, d'you understand."

Anya said: "Darling, I am so afraid."

"What, now?"

"Now more than ever. I have so much more to lose."

"Yes. . . . I felt that this morning."

"Did you? I didn't know."

"Happiness is a maker of cowards. Who cares what you lose if you've nothing to lose? But maybe it also makes fighters who fight longer in the end."

"I feel over-burdened, frightened of the danger around us—now, at this moment."

"It's not likely to have changed in two hours."

"It has for me."

"I mean literally."

"I wish you'd put the telephone back."

"Soon."

In the flat on the opposite side of the street someone had switched the radio on, but the music came to them diffused by distance, disembodied, remote.

She stirred restlessly. "It is strange to be so happy and so unhappy at the same time. The heights are no higher for the existence of depths. I want no more than Parnassus."

"What's that thing of Flecker's? 'We stood at last beyond the golden gate, Masters of Time and Fate, and knew the tune that Sun and Stars were singing.' "

After a pause she said: "This afternoon several times, you have spoken to me in Greek. It was like something within yourself speaking, something deeper and more instinctive than your own tongue. That, I think, convinced me more than anything. . . ."

"Of what?"

"Of what I was most anxious to know. Gene."

"Yes?"

"How will you ever clear yourself even if you do get away? How *can* you? It is impossible without some help from this girl. Even then you would be guilty as an accessory. Will she be out of the country yet?"

"Today, I should think."

"I have this feeling, as if something terrible is going to happen, as if our happiness is already fated. It's a premonition. God, that one should be so morbid! It must stop." She raised herself on one elbow and kissed him. "Tell me this fear is not true.' "

Holding her, he said: "Darling, it's not true."

"I wish we could escape together."

"So do I."

"Do you know the Cyclades? I believe we might be forgotten

there. They are hard and windy, but so beautiful. Hot with a lovely sea-heat in the summer, and shell-clear water, like Sounion. One can fish and swim and sit in the sun all day. I think there one could lose ambition, which destroys so much of the world."

"Do you like sailing?"

"I have never done as much as I would want to. And you?"

"We might try together."

"First we must get you out."

"And then you will join me."

She sighed. "It sounds so easy. But I think it will be safer in the South Seas."

"Yes, I might not need to wear a beard there."

She said: "Oh, Gene, there is *no* way, there is *no* way. . . ."

"There is, there is," he whispered. "We will find it."

After a while she murmured in his ear: "The telephone."

"Right, soon."

"Now."

"Right." The telephone by the bed did not work unless the other was connected, so he slid to his feet and padded out into the next room, put the telephone back on its rest, peered through the blind. The street was quiet but there were a few more people about, and cars moved up and down it. The sun was slanting, falling full upon the blinds, and the sala was warmer than the bedroom. The remains of the lunch they had eaten looked untidy and desolate. The little French clock said twenty-five minutes to five.

He went back into the bedroom and found Anya dressing. He interrupted her.

"So soon?"

"I—yes. I feel safer. Is there anyone in the street?"

"Not anyone who shouldn't be there."

He held his face against hers. Her hair touched his forehead and he blew it away. She laughed.

"We must have a wonderful dinner tonight, Gene."

"I'd like that."

"I will devise a menu. My mother taught me to cook, you'll be surprised to know."

"Give me the key to your wine cellar," he said. "Or have I already seen it?"

"What?"

"Your cellar. That's where I hid on Tuesday night? I thought the white wines were rather warm."

She said laughing: "I bought a lobster this morning. With pâté before it. Or is that too rich? A good soup. . . ."

"I'll risk the pâté. Darling, do you play that great piano in the next room?"

"Of course."

"Then will you do that?"

"Now?"

"Sometime soon. You see, I don't know you yet, and I want to get to know you."

She said: "And there are those things from the excavations at Sounion. I promised to show you them."

"We mustn't over-crowd the evening."

She put on high-heeled mules of fine kid. He watched her.

"Why not those bedroom slippers?"

"I cannot bear to be sloppy."

He laughed. "But *I* am sloppy."

"No, you're not. Not in the ways that matter. Your shirts, your shoes. . . ." She stopped. "Seriously, Gene. . . ."

He laughed again. "How often have you said 'seriously' to me already?"

"If you would speak Greek to me I should not have the habit. But Gene, this is really serious, really important. Last night, talking about the arrangements I had made for your escape, you said to me, 'if you can do all this for me in a day, I wonder what you could do in a lifetime.'"

"I meant it."

"But I want to say this now: if we have luck, if we have some life together even for a short time, I shall not try to organise it—not even with the help of Mme Lindos."

He said: "And in reply, seriously, if that happens, you can dictate your own terms. I shall be in no mood to bargain."

She stood up and buttoned the back of her dress. He went again to the window. The palm outside was rustling its leaves like a great elephantine fern; one huge frond almost brushed the window. On the other side of the street people were opening their shutters as the sun left them. The shutters immediately opposite were pale grey in a pink-washed house. A woman was brushing her hair, just seen as a pale arm moving regularly in the dark room.

He turned and found Anya smiling at him. She said: "You're wondering how I could live simply on an island if I can't bear to be sloppy?"

"I wasn't, but I can if you want me to."

She said: "It is not what one wears, darling, it is an attitude of mind. I'm sure I should not disgrace you in Tahiti."

He said: "You have very quaint ideas of who is conferring the favour in all this. All I ask, when I write to you, is that you should come."

The telephone began to ring.

They looked at each other. She slid out of his arms and went into the other room. From the doorway as he dressed he watched her.

"Yes. . . . Who? . . . Oh. . . . Yes, he is here What is it?" All the laughter had gone from her face. She held out the telephone. "It is Mme Lindos. For you."

He took the phone, his mind registering the incaution of these women. Then he heard that unmistakable dry voice, rather masculine over the phone.

"Gene?"

"Yes."

"You must go. The—the people who called for you on Tuesday night are coming for you again."

He felt what he had never felt before on his own behalf, a qualm of panic.

"When?"

"The message was a little indefinite—naturally. But I think immediately. I have been trying to telephone you for fifteen minutes.

I think they will be round any moment. Now listen. Understand this carefully."

"Yes?"

"In five minutes—if these people who are coming for you are not there before then—a taxi will draw up at the door. I do not know what sort it will be, but the young man driving it will be looking for you. Be in the doorway ready. The taxi will not stop its engine. As it draws up go out and jump in. The driver will help you as best he can. Is that clear?"

"Yes. What are you——"

"It is the best I could do in an emergency. It may already be too late. If my maid comes with a note before then, tell her to come straight back to me. I——"

"Sophia, I cannot let you——"

"You must be there waiting, for my friend will not stop. That is asking too much. He will tell you the rest. God go with you."

He spoke again but she had rung off.

He put the phone back, turned to look at Anya who was standing tall and straight watching him.

"I'm on my way out," he said.

He dressed like lightning, fishing out the old gladstone bag with his own clothes still unjettisoned, put on his spectacles, hat, talking to her. . . .

"Don't worry about me. Clear these things. Wash the glasses or break them. If they——"

"*Gene*, what when you get in the car? Did she say nothing? . . ."

"It's up to me. And looking after yourself is up to *you*. If they find no traces of me here they can do *nothing* to you. Understand? Nothing. So don't come down with me. Cigarette ends, remember. The newspapers on the piano. Look round the bedroom——"

"What do I care about myself? How shall I hear from you? How shall I know you're safe?"

"No news, good news. But I warn you of one thing. If I get out you'll hear as soon as I can let you know. You'll *never* get clear of me now. *Never*. Understand?"

She said indistinctly: "Food, wine; take something with you in that bag. Here, give it to me. . . ."

While he unlocked the outer door and peered cautiously up and down the stairs she flew to the kitchen, found a small bottle of brandy—that and half the chicken and a piece of cheese and a stick of bread went in on top of the clothes. He was back at the window looking out. There was still no sign or sound of the police. But Mandraki was there now, leaning against a wall about thirty yards away on the opposite side.

He took the bag from her and they went to the door.

"No further. Wash those plates. Darling, darling, I must go."

"Remember me," she said.

They kissed. He said: "Anya. . . . Good-bye."

She kissed him, but couldn't speak. Then he was gone, pattering down the stone stairs.

Chapter Thirty Two

Wait at the door. How long to wait at the door? Four minutes exact had passed since putting down the receiver. No taxi. Street empty. So it was a question of waiting. But which would come first, the taxi or the police car?

Every second made danger more extreme. If the police came first he was caught without a hope. Sophia Lindos's friend might not be as brave as she thought. Getting the request from her he would no doubt decide with a typical shrug: better have a breakdown, apologise to her afterwards, not really worth the risk of falling foul of the police. Perhaps he was smoking a cigarette now in his garage; pity, he'd think, I'd have liked to help the chap.

Anya's risk was increased too by this wait. They must accuse her if they found him here, on her doorstep. Better if Sophia hadn't made any plan, left it to him. At least now he would be on his own. He wasn't afraid of Mandraki. Shake him off. Or push him under a bus. He could fend for himself. Athens was his native ground. A dozen holes.

A gypsy was coming down the street leading a brown bear on a chain. When he stopped, people at once began to gather round to watch. The *romvia* was still an attraction when he ventured into the city.

Outside the taverna a lorry was delivering a barrel of resinated wine. A car came down the street, swerving round the lorry, and seemed about to stop. But it went on again, gears whining, turned a corner on its brakes. Someone in a hurry, but not for him.

The gypsy wore a leather waistcoat over a green shirt with old brown breeches. He beat on his tambourine and the bear hoisted itself on its hind legs and began to shuffle laboriously round its master. A crowd was the perfect cover; but this crowd was too far away. But for Mandraki, of course, he could have gone across, and waited with the watching people, inconspicuous and fairly safe. To stand a chance he *must* go; it was suicide to stay in this doorway——

. . . An elderly black taxi with yellow artillery wheels and yellow doors came purring up from the opposite direction. It slowed and almost stopped, moved on and came to a stop in front of the *romvia*. The driver was peering up at the numbers above the doors.

Gene slid across the pavement in one streak and got in. The young man driving had curly brown hair and was wearing a boiler suit.

"M. Vanbrugh?"

Gene nodded and slammed the door and fell into the back as the car jerked violently and screamed out into the centre of the street. He didn't look out of the back window but lay on the seat until the taxi had turned twice and was making downhill towards the centre of the town.

When he looked behind there was nothing following. He leaned forward and said to the driver in Greek: "Thank you."

The driver grinned and switched down the 'libre' flag. "Think nothing of it."

"Where are you taking me?"

"Where do you wish to go?"

"To Piraeus."

"Mme Lindos thought otherwise."

"What did she suggest?"

"Nafplion. She said ask for Constantinos Salamis in the square beside the cinema."

"We can't go all the way there in your taxi."

"It's not my taxi. I stole it from the rank while the driver had gone to ease himself."

"You're a man of resource."

"But naturally."

They were coming rapidly into the busy section of the town.

Gene said: "Then what are your plans?"

"Soon, when we have gone a little further, I will get out and leave the automobile to you. What you do with it then is your own concern; I am glad I shall not know. You are right that this taxi will be noticeable if you drive in it all the way to Nafplion."

"It will be noticeable before then," said Gene, thinking of Mandraki.

"There is a train leaves the station for Nafplion at six."

"And the station will be very carefully watched by the police."

"Maybe. But there are other stations. The train stops at Eleusis and at Megara. They are not so many miles out of Athens, and I do not suppose they will be picketed."

"I think Corinth will be watched."

"Maybe. But by then you should be on the train." The young man, having exhausted his ingenuity, was becoming slightly less interested.

Gene glanced behind. It was impossible to be absolutely sure in this busy street, but he could see nothing suspicious.

The young Greek mopped the back of his neck. "Do you know your way out of Athens?"

"Yes."

"Then I will turn down at this next corner and leave you. It is best to do it in the centre where it will not be conspicuous."

They swerved into a side street and stopped. The driver jumped out and made a pretence of going round and examining a rear wheel. Gene got out and joined the driver. They put their heads together a moment, and then Gene straightened up and in a leisurely manner strolled to the driver's seat and got in. The other man kicked the tyre a couple times and presently went into a shop for some cigarettes. Gene felt for the pedals, restarted the motor glanced behind him, then drew out into the traffic and moved off.

A hunted man is like a man at the centre of a cyclone; there are periods of calm when it's impossible for him to assess the strength of the storm around him. Gene tried hard to take an impersonal view of his chances.

Police of course would keep a special watch at docks and stations and airports. What else? Road blocks? Trains stopped and searched?

Special checks at appropriate places on identity cards and passports? Hardly likely unless he was deported on a particular route. For a man in his position it was almost as dangerous to take too few risks as too many.

The homicide rate in Athens was probably the highest of the European capitals. But this was a special murder, of a statesman and a millionaire. How far could EMO put pressure on for extra measures?

The taxi had to go early. Mandraki would soon let the police know how he had left. But again, to be too timid would be to lose an initial advantage.

This was the same road so far as they had taken to Delphi cutting across the peninsular through Daphni. He was well away from the railway line now but the two ways would converge at Eleusis, as the young Greek said. Already one or two people were staring at the old taxi. Not that this mattered much—people always did stare in Greece—but if one of them remembered. . . .

Short of Daphni he slowed to a crawl. Two or three kilometres beyond the little town he remembered there was a fork in the road: if he turned left there he would be doubling back to Piraeus. The police might expect him to do that.

Almost in sight of Daphni he saw a side-lane turning sharp to his left and climbing up into the narrow mountain range separating the road from the sea. He swung the car up it and changed down, grinding the unfamiliar gears. The old taxi began to lurch and grunt up the hill.

It was half a mile before he came to cover, and he beat the guts out of the engine getting there. Thin low scrub of laurel and myrtle grew beside what in wet weather might be a rushing stream but now was a rubble of small stones, white and smooth as skulls.

He drove the car off the road, bumping between two boulders, and grounded it hard in the middle of the river bed. When he got out he found it was hidden from the road. He tipped his own clothes out of his bag, dropping Anya's bread, rolled the clothing in a ball and hid it under a rock, retrieved the bread and shut his bag.

He ran back as far as the main road, then walked more slowly through Daphni. People in doorways stared at him, but unspeculatively, as they would have stared at any moving object that came into their line of vision. Once out of the town he went on more quickly. It was ten minutes to six and his chances of catching the train at Eleusis—even if he decided to take the risk—were small. Eight or ten kilometres yet.

The road here was downhill and uninteresting but in a little while would run beside the sea. A peasant cart turned out ahead but it was moving no quicker than he was walking, in fact he began to catch it up. Then he saw a little knot of people standing at the side of the road, two or three of them carrying baskets and one with a child in arms. He joined them. Several of them stared and two nodded a good evening, but everybody was talking too animatedly to notice him for long. Not that there was anything in their talk to get animated about, but it was their nature to make the best of indifferent material.

Roads were so few that no vehicle going in this direction could be making for anywhere but Eleusis; but when the bus came up five minutes later it was marked Megara, which was 20 kilometres beyond.

He crowded into it with the others. He stood near the back between two black-dressed women, one with a basket with live fowls. A man in a sombrero hemmed him in in front and a boy with a dog rubbed against his legs. Everything smelt of garlic and old sweat. The bus jolted into movement and the conductor fought his way through to get his fares. Everybody was talking, and somewhere at the front a young man was trying to play a mouth organ. Gene took a ticket to Megara. He worried for Anya, how she had faced the police when they came, what she was doing now.

At ten past six the bus lurched into the narrow streets of Eleusis. It stopped near the waterfront while sixteen people fought their way off and another twenty got on. There was a policeman at the stop watching the crowd but he took no special interest in them. Gene thought of the Greek phrases, 'It does not matter. Let us do it tomorrow.'

A hand touched his arm. "Are you from Argos, *patrioti*?"

He looked down at the man with the sombrero, who was peering up at him. "No, from Lavrion." It was his usual reply, to pick the opposite side of Greece.

"Well, well, I thought your cloth came from Argos. I am a tailor there." He looked more like a brigand with his fat body, a nose jutting like a scimitar from under his hat, a stubble of beard.

"It may be that it did," said Gene. "My own suit was damaged in an accident and I bought this second hand in Athens."

"Ah, that explains it, if you will pardon me. The *koukoulariko* comes of course from Kalamai, and I rather think. . . . You'll pardon me." The Greek put out a black-nailed finger and thumb and felt the edge of the cloth "Yes, that's it. There was not much of this heavier type, and it was made up locally."

Everyone in the bus lurched as it began to move. A faint welcome air stirred the heat and the smell.

"Are you going to Argos tonight?" Gene said.

"I hope to. I have something to pick up at Megara and then I intend to catch the automotrice."

"That's the diesel train?"

"Yes." Swinging and lurching, the little man got out a watch. "One has to be hasty but I have caught it before. I am in Argos then by nine-thirty."

Gene said: "I too am going to Argos—or near there."

"By the train?"

"I had thought so. But I have never been before. That's the best way?"

"It's the only way if you wish to get there tonight. And the steam trains tomorrow morning—they barely crawl."

"I am a radio mechanic," said Gene. "I have business ultimately in Nafplion."

"Well, the train will take you there tonight. You will be there before ten. Permit me to introduce myself. My name is Diomedes Cos."

Gene gave a name he had used during the war, and the bus lurched on towards Megara. Everybody talked, and M. Cos was full of information. He was also full of curiosity about Gene—a common characteristic in the country districts; it was a candid, unassuming curiosity, giving and expecting to receive a free exchange of information as a way of enlarging one's acquaintance and passing the time. Gene was forced to keep his wits at stretch.

The sun was low in the sky, and the water of the bay had become a willow pattern blue, brimming so full it seemed as if it was going to over-spill and flood the land. Megara loomed up climbing its two low hills; they bumped and rattled through the squat white concrete hovels on the outskirts and then lurched through the town and came to a stop in the main square. The doors of the bus opened and people were spewed out upon the cobbled street. Children cried, dogs barked, street sellers offered sweetmeats in bags and grilled mutton on wooden sticks.

"The station is over there," said M. Cos. "I shall hope to join you in a few minutes." He went off across the square on fat purposive legs.

Soldiers here, talking in listless groups, squatting around some sort of a gambling game, sitting on the walls. Gene walked to the station. He was in time for the train. There were a few people on the platform and a number around the booking office. No evidence of police; but one couldn't be sure. He didn't go in.

There was a kiosk near, and he bought a bottle of wine, a *baclavá* cake, a magazine about radio. He was still reading when Diomedes Cos came hurrying back across the square with a big parcel under his arm. Gene followed the tailor into the station and caught him up at the booking office. They exchanged nods and Gene said: "I was hungry but I was afraid there wasn't time before the train came in."

They bought tickets. There were two men in the booking office but neither had the interest to raise his eyes. They pulled tickets out of cubby holes, accepted money and shoved masses of dirty small notes back through the grill.

On the platform Cos said: "You see, there was just time. The train is signalled."

Two crones whispered together in the long slanting sunlight. A priest with a black beard paced up the platform ostentatiously reading his Bible. A small almost yellow-skinned boy clung to his mother's skirts waving a blue and white Greek flag. At the end of the platform an oleander tree gleamed, its leaves brilliant and undusty. There was a hoot in the distance, and a small diesel train slid into the station.

Only two carriages, and those connected with a continuous passage down the centre. Gene stuck close to the fat little tailor; a man on his own would be more to look at. There were a few seats and they got two with their backs to the engine near the middle of the train. Opposite were a young man and a girl.

The train moved off at a good speed, whining like a big vacuum cleaner. After a time Gene offered Cos wine from one of the two cardboard cups he had bought, and felt for the penknife he'd been presented with at the *Aegis* offices. But he couldn't find it.

"I'm sorry. I thought I had a corkscrew."

"No matter. We will ask the guard. He will have one."

The guard had not got one, but he said he would ask the driver who always carried one.

As they neared Corinth the sun dipped flaming behind the great Peloponnesian mountains. The light flared from behind them; rocks and cliffs and cypresses stood up with startling blackness against the glow; for a few minutes it was unearthly, as if the events of four thousand years were burning behind the hills—Hercules was hunting his lion and Agamemnon riding out to war. The train stopped at a squalid station and then moved slowly off and crawled across the viaduct spanning the Corinth canal. Almost every passenger in the train stood up to peer out of the windows at the long narrow slit of water. As they ran into Corinth station twilight was already clustering over the lower hills.

Bustle and movement. Gene saw two policemen walking slowly along the platform peering in the train. This was the testing point, the obvious place to come in, asking people for their papers.

The policemen came down, revolvers tap-tapping in holsters. The child with the Greek flag waved it at them. Gene poured more wine into the tailor's glass. Cos was a supporter of Karamanlis, and Gene asked him whether he thought the government would go back. That gave them conversation while the policemen went past.

The train began to moan again, and moved off. Gene leaned back and slowly allowed his grip to relax on the cardboard cup. 'It does not matter. Let us do it tomorrow.' He bit into the almond cake. It was very sweet and rather dry.

He wondered if Anya was all right. The loss of the penknife worried him. Already this afternoon seemed a week ago. Now the recollection of it came back like a floodlight on a dark day.

Everyone still talked in the train, talked in high voices above the whine of the diesel; but Gene found his eyes shutting. He tried hard to hear what the fat tailor was saying but the words began to blur. He nodded and came half awake to look through bleared eyelids and see Mandraki sitting opposite him.

He jerked his head up, fighting something stronger than sleep, drugged wine perhaps; shook his body, tried to get to his feet, was bound hand and foot, struggled, raised his hand to strike; and then the fat white face blurred again and became the bristly chin and hawk nose of the tailor.

Night had fallen while he dozed. The train ran along swaying gently, a ship on a dark sea. There was a feeling of ostracism, and of being exposed to peering faces that could not be seen.

Half asleep, half awake, he thought of Maria Tolosa. With a mixture of illusion and clairvoyance, he saw her on a small Turkish steamer, sitting in the steerage holding some bundle of clothes she had got together, lonely like himself and lost. The memory of her as a talented vulgar good humoured night club singer and dancer was overprinted by the memories of her since the bereavement, the tight dragged head shawl, the determination and the bruised face.

Through the rest of the journey he talked and dozed. They stopped two or three times at tiny wayside stations. The Greek tailor talked animatedly to the girl opposite him who, young and pretty though she was, already had the beginnings of a dark moustache. The train hooted and began to slow again.

"I leave you here, *patrioti*," said Cos, breaking off suddenly and speaking to Gene. "In a little while now you will be in Nafplion. Remember the restaurant where I recommended you. And when you want silkcloth like that again. . . ."

Gene shook hands with the tailor and also with the young man and the girl although he had hardly spoken to them. It was all very friendly and homely; the alarms and pursuits of Athens were far away. It had been a feeling he had often known before, as if Athens were a state within a state, having its own frontiers and its own aggressive tin-foil civilisation; outside the city and beyond its boundaries one came into the essential eternal land of Greece, slow moving, warm-hearted, hard, convivial, courteous, sincere. One was already beyond pursuit.

The train stopped and his friends got out. He waved to them through the window. Many people were leaving the train here, and the guard said there would be a ten minutes stop, so he got out and walked slowly along the platform stretching his legs and trying to blink the sleep from his eyes. Another train came muttering in on the opposite platform, a steam train going the other way. The engine had been built by Krupp's, probably for shunting work, seventy-three years ago. The carriages might have come from an old nineteenth-century print. As it shuddered to a stop, doors opened and crowds streamed out, many young people laughing and joking, a few carrying blowers and wearing paper hats.

As they went past, Gene said to the guard of the steam train: "What is it? What has been happening?"

"The festival at Nafplion. It's held every year." He moved on, furling his flag.

"Those police on the platform," said a girl laughing as she went past. "Why were they there?"

"To look after us," said her boy friend, and blew his paper blower in her face.

Gene stood still. There were a lot of children on the train and they were taking a time to be got off. Police on what platform?

he wanted to hurry after the girl and ask. But did he need to ask? Like a lump of heavy driftwood in a shallow stream, Gene began to move slowly with the crowd. As he did so he saw two men making for the waiting automotrice. They were not in uniform, but you couldn't mistake them. They stopped at the centre door of the train and one of them drew back and glanced up and down so that he could keep the whole train in view. He had his hand in his pocket. The other man got on the train.

The driftwood, as if it had come into deeper water, began to move more easily with the stream. At the barrier there was a cluster of people waiting to go through, children, black-clad women, boys laughing. It was a toss up—either that way or a dart across the railway lines. But always he had avoided the panic move.

The man at the barrier was snatching tickets as the people went through. There did not appear to be anyone with him, anyone watching. Gene went through squeezed between a fat woman with a basket of oranges and two short-trousered bare-legged boys. The ticket was taken from his hand. He glanced over his shoulder and saw that one of the men who had gone to the automotrice was walking back to the barrier.

Outside the station dim street-lights and a narrow rutted square. Walk in the same direction as most of the crowd. A man in a taxi, seeing him better dressed than most, called out to him but he hunched his shoulder and went by. It seemed a long walk but he did not look round again. Twenty steps to the corner, ten, five. A long street. People were spreading out, this way and that, giving him less chance of cover. A darker street to his right, leading back in the direction of the railway lines. He took it.

Chapter Thirty Three

He got to Nafplion just after midnight. He had walked all the way. In the dark and along the country roads there was little danger; even if the police were sure he was in this area they would not have great forces at their disposal. No doubt the taxi had been found, and at once the police had been alerted along the various routes he might have taken, south towards Piraeus, north in the direction of Levadhia and the main railway line to the Balkans, west into the Peloponnese with obvious attention to the only train feeding the area that night. It was his luck that he had got so far.

He had left his bag on the train. It held nothing of value except the food and brandy that Anya had put in; but for the police, if they identified it with him, it was proof he was in the neighbourhood and only a step ahead of them.

The town of Nafplion was still lighted. He came in along the Tiryns road; cafés were open and music came from one or two. He passed the bus station, where two crowded buses were just leaving, and made into the centre of the town. He had never been here before and had to ask his way. He found the cinema, which had clearly changed its religion, having begun life as a mosque: a few tattered posters hung outside, three photographs of film stars fly-spotted and faded in the sun.

"Constantinos Salamis?" he said to a passer-by.

The first did not hear him, but the second pointed back to a lighted doorway and went on his way trying but failing to walk straight. It was a taverna, bigger than it looked, music came from it as well as stumbling men. He went in and groped a way among smoke and feet and talk and the braying of an accordion; found a seat, slumped into it, for once near the end of his tether. He needed a breathing space and food and rest.

In the middle of a group three men were prancing rounds one other who, middle aged and thin and bald, was twisting himself into wild contortions and leaping into the air while the audience roared and clapped in time. Everybody had had plenty to drink.

"Sir?" A slim dark young man had come to the table, clearing an empty mug and wiping a dry patch on the table.

"Have you food?"

"No, sir."

"Wine, then. And I want to see M. Constantinos Salamis."

"I am Constantinos Salamis."

Gene glanced at his neighbours. But they were all watching the dance and roaring witticisms and advice. "Mme Lindos has sent me."

The young man bent to wipe the table again. "I do not think we can serve you."

"Why not?"

"We were not expecting you until tomorrow, and—it is difficult."

"I can pay."

"So would we, if we were caught. It is not the money."

"Then I'll go."

"No, wait, I'll bring you the wine."

He went off and Gene stared at the dancers. At length one of them slipped and fell and there was a howl of laughter and applause.

Salamis came back. "If you are hungry there is this cold, *katsiki*. It is all we have."

"Thanks."

"And stay a while. This is a bad night. We will see what we can do."

The man who had fallen had sprained his leg and they earned him to his chair laughing and cursing. Then two other men, without much urging from their friends, got up and began to sing an unaccompanied song which seemed to derive, as the cinema did, from the Turkish occupation. It was a love song hung with quavering trills and appoggiaturas, nasal, oriental and sad.

The cold kid, helped down with strong red retsina had a tonic effect. He began to recover, to look around. Salamis came back.

"When you go out," he muttered, "go to the back door. You will be let in."

As soon as he had finished Gene paid his bill and left. This taverna was just the sort of place the police would come to. The sooner he was out of sight the better.

Mme Salamis said: "He must stay here tonight. There is not much risk and we can do no less."

She was a pretty young woman except when she showed her teeth, which were decaying.

Salamis shook his head. "I have seen too much of this during the war to risk it all again—my business, my wife, my baby son, even for Mme Lindos whom we owe so much to."

Gene said: "There's still six hours of darkness. I can be miles away by morning."

"No, do not misunderstand me," the young Greek said. "I will take risks but not by keeping you here. That is too much. Let me think. There are better places to hide."

"It's not merely hiding," said Gene. "I want to get away."

"Oh, I think that is the lesser part. We had begun to make arrangements for that. Carlos has the better boat and he thinks nothing of being away a week. No, it is not that. It is keeping you until tomorrow night when one of the boats has the right excuse to go."

"Let me fend for myself till then. I can meet you by arrangement."

"Was that someone in the shop?" said Salamis. "Wait, I must see." He went out.

Gene looked around him, at the cradle beside the girl, at the low wattage unshaded electric light, at the triptych in the corner with a red-glassed oil lamp burning before it.

"Do not worry," said Mme Salamis. "He will look after you."

"I don't think I want to be looked after," said Gene.

She smiled and went on with her sewing.

Salamis put his head round the door. "It was no one. But wait, I have an idea and wish to telephone."

After a while Gene said to the girl: "Your husband speaks as if you were in the war. You look too young."

She smiled again. "We are Cretans. During the war my husband fought—and then he was captured. The Germans left him and his fellows in the prison starving. I and my friends used to go down and feed them. We met then and fell in love and promised that if we lived through the war we would marry. Afterwards he was taken from the island and then I did not see him for six years. I thought he was dead."

"You must have been very young."

"My husband was eighteen when we first met and I was thirteen."

For ten minutes or so Gene leaned with his head against the wall, half awake and half dozing. It was three o'clock and the lethargy and fatigue had come back to his limbs. He had had only broken and short sleep for the last four nights.

Sounds and memories adhered to his brain like strips torn from a complete pattern; the day's events had been blown to shreds and left only these defeated flags fluttering. The voices in the train, the grind of gears in the old taxi; Mme Lindos said: "You've got to go; the police are coming." And Anya: "Tell me, this fear is not true." "Those police on the platform," said a girl's voice. "My spanner's too big," he said. "I thought you might have a smaller one." He could not find his penknife; there should have been a corkscrew on that. And Anya said: "Take off the phone. Take off the phone, Gene. Take off the phone."

He started up as Salamis came back into the room, his pale sallow sad face expressionless.

"Do you know the town?"

Gene stared at him, then shook his head.

Salamis said: "There is an island in the bay. Bourtzi. You have heard of it?"

"No."

"There is a castle on it. Very small. The owner is away and there is no one there. The caretaker lives near here. I have been to see him. It would be a place to hide."

"You can trust him?"

"Angelos? Ye-es. It is not our way to sell our friends."

"I am not your friend."

"You are Mme Lindos's friend."

Gene said: "Do you know what the police want me for?"

"It's of no importance."

"Do you know that they are offering a reward of 25,000 drachmae for my capture?"

"Money is not everything."

"Thank you."

The Greek glanced at the cheap clock on the mantelpiece. "It is time to go. The moon has set. You will need food and drink for at least twenty-four hours. I will arrange that with Angelos in the morning. There is danger tonight: first the risk of being seen in the streets now, which are empty; second of being seen going out to the island."

"How far is the island from the shore?"

"Oh, no distance. Six hundred metres."

"Then I can swim."

"I hoped you would suggest it."

The girl made a movement. "You should take him by boat, Tinos."

"It was partly of his own safety I was thinking," said her husband. "This is a small town, monsieur, and very little can happen without others knowing of it. The quay will be empty and dark, but I know from experience that we should be lucky if we were not seen using a boat."

"I'll swim," said Gene.

Salamis took a heavy key out of his pocket. "This will let you into the castle. Inside you'll find a bed. Angelos will come in the morning. Now I'll take you as far as the quay."

"There's no need. I'm used to finding my way in strange towns."

"That may be, but it is necessary to know which parts of the quay to avoid. Also, in this case, two men are less noticeable than one."

The girl got up and went to the door and opened it to put an empty tin out. "There is no one about."

Gene got up and held out his hand to Mme Salamis. "I have a feeling that your husband won't allow me to pay him for his help."

"Your feeling is right," said Salamis.

"But you have a child?"

She looked up at her husband who frowned and then shrugged. Gene said: "No parent would deny his son. . . ."

The girl said: "Thank you. If Tinos will allow." She accepted money and folded the notes slowly into a small bundle.

"Thank you," said Salamis. "Now come. . . ."

"It is quite safe from here if you can swim well. Do not lose the key."

"You'd better burn the suit."

"No, no. Angelos will bring it over to you in the morning. He will also bring you word of arrangements for tomorrow night."

"We shall not meet again?"

"I hope not." Salamis's teeth gleamed briefly in the dark. "For our own sakes, I mean."

"Then good-bye. And thank you."

"Down these steps. There should be nothing to run foul of between here and the island. God go with you."

"And with you," said Gene.

He found water at the eighth step, slipped slowly into it and began to swim. The water was quite cold but refreshing. There was no risk of missing his mark: boats and the harbour end stood out clearly in the starlight, and right ahead of him a black hump shaped like a coconut cake showed up between the jaws of the bay. Apart from the harbour light some lights still showed in the town, and there were evidently high cliffs to the east.

A few minutes brought him to the edge of the rocks. He had no difficulty in finding the landing quay, which was just a concrete step running out into the sea; but as he climbed up, a sharp pain went through his stockinged foot and he knew he had cut himself on something.

Twenty yards across a fiat sanded surface took him to the door of the keep. He limped up the steps, took the key from his belt and pushed it into the door.

He had little enough energy to look round the place. There was a courtyard and various other doors, one of which he found unlocked. It led into kitchens and then downstairs into queer cell-like rooms with the sound of water lapping close under the windows. In one of the rooms was a bed. He stripped off and lay down on the bed. In a few minutes he was asleep.

Chapter Thirty Four

He woke to the sound of someone whistling. It wasn't a jolly tune but three or four notes repeated over and over again in a monotonous and depressing way. He got up, knowing at once where he was but not realising it was full daylight. He pulled on the clothes he had, which had lost some of their wetness in five hours.

A man was coming down the steps carrying a bag. He was short, square shouldered, red haired and walked with a limp. He didn't seem to notice the eye at the door, but when he got to the bottom step he put his bag down and said:

"Your health. There's clothes here and food. And Carlos will be here for you tonight."

Gene came slowly out. "Your health. What time is it? My watch has stopped."

"Nine o'clock. I'm later than usual, but last night was the Festival, so one is up later today."

The man had a queer neck as well as a limp; the bones were deformed and he held his head as if looking round a corner. Gene bent to the bag and pulled open the string.

His suit and his shoes were inside.

"The food will cost you eighty-four drachmae. Meat is not cheap in Greece today. And there is bread and fruit and wine."

Gene gave him two hundred. "I should not have heard you but your whistle woke me. . . ."

"You slept well?"

"Like a log."

"Just so. Just so." Angelos gave him a peculiar smile. "You a foreigner?"

"Why d'you ask?"

"It says so in the paper."

"I have some Greek blood."

"Ah. But your eyes are too light."

"What about your own?"

Angelos laughed. He laughed silently with his head on one side and his mouth open. It was like a man having a fit.

"The police are looking for you, *koubare*. They've not found you yet. You were last seen at Argos. That true?"

Gene nodded as he got into his suit. He was used to summing people up quickly. Young Salamis had been as clear as day. Not so this man. One was in muddy water from the first word and the first glance.

"Have you looked around the castle?"

"No. I came straight in here."

"Instinct—that's what it was—instinct." Angelos had his convulsion again. "Well, there's nothing to the castle. But I warn you if you move about keep off the skyline, for someone will be sure to notice you, and the police don't believe in ghosts even if we do."

Gene followed the man up the stone steps. Outside the sun was blinding. They were not on view in this enclosed courtyard.

Gene said: "Someone is coming for me tonight?"

Angelos looked at him round the corner of his shoulder. "Tomorrow morning. Carlos will pick you up, and I shall be glad to see the back of you, I can tell you; but he cannot do so till the moon has set, which will be at four. You'll see his boat leaving the harbour at sundown. A handsome boat. I wish I had one like it."

"You do?"

"Yes. It's a blue one, and if there's a breeze 'twill carry a red sail. In the night 'twill come back for you. You'd best be ready on the little quay. There'll be no light but you'll hear the engine. Once you're off you'll be in their hands."

Gene walked with the man across the courtyard and found himself limping in company. Angelos looked at him suspiciously and Gene had to say: "I caught my foot on the rocks when I landed." He slipped his shoe off again and looked at his heel.

Angelos twisted himself with laughter. "Sea urchins. They're all over these rocks. They'll give you trouble. Once in they'll never come out. They'll fester and weep. Only way is to cauterise 'em. Red hot needle. Something for you to do this afternoon."

"I can't wait to try," Gene said.

As they came to the outer door Angelos stopped again and looked at Gene over his shoulder like something he'd forgotten. "I'll have to have the key, mind. Leave the door unlocked when you go. I'll come early tomorrow morning and lock up."

"It's a queer place to live."

"Think so? Oh, some people like it. My uncle liked it."

"Was he the owner?"

"He lived here. He was called Angelos too. On the side of the angels, eh? That's what I always say."

"Have you ever lived here?"

This amused Angelos. "No. It was all finished before I grew up."

"What was?"

"This place. You know what it was?"

"No."

"I thought not. Some people don't mind. Some people do. Hundreds of years ago it began. This part belonged to the Italians. Venice, you know. Up there, on the cliff, that's the prison, see? They had a hangman, of course, ready when needed. But we Greeks didn't like a hangman in our midst—and a foreigner at that—in the town, hobnobbing. Wasn't nice. And dangerous for him. He'd get his throat slit. See? So he lived here. Lived here for centuries. And even when there was independence, when Greece belonged to the Greeks, they still kept the hangman here. This was his house. And this was where they did the dirty work. That was where the gallows used to be—up there. My uncle was the last executioner. They've moved it away from here now. Pity, for by rights the job would have been mine."

"Pity," said Gene.

"Yes. Comical you being here really, considering what you're wanted for. Very apt when you think of that room you slept in. I suppose you went there just as if you'd been guided."

"Guided to what?" said Gene.

Angelos opened his mouth and laughed silently sideways. "That used to be the condemned cell."

Gene lay in the hot sun, his damp shirt steaming, and watched Angelos row away across the pale water of the bay. Gene was no surer of him than after the first word. He had gone off limping, sly, peering, gusty, lustful, full of slightly obscene laughter, leaving his prisoner where he could get at him any time. There were eighteen hours yet during which Angelos might call at the police station and earn the reward. A sobering thought.

As the heat of the day grew, the prickles in his foot began to throb and he tried to dig them out. The sea urchins clustered all round this island like a second fine of defence, evil black pincushions showing through the glass-green water. Perhaps one had grown for every man hanged. Difficulty about getting the prickles out was that they constantly broke, and he gave it up half done to eat some of the food Angelos had brought.

After he had eaten, and with a rag round his foot, he looked over the castle. The island was tiny, no more than a rock jutting out of the bay, the castle a round keep with a central tower, a few dungeons, an enclosed parade yard. He went down again to the room where he had spent the night. It was only six or seven feet above the sea. There were still the marks to be seen where the window bars had been removed. The walls had been re-plastered, and he wondered what scrawls and last messages the new plaster covered up.

It was cool here after the heat upstairs and he felt sleepy again. The bed still bore the impression of where he had lain almost unmoving through the night. He lay down in the same place and allowed his mind to slip back into its preoccupying groove. Everything in his life and future seemed now to be coloured by thoughts of Anya.

Presently he fell asleep.

He got the last prickles out of his foot just before the sun set. He bathed his swollen heel in cold water, wrapped it in a strip of handkerchief and then limped to a point of vantage to watch for his boat. He saw it leave just as dusk was falling; there was a little wind and the red sail was set aslant. As it went out, its engine chugging, it came quite near the island and Gene saw two men aboard. They didn't glance at the island. He watched the boat until it was out of sight round the south headland, then he crouched where he was for another half hour watching the lights winking on all over the town. Some broken cloud had drifted up just before dark, but the moon, now three quarters full, was brilliant.

Dry clothed and rested, he went back to the kitchens and ate some supper. He saved some of the wine for later. He had slept so well that there was now no sleep in him; in any case, although there was still seven hours to wait he could not take the risk of lying down again. This especially so because of the onset of cloud and an increase in wind. If the night grew dark enough they might come for him before his time.

Or if the wind grew strong enough they might not come for him at all.

By midnight there was no moon and a light drizzle was falling. The wind had veered and freshened but was still nothing more than a strong breeze. The water slapped against the rocks in little spiteful wavelets as if the castle were a ship pushing against the tide. He wandered occasionally about the place, but after sitting for an hour in darkness in an easy chair in one of the two living-rooms he found the moon cast disturbing shadows, so he went quietly down to the kitchens and thence into the condemned cell. He had six cigarettes left but he would not light a match in case some reflection showed.

Then when lying on his bed in the cell he heard what sounded like a footstep outside. In a quick but silent movement he was up and had opened the door, and for a moment thought he glimpsed some shadow of a figure at the top of the stone stairs. He went after it, but when he got to the enclosed courtyard there was nothing to be seen. Then the door of the cell below creaked as the wind pushed it to behind him.

Thereafter he began a systematic search of the place. Through shadowed rooms constantly lit and darkened by cloud and moonlight he made his way, backwards and forwards, backwards and forwards, watching and listening.

Eventually satisfied there was nothing inside at all, he began a tour of the few battlements, crouching whenever the moon shone, moving again at the next cloud. The drizzle had stopped and shadows were lengthening; he looked at his watch. If they were prompt only another seventy minutes. But they might not be prompt. They might be hours late.

He squatted beside the place where the gallows had been, a cigarette between his lips for company, though unlighted. Maybe the footsteps he had heard were echoes of an earlier time, someone leaving the cell and climbing the stone steps. Through the generations, through the centuries, this island had borne its one-way freight. All had come here for the axe or the hangman's rope: the patriot, the criminal, the fanatic. Walking courageously, dragged here fainting or screaming, head on block or head in noose. If anything lingered here, an ambience, a flavor. . . .

The moon went slowly down, swelling as it neared the mountains. A great black canopy of cloud stretched almost across the sky, and it was from under this that the moon flung its last light slantwise across the bay and town. The houses climbing the hill on one side were white as if caught in a car's headlights. As one watched, the reflected light faded as the moon was misted by the vapours from the land and turned yellow and then orange.

Gene stirred his cramped limbs and moved to go down. As he did so somebody whistled faintly, a flat two notes, cautious, inquiring.

Not only were they prompt, they were a few minutes early. A Chinese lantern shaped like a deflated football was still showing between two humps of the land. Gene moistened his lips and whistled back.

The boat had come in under sail, gliding undetected across the bay, making use of the breeze and the slap of the sea to come alongside the jetty without even Gene noticing it, though he had been on the alert.

He slipped his heel in his shoe, fastened it, and then padded down the steps to the stone courtyard, opened the great door and stepped through on to the rough gravel approach to the tiny quay. The boat was there and the two men were standing beside it. Gene walked up to them. As he got near he saw the vessel had a short stubby mast, and his eyes, acute beyond ordinary because of the long hours in the dark, saw two other men crouching in the shadow of the jetty.

So Angelos had earned his new boat.

Gene turned to run, to jump off the low rocks into the sea, but one of the policemen, nervous in the dark, stood up quickly and shot him in the back.

Chapter Thirty Five

The small whitewashed room had tumbled down upon him in irregular intervals of consciousness throughout the first thirty hours. Walls moved in landslides over continual precipices that hurt his eyes and his back and left him glad to return to the darkness of the pit. Only in the daylight of the second day did he recognise his identity again and the separateness of movement about him. A woman was with him, an old woman and sometimes a man, inside the cage that the whitewashed room periodically became, a wire fence woven between castle turrets; attention reaching him through it like messages passed into a concentration camp.

At the foot of his bed was a slip of paper that the man sometimes wrote on and then put back, some record of progress or betrayal. The woman washed him and gave him liquid to drink; even her hair was like wire, rusted with streaks of grey. Once he heard what the bearded man said. It sounded like 'he'll do' or 'we'll do.'

Thereafter a period of sleep, and it was waking fully conscious and completely aware of his position for the first time that he saw the bars across his window as the cause of the illusion of the cage. . . .

After that it was dark for a long time, and the unshaded electric bulb hurt his eyes when someone switched it on. The nurse came in, and with her were the doctor and Major Kolono.

The doctor said: "I'll give him another transfusion in the morning. It will strengthen him for the journey. More than anything it's a matter of rest and recuperation now."

"Can he walk?" said Kolono.

"I suppose he could, well strapped up. It's chiefly weakness now from loss of blood. But the obvious thing is an ambulance if you intend to take him tomorrow."

"He's got to go tomorrow," said Kolono, fingering his moustache. "We want him for interrogation."

"I shouldn't advise interrogation for a day or two. It might cause a relapse."

"We want him for interrogation," said Kolono. "It makes very little difference to us whether he has a relapse or not."

"That's just as you say," said the doctor, looking annoyed. "It's my duty to point out these things."

He left the room, but Major Kolono went to the window staring out with his hands clasped behind his back. The nurse gave Gene a milk drink in which some drug was rather unsuccessfully disguised. Then she asked him if he could eat anything and he said he could. When the nurse left the room to get him food Kolono came and stood by the bed. He watched Gene for a while in silence.

"So you are still alive, eh?"

Gene didn't answer. His strength needed conserving.

"The bullet missed all vital parts," said Kolono. "Pity. It might have saved us the trouble of taking you back for trial."

Gene said: "I thought—you would enjoy that."

Kolono took out a cigar and fitted it into a short yellow holder. "It is my duty to tell you that the woman calling herself Maria Tolosa has been arrested in Thessaloniki."

"What? . . ." He was too weak even to pretend. "What are you talking about?"

"She was taken on Saturday as she was trying to board a ship. We have been on the look-out for her, you know. She was seen leaving Heracles House on the night of the murder."

There seemed to be grit in Gene's teeth. He tried to speak but could not. Kolono's words carried conviction, and they carried defeat too, ultimate defeat, turning to mockery all his efforts of the last five days. After this nothing was left, not even credit, not even a justifiable memory.

Kolono said: "Of course it will make no difference. Whatever her testimony may be, we shall make specially sure of convicting you. Whichever of you actually used the knife does not matter. You will be charged jointly. Our taking her won't have helped your case at all."

Through the day that followed Gene gained strength, but it was slow, and in a way it was like the recovery of a very old man: one climbed laboriously back to life only to find that life had nothing left. He had never felt so down. There was a gap in his usually purposive mind, like a rift caused by an earth tremor, across which as yet the usual communications did not reach.

The nurse, who was under orders not to talk to him, told him only that it was Monday, that he was still in Nafption, in the prison on the hill, and that so far as she knew he would be leaving that evening for Athens. At noon he was able to sit up and eat the meal that she brought him, and from then, almost in spite of himself, his strength came back quickly. During the afternoon he slept a little and dreamed of Lascou's death and the gallows at Bourtzi and of Anya calling to him from far off.

The doctor came in at four and inspected the two wounds in his side. He prodded them a good deal too much and then injected Gene in the thigh. From the feel of things it wasn't the first injection he'd had there. Another official came in and they talked in low tones in a corner of the room while the nurse re-dressed his side.

The slanting sun was falling in through the window, and the bars were shadowed like a prophecy across the floor. The nurse's sunken eyes followed the movement of her hands, which were gnarled and whitened with work, as if they had spent long years over a scrubbing board. She was not good at her job and fumbled and let the bandage slip.

The official was signing something. Signature, gaol delivery, passing of custody, of responsibility from one official to the next; the death penalty still existed in Greece, but life imprisonment was probably as likely; strange if he came back here to serve it; he'd already seen the inside of the gaols of Athens; the Germans had crowded them with offenders; so had the revolutionaries, so had the counterrevolutionaries; it was Mr. Wet—Mrs. Fine during the years after the war. Would they allow him to choose his own defence lawyer? Anya must keep out of this. Contact with him now would ruin her. He must get her word, through Mme Lindos perhaps, warn her she could not help now and must not try.

Major Kolono came into the room and the conference continued in the corner. Presently the two other men left and Kolono waited until the nurse had done. When she too had gone he stayed by the window for a while, hands behind his back in his favourite attitude, the sun glinting on the bristles of his moustache.

Gene waited. Several minutes passed in complete silence. Kolono turned, his face half-lit now, the other half shadowed. He said: "You will leave at seven this evening for Athens."

"Whatever you say."

"Can you walk?"

"I haven't tried."

"I will drive with you personally. Then there will be no chance of escape."

"I couldn't get far at present."

Gene watched the man's regular false teeth gripping the cigar holder. He badly wanted to smoke.

He said: "I don't know if it's any good appealing to your sense of chivalry, Major Kolono."

"What d'you mean?"

"Well, why don't you drop this charge against Maria Tolosa and let her go? She's not much more than a girl and it's me you want really, isn't it."

"It is you we want really," Kolono agreed.

"She saw her own husband killed. She was half crazy with grief. She didn't know what she was doing. Why can't you be lenient with her and concentrate on me? I came to Greece to get Lascou and I got him. Isn't that enough for you?"

"What is enough for me, Vanbrugh, is beside the point. The law of the land must now take its course."

"But you're not without influence. The prosecution might even refuse to believe her story, turn her off without bothering about her. I'm quite willing to make a full confession."

"That you did it?"

"That I did it."

Kolono's eyes were like dark olives freshly moistened. "I wish I could make use of that."

"Can't you?"

"Unfortunately, no."

The spiral of smoke was going straight up. Kolono did not seem to be drawing on the cigar.

Gene said: "Put it to your superiors. It would save time, trouble, publicity. On the one hand you'd have two people in the box fighting all the way; you'd have us both making accusations—it wouldn't help. On the other you have one man with a full confession, trial over in a day, and the Spanish woman shipped off without being allowed to become a nuisance. Don't you think that's worth considering?"

Silence fell.

Kolono said: "Unfortunately I may not consider it. I have another proposition altogether to put to you."

"What is that?"

"What would you say if we offered you your freedom?"

Dressed in the now frayed and stained suit he had bought in the Plaka, Gene was helped to the door of the ambulance and got in. He was glad enough to lie on one of the bunks after the effort of getting there; but on the whole his strength was not bad. Major Kolono climbed in and sat on the opposite bunk, and the ambulance drove out of the gates of the prison. It was not quite dark yet but the sun had set.

Gene said for the fourth time: "What's the catch in all this?"

Kolono lit another cigar. "In a few minutes from now this ambulance will stop with engine trouble. While we are stopped you will leave the ambulance and go."

"D'you like it better that I should be shot again while trying to hobble away?"

"It would give me great pleasure to be able to do that personally."

"And that's the arrangement?"

"I am here to tell you the arrangement. Where we stop will be at an inlet on the coast between—well, no matter—at an inlet. A boat is waiting there to take you to Brindisi. Once you reach Italy it will be your personal concern to return to Paris."

"I don't understand."

"Maria Tolosa has not yet been publicly interrogated. But she was privately interrogated by me this morning. She is prepared, under pressure from us, to swear that the man who was seen leaving Heracles House with her on Tuesday night was her brother-in-law, Philip Tolosa."

"Philip To . . . But he's . . ." Gene stopped.

"He is dead."

There was a pause. Gene said: "Do you mean you intend . . ."

"I can promise you nothing absolutely—except your freedom tonight. And that on conditions."

Gene said: "The boy——"

"I am not Chief of Police. I am not the Public Prosecutor. I cannot influence them. But I am in charge of this case, and I will do what I can. On conditions, we are prepared to prove that Philip Tolosa, not you, killed Lascou. It can be done. You are alike in build, figure, colouring. Manos, who was in the flat within three minutes of the murder, and M. Lascou's secretary, are prepared to identify Philip Tolosa as the man who committed the crime. It is a case of mistaken identity by a boy of eight. From there on you will be free."

After a time Gene said: "That may be; it may be possible, what you propose; but I don't begin to understand why you're proposing it. Who is behind this?"

"There are two conditions, as I have said. One is absolute secrecy. You return to Paris and keep your mouth shut. No reporters. No interviews. No idle talk with friends. In no circumstances do you say anything about your visit to Greece."

"And the second?"

"The second is that in no circumstances do you ever return here."

"That's more difficult."

"Murderers can't be choosers."

They jogged along for some way in silence. Gene felt glad for a moment that the conversation had stopped; it gave him time to relate it to common sense, to breathe.

"And Maria Tolosa?" he said.

"That is for the law to decide. If this proposition is carried through, she will appear rather as a witness than as a collaborator. That is not because we care what happens to her but because it is necessary to our case. She might get off; she might at worst go to prison for a few months. Again I cannot promise anything."

"And if I refuse to go?"

"It will be very much worse for Maria Tolosa if you stay, since the need for us to use her mainly as a witness will have disappeared. Just as I have pointed out to her that it will be much worse for you if she insists on telling the truth."

The ambulance lurched and rattled over the rough road.

"Why am I so dangerous to keep?"

"Perhaps you will learn that before you leave."

"From you?"

"Not from me."

"We are meeting someone?"

"It maybe."

"Who?"

"You will see now," said Kolono, stubbing out his cigar and putting away the end in his case.

Chapter Thirty Six

The ambulance came to a stop. The driver got down and opened the doors. It was clear that he was a party to the arrangement. Gene pushed himself into a sitting position and allowed himself to be helped out. Kolono followed.

The moon was full. They had stopped in a side road. A low wall bordered it, with pine trees on one side and on the other the sea. Low jagged rocks hemmed in the narrow mouth of the bay. Every now and then in the distance a lighthouse winked. A flock of dark sea-birds was winging silently across the sky.

In the lane a few yards ahead of them an old Buick was parked. Two people were standing beside it. Gene recognised them at once as Jon Manos and Anya.

Getting to her he almost forgot the pain in his side. She did not come to meet him. Kolono followed close behind, and in a minute the four were grouped together out of earshot of the soldier standing beside the ambulance. No one seemed to want to be the first to speak.

Then Kolono said: "Well, here he is."

Manos said: "Do you agree that our part of the bargain is now fulfilled?"

Anya said: "It will be when he reaches Paris."

"Anya," Gene said.

"Is your—wound bad?"

"No, nothing. Why are you here? What is this arrangement?"

Anya's voice sounded tired and hoarse. The colours and of their last two days together had quite gone from it.

She said: "I want five minutes with him alone."

239

Manos said: "Be hanged to that. Get him on the boat."

She said; "I want five minutes with him alone."

"No!" said Kolono. "Anything you say must be said in front of us."

After a minute Anya said: "I have made a bargain with these gentlemen, Gene. For a certain consideration they are prepared to see you out of the country. That is all. It is as simple as that."

"I don't understand you," Gene said.

"You did not finish reading the letters from Anton Avra to George Lascou?"

"No, I thought you'd burned them."

"In the haste that first evening I put them between the music inside the piano. After you left I couldn't remember at first—then I found them. In the last two letters there were other names mentioned besides his own. Six names in all. Two are here with us tonight. . . ."

"And?"

"I realised the letters were still not quite useless. I took them to the Bank of Greece. They are now in its vaults with instructions that in the event of my death—or yours—they are to be delivered personally to the editor of *Aegis*."

Gene leaned against the wall. In the reaction and in his weakness the importance of what she said kept escaping him. He would grasp it and then it would slip away from him.

"Anya—"

"Come, we've wasted long enough," said Manos coldly. "The boat is waiting."

Gene did not move. Some machinery of warmth had begun to work, but surrounding it was a block of ice in which all his ordinary feelings were still congealed. He tried to shake himself free of it.

"And what happens to the letters when I reach Paris?"

"They stay where they are," said Anya.

"And you?"

"I too stay where I am."

The birds were winging overhead again, wheeling round as if disturbed in their privacy.

"So that's it," Gene said. "Then I'm not going."

For the first time Anya moved and be saw her expression there had been hard bargaining and a hard fight and it had left its mark; in the moonlight her face looked drained of blood but not of feeling.

She said: "It is a fair arrangement, Gene. Otherwise they will not play their part."

"What difference would it make?"

"They do not trust you, my dear. I will stay as their security."

"Come if you are coming," said Manos impatiently. "We are not on a deserted island."

Gene said: "Is there more behind the bargain than this?" He looked at Manos.

Anya took his arm. "There is nothing more. I promise you. Can you not believe that?"

"Normally. But in this this case I . . ."

Manos turned on him. "Listen, man; you're lucky to have had this woman to fight for you! Well, now we *have* fought it out, round a table for five hours, while you were lying in your bed in Nafplion. You were not consulted in this and you are not being consulted now!"

"That's what you may think——" Gene stopped because Anya was pulling at his arm.

Manos said: "For a certain consideration we are prepared to pay. We are prepared to pay by misrepresenting the evidence in this case to make it appear that George Lascou was murdered by Philip Tolosa, who committed suicide on the following day. In doing this we are taking a considerable risk. In particular Major Kolono is risking his whole career. If this goes through you will be free, completely free. But we do not trust you. Once this case is closed we shall have no further hold on you. Well, you have your hostage, these letters. We shall have our hostage, this woman, who has worked in our midst all these years."

"And d'you think I'm willing to get out on those terms?"

"You've no choice."

"If Anya joins me in Paris——"

241

"If she were to join you in Paris, what guarantee would we have that you would not at once give an interview to the reporters? Your word? It's not worth a spit. *But* if Anya stays here, then if you have any care for her safety, as she says you have, you dare not talk because of what we would do to her. The bargain has been struck. Now get out and never come back."

Quietly but insistently Anya began to move him towards a break in the wall where a path led down to the beach. Kolono turned to speak to the soldier, and Manos momentarily turned with him.

She said: "Gene, it's the only way. . . ."

"But it's impossible——"

"I tell you it's the *only* way! Later——"

"What other conditions are there? You—Manos?"

"No. I am quite free so long as I stay here——"

Just before the others caught up with them he felt her slip a small package into his pocket. They went on. The moon was still low and the moonlight only caught one edge of the bay like a bar sinister on a crusader's shield. A fishing boat moved quietly at a jetty even smaller than the one on Bourtzi. A man swung along the deck, strap-hanging by various ropes attached to the mast. The sea was quiet.

Anya's hand was on his arm. He held it to him, his mind tingling from the impact of her last action—groping, trying to see its way.

To gain time he said: "And how long has this—bargain to last?"

"Five years, ten years," said Manos venomously. "What does it matter?"

"It matters everything——"

"Listen, Gene," said Anya, squeezing his arm warningly. "We have fought this out and fought this out. You must see their position. Talk from you in Paris would still damage even with no proof. Accusations from me would be much worse. After all I was George Lascou's mistress. Until the election's over they *must* keep us quiet. After that, each month that passes will slightly reduce the harm we can do by talking. As George is—is forgotten, so anything connected with him will have less news value. The letters will always remain just as dangerous for them, but our unsupported word will carry less and less weight. In time——"

"But how much time?"

"We cannot decide that now. But perhaps—though I don't want it—some interval is the right answer for us. In that way we can prove something to ourselves." She stopped. "But that is for the future. I believe, if it is everybody's wish, a settlement can be arranged. They cannot feel safe with the Avra letters still in existence. I might die accidentally and then exposure and ruin would come for them. Sooner or later we can make some arrangement for the exchange of the letters. And part of that arrangement could be that we can come together again—if you are still of the same mind."

"I haven't any other. Believe that."

She said: "It will be for you to choose. . . ."

"If you are going," said Manos, "get on that boat. Otherwise the bargain ends here and now."

Anya said: "Jon, *our* bargain stands. But he must reach Paris in safety. These men will look after him?"

"Of course they'll look after him——"

"I promise you," she said, "if this man dies, you and your friends will go before a military court on charges of treason within a week."

"Here!" called Manos angrily to the boat. "Here's your passenger."

One of the two figures on the boat stepped on to the jetty and came down to meet them.

Anya said: "Gene, write. . . ."

"Writing won't be enough."

"But it will help—for a time. And remember—I have done what I can. It is now for you to choose as you think best."

She had said it twice. He had to answer. Picking every word with care, for every word must carry its message to her and not to them, Gene said: "You must realise that if it comes to me to choose, I am not interested in these men and what their past histories were. They are small fry. George Lascou was the only real threat to Greece, and that threat is gone."

She said; "Yet I have tried to—what is the expression you would use?—to put the ball back at your feet. That is how it should be. Never forget that you have freedom to change your mind."

"Never forget," he answered, "that I shall never change it. There will be no conflict over that. I am not interested in these men."

Manos was listening suspiciously. The sailor took Gene's arm. Gene made a pretence of trying to free himself. But his next words were not spoken in pretence. "To leave you here like this with such men——"

"I have been in the company of such men all my life."

"I know. But there must be some other way——"

Anya said: "If you refuse to go you will be taken on board. This far I am quite prepared to—arrange your life."

The sailor's grip tightened. So did Anya's for a moment and her cold soft lips brushed his cheek. Then her fingers sharply relaxed as if quick now to have done with the moment of parting. He let her fingers fall one by one. Then she was a foot away. Then she was standing between the two men, the moon shining on her face. Then she was one of three figures in the distance.

Gene sat crouched over the gunnel in the stern of the boat. He fingered the Avra letters she had given him but did not take them out. The strong smell of petrol came up to him as the old four-cylinder motor began to chug its way out to sea. A sail flapped above him but as yet caught no wind. They'd gone, the two men, but she still stood there. He raised a hand, hardly capable of the gesture because, whatever the promise for the future, however much through her great courage it might now lie again in his hands, this was for the present a gesture of good-bye. He did not expect her to see it, but she saw it and waved back. Then after a few minutes he could no longer see her figure but only a mark on the beach which would have moved had she moved. He persuaded himself of this long after his eyes could see nothing against the dark land.

They reached the entrance of the bay. The opening was only thirty feet. They slipped through like some slow-moving aquatic animal avoiding the claws of a crab. The sail flapped above his head and the boat listed gently, quivering with a different and more sensitive life. On the port beam a lighthouse winked. A few lights showed here and there round the ancient coast, but ahead it was quite dark.

A hand touched his shoulder.

"Come below, sir," said the sailor. "We've orders to see you come to no ill."

Lightning Source UK Ltd.
Milton Keynes UK
UKOW03f2328251116

288548UK00001B/258/P